RA
SU

WHITE DECEPTION

"A suspenseful mix of western and Native American romance, with an intriguing paranormal element, this book promises to be one of the best in Edwards's popular White series."

—*RT BOOKclub*

WHITE SHADOWS

"One of the best books of this genre I have read in a long time. I look forward to reading many more of Susan Edwards's White series.... I wholeheartedly recommend *White Shadows*."

—*Romance Reviews Today*

WHITE DUSK

"The wonderfully poetic prose captures the naturalism of the traditional Sioux.... A compelling story."

—*Romantic Times*

WHITE DAWN

"The story had me riveted from the first page to the last. Susan Edwards packs this story with passion and emotion."

—*Romance Reviews Today*

WHITE DOVE

"A beautifully written tale. Ms. Edwards has a way of enchanting readers with her characters."

—*Romance Reviews Today*

MORE HIGH PRAISE FOR SUSAN EDWARDS!

WHITE DREAMS

"Susan Edwards has the talent of hooking her readers in the first paragraph and selfishly holding on to them until the last page has been turned! Highly recommended reading!"

—*Huntress Book Reviews*

WHITE NIGHTS

"Tender, heartwarming, touching, *White Nights* is a story you can savor."

—Connie Mason, *New York Times* bestselling author

WHITE FLAME

"Susan Edwards has penned another winner… Her sensual prose and compelling characters are forging a place for her at the forefront of Indian romance."

—*Affaire de Coeur*

WHITE WOLF

"Ms. Edwards's words flow like vivid watercolors across the pages. Her style is smooth, rhythmic and easy to read."

—*Rendezvous*

WHITE WIND

"Talented and skillful, this first-rate author has proven her mettle with *White Wind*. Ms. Edwards has created a romantic work of art!"

—*The Literary Times*

A TASTE OF PASSION

"Swallow that damn pride of yours," Tyler said.

Renny tipped up her chin. "Pride kept us together. You would have torn us apart."

"I wanted what was best."

"What you wanted was wrong." Renny's mouth firmed into a tight line. "The only thing that you care about is Sheriff Trowbrydge Tyler Thompkins Tilly."

Frustrated, Tyler felt like shaking her senseless—or better yet, kissing her so. As he stared at her full, lush red lips, Renny said, "Now that we've had this little talk, get your hands off—"

Tyler covered her mouth with his. All anger melted at the touch, the feel and the taste of her. She didn't fight. She gasped, and he drew her breath deep into him.

Other *Leisure* books by Susan Edwards:

WHITE DECEPTION
WHITE SHADOWS
WHITE DUSK
WHITE DAWN
WHITE DOVE
WHITE DREAMS
WHITE NIGHTS
WHITE FLAME
WHITE WOLF
WHITE WIND

WHITE VENGEANCE

SUSAN EDWARDS

LEISURE BOOKS NEW YORK CITY

This book is dedicated to all
my family and friends and faithful readers.
Thank you for your support.

A LEISURE BOOK®

January 2006

Published by

Dorchester Publishing Co., Inc.
200 Madison Avenue
New York, NY 10016

ISBN 0-8439-5334-9

Printed in the United States of America.

Visit us on the web at www.dorchesterpub.com.

WHITE VENGEANCE

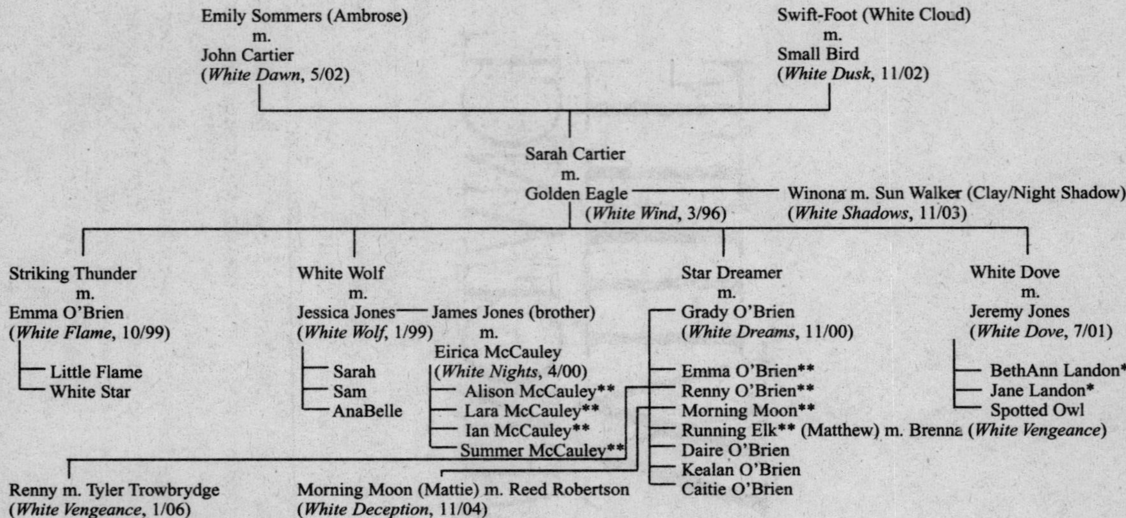

* Indicates adopted child
** Indicates child from previous marriage
Note: Not all children are listed

CHAPTER ONE

Mazaska Wicahpi raced across waving spears of crystal-green grass. Named for the silvery stars that graced the night sky, the horse spirit rode as one with *Tate*, Spirit of the Wind.

They kissed the ground, one with hooves light as air, the other with breath warm and soothing. Beneath them, blooms of purple, yellow, orange and blue harmonized with carpets of green.

Silver Star shifted and dipped her hooves into the stream as she gave herself over to the simple joy of being. Her long, moondust mane and tail floated behind her and around her and her eyes matched the blue of the heavens. She was fluid; molten silver streaking above the fast-moving river. Water sprayed into the air, glittering like diamonds in her wake.

Tipping her head up, eyes fixed on the far horizon, Silver stretched out fully, her hooves gracefully leaving the confines of *Maka*, the earth.

She soared high into the sky toward the setting

sun, which flowed across the heavens like a spill of red wine and liquid gold.

Higher she flew, blending with cool, pure air, a crystalline shimmer among the wisps of clouds. Descending from a cloud above her, the spirit *Wambli* joined her in soaring across the sky as they honored the end of day, the beginning of night.

She opened her mouth and sang, her clear, pure voice spreading joy across the earth on the wings of dusk. *Mahipiya,* Spirit of the Heavens, Clouds and Sky, had gifted the world with a sunset of bold, harsh color. No soft, pretty pastels to lead the land gently into night. Tonight, dusk struck as a raging fire across the sky, lining the edges of the puffy white clouds with gold and red.

In silence, the two spirits, one dark as the forthcoming night, the other nearly translucent, floated on the unseen breath of *Tate.*

Far below them, the prairie rolled, rising, then dipping into shallow valleys where streams of blue water sparkled in the waning light. Movement below caught her eye. Silver swung around and watched as a young woman passed beneath her.

The woman's feet dragged over the grass. She walked with shoulders hunched and head bent as though a great ball of weight made moving difficult. Silver Star sighed sadly, her joy fading into worry as she dropped gracefully from the sky.

Humans had spirit helpmates to guide them in their lives' paths. Many years ago, Silver had walked beside the child this woman had once been, had watched out for her, talked to her, taught her.

But no more. Renny's eyes were now blind to the spirit helpers who walked beside her, her ears unhearing of whispered words of comfort, her soul cut off from beliefs that had once given her great joy.

Renny no longer believed in what she could not see or touch. Her faith lay in shattered ruins.

Tate's touch curled around Silver. "She walks her path unaware, my friend. The human does not see."

"Or remember," sighed Silver Star as she studied the red-haired woman standing at the foot of two graves. Her attention was so fixed on the tall wooden cross that she didn't see a tiny bird hovering to her left, its tiny wings beating so fast they blurred.

The hummingbird rose a bit higher, staring intently at the human, willing the human to turn and see. But the troubled woman turned her back on the ruby-throated bird.

Silver watched Renny O'Brien shove her hands deep into her worn denim pants and back away. The tiny bird hovered for a few more minutes before giving up.

Silver shook her mane sadly as she watched the bird fade from sight. To have a hummingbird fly close enough to see into its eyes was an honor.

The tiny bird represented tireless joy and the nectar of life. Those who saw it were reminded to find joy in all they did and sing it out.

Silver Star drew in a deep breath as she focused again on the young woman. Renny's aura was a dull, sad gray. Much of Silver's joy in the evening vanished as she too became sad.

Renny had lost the joy in her life; she no longer celebrated the miracle of life as she once had done. Silver snorted out a breath of distress. She clearly remembered Renny as a child. She'd been drawn to the small human girl and her zest for living.

Even as a captive of the *Ikce Wicasa*, the Natural Humans, the free wild people, Renny O'Brien had found joy in living and learning about a life so different from her own.

"*Weshawee* no longer sees as she once saw. Or believes," Silver commented, her voice filled with sadness and regret.

Tate's gentle breath of air ruffled Silver's mane. "Then it is time for her to return to the world she once loved. Only there will she find the child within."

"Without the child within, she will never find true joy." Silver pawed at the air. "Many times I have tried to talk to her but she no longer sees me or hears my voice."

"Then you must *make* her see and hear you," *Tate* said. The words vibrated, a low rumble of sound. A burst of wind swept over the grass, bending the tall blades.

Silver felt her fellow spirit's frustration. She knew it would be up to her to bring this woman back to a world of light and knowing, of happiness and much needed inner peace. It was a task that would not be easy. Healing wounds of the heart and soul was never simple.

As a girl, *Weshawee* had once been full of life and energy with a child's simple acceptance and innocence. But that child was long gone. *Weshawee* was no more. The girl-child had become a woman who'd forsaken the child within.

Sighing, Silver dropped back to earth gracefully and fell in step with her human charge. She called out in a compelling voice that was light as air and rich as cream. Each evening she tried unsuccesfully to reach Renny.

Tonight was no different. *Weshawee* still did not hear, did not see her spirit helper walking beside her, eager to help guide her steps on the path of life.

Silver rose up onto her hind legs and tossed her mane as she came back down onto all fours. Silver's heavenly blue gaze turned thoughtful as she studied her charge. After a moment she smiled.

"I am life. Life flows within me," she murmured, determined to use all she had, all that she was. She'd vowed to help this human find the spirit of the lost child and carve herself a niche in the world.

Only then would she know the peace and happiness she'd once known as *Weshawee*, adopted into the Sioux family.

The beauty of day cocooning into night went unnoticed by Renny O'Brien. The colors in the carpet of grass softened, trees and brush faded into one another and the bold sunset faded slowly from the sky.

Night held its own beauty; shadows, shapes and sounds and hidden treasures. Standing completely still, as frozen in place as a majestic hundred-year-old oak, Renny became part of the night.

With her sight and thoughts turned inward, she was oblivious to the changing of the guard. She didn't hear the soft rustle of a mouse peeking at her from beneath the tall grass, didn't see the unblinking stare of the owl above her head.

She only saw the cross bearing the names of her parents. Dropping to her knees, she brushed her hand over the blanket of grass and wildflowers that she and her siblings had planted. In the shade of the lone oak, the bodies of her parents rested.

Around her, nature began tuning up her orchestra, the soft whirs, buzzes and chirps sounding off as if answering to roll call.

Renny no longer had use for the magic of night or the beauty and power surging around her. Feeling a slight tickle on her cheek, she reached up to brush away the irritant. It came again; something skimming against her cheek, like an invisible hand caressing her face.

Scowling, Renny ran her palms over her hair to smooth back any strands that might have come loose from the single thick braid hanging down her back. The faintly irritating and annoying sensation persisted.

Jerking around, she waved her hands. It stopped, replaced by a feeling that she was not alone. She narrowed her eyes, repressing the urge to move deeper into the shadows.

"Stupid," she muttered as she scanned the gentle rolling prairie surrounding the O'Brien homestead. All seemed normal, quiet. Even peaceful. There was nothing to fear out here.

Renny absently rubbed at a small lump on one side of her head. The healing scab and the dull, throbbing pain were reminders of the injury she'd received several weeks ago.

Taking a deep breath, Renny inhaled and exhaled several times. Her close call with death was making her edgy.

"They are safe. We are all safe," she murmured, hoping that by hearing the words spoken aloud she might believe them.

In her mind, she knew that the danger to her and her family was gone. There was no reason to be afraid. But she was.

Clenching her jaw tight, she fought the anxious fluttering of her heart and the nervous waves roiling in her stomach as she turned away from the wooden cross and walked backward for a few steps. Her gaze scanned the shadows creeping across the land.

Once, a short time ago, she'd loved the night, enjoyed the quiet and calm, and found its secrets intriguing. Nowadays, she was afraid of what she could not see or control.

No matter how many times she told herself that the trouble of the last year was gone, she was afraid not to be afraid. She remained watchful, and fearful.

Fear kept one's instincts sharp and honed. The day she'd buried her parents, she'd vowed to be vigilant, to protect her siblings from harm. But she'd failed. And they'd all suffered.

Renny rubbed her eyes, then dropped her arms

down. She was so tired; weary of heart and mind and soul. Reaching the river, she kicked angrily at a large stone. It hit the stream with a splash.

"There is nothing more to fear," she whispered. The lure of the gently moving water tempted her for just a moment into sitting on her favorite rock.

She used to come here, to sit and daydream the evening away. It had been her father's favorite spot and many an evening, the two of them would sneak out of the house to come sit in the quiet solitude.

Her father was gone now, murdered with her mother a year ago, yet Renny still came out here trying to find peace and solitude, seeking comfort in her cherished memories. She had always loved the outdoors, especially the peace and quiet of nighttime.

She rubbed her arms vigorously as images of being ambushed along the river a few short weeks ago intruded, keeping her from relaxing and enjoying what she'd once treasured. She closed her eyes, her hands forming tight fists. While traveling along the river, she and her family had been attacked. She'd taken a blow to the head, her brother Matthew had been shot, and both of them were left for dead while two of their younger siblings were kidnapped.

Her breathing growing harsh, Renny quickened her pace along a path that led not back toward home, but away. She couldn't face her brothers and sisters with mounting fear and anxiety. Her siblings knew her well and would sense it. And worry over her.

She was the strong one, the one they all looked to for advice and help. She could not allow them to see her fear. Over and over she'd reassured them all that they were now safe.

If only she could believe her own words, but fear for the safety and happiness of her siblings remained stronger than the voice of reason.

Renny followed the gushing river. Framed by shades of green, scattered bushes and tall cottonwoods still drooping with their cattail-like blooms of pink, this spot had always been one of her favorite places to come and think.

The beauty and quiet had always provided peace and contentment. But not today.

Climbing up a small rise in the land, she caught sight of home. Seeing the tendrils of smoke curling lazily from the chimney, the antics of the horses in the corrals, should have brought a happy glow to her heart. But not today. Nothing seemed to ease the ache that had settled deep within her. It was a wound that refused to heal.

Wearily, she trudged across the damp earth, making her way toward home. Toward what had been her home, until she'd decided to move out. As she drew nearer, her gaze fastened on the closed door of the cabin.

"Open," she breathed. She needed for her young siblings to spot her from the windows and come running out to greet her.

But as it had been for the last week, there was no movement from the house. Reaching the bottom step leading up to a wide porch, she heard laughter. She paused to listen to the giggles and high-pitched shouts of glee.

She forced a smile and opened the door, praying to find relief from a deep ache that hurt worse than her head wound.

Renny stepped inside. Her smile died slowly when no one appeared to realize she was home. Mattie was mixing flour for biscuits. Caitie and Kealan wrestled on the braided carpet with Reed, Mattie's new husband of only a few weeks.

Nine-year-old Daire sat in the chair that had once belonged to their father, hooting with laughter and calling out encouragement to his younger brother and sister. The large room, the heart of the house, rang with laughter, love and warmth, yet the scene chilled Renny. Inside, she felt as though a ball of ice had lodged in her very soul.

Renny felt her eyes dull and fought resentment and anger. She tried swallowing her disappointment and hurt. Before Reed had come into their lives, Renny had clung to the exuberant welcome of her siblings after a long day working the land. It got her through the next day. And the next.

No matter how tired she was, *she,* Renny, had always found a bit of energy in reserve to play and wrestle with her much younger siblings.

A small sound of distress must have escaped because Mattie turned to her.

"Don't blame them," she said softly. A small smudge of flour streaked one cheek.

Renny walked over to her sister, younger by only a year. Using the hem of Mattie's apron, she wiped the flour from her face. "For someone who is blind, you see an awful lot." There was no anger in her voice. Although she was her sister by marriage, Mattie had been Renny's best friend since she'd been nine and Mattie eight. They'd been soul sisters before their parents had met and married.

"You know I don't blame them." Renny sighed. "For a while I was afraid they'd never laugh or play like this again. I'm grateful that they've recovered as well as they have and are getting back to being themselves."

Renny meant every word. Sights like the one before her meant that time would heal the wounds fate had inflicted on them all.

Her gaze rested on Caitie, who still woke screaming in the night. Her kidnappers had paid—with their lives—but there were times when Renny felt that death was not punishment enough for those who'd brought death and terror into their family.

Mattie stroked her hand along Renny's arm. "The children love you. Nothing has changed, my sister."

Watching Reed rise up on his knees to give a big roar as he grabbed Caitie and hugged her until she squealed, watching Kealan jump onto his back as he tried to wrestle his much older, and much beloved brother-in-law, Renny shook her head. Everything had changed that day, nearly a year ago, when she'd found the bodies of her parents, murdered, shot in cold blood.

She forced lightness to her voice. "Don't fret, Mattie. I understand. Truly. I'm so happy for you. All of you. Reed is good to them and they love him."

Compared to what Mattie had suffered through, Renny had no business complaining. Shortly after losing their parents, Mattie had gotten married. Fate had cruelly taken her husband of only a few short hours.

Trapped in a burning barn, he'd died trying to get Mattie out. Mattie had survived, barely. But she hadn't come away unscathed. A blow to her head had left her blind.

Yet Mattie remained strong, never growing bitter. She'd adapted to her limitations, refusing to be a burden. Renny had admired her sister then, and still did. She was grateful that Mattie and Reed—and all of her siblings—were safe, loved and content.

All was right with their world. Or nearly, Renny corrected, thinking of Reed's need to return to the home of his parents, who were taking care of his children. But for now, all was as it should be. It was only her own life that seemed so bleak at the moment.

Mattie gave Renny's dangling braid a tweak. "Stop torturing yourself, my sister."

Renny rolled her eyes. She'd never been able to hide her thoughts and feelings from Mattie.

"I saw that," Mattie said.

Renny couldn't help the small laugh. "Saw what?" Mattie smiled back. Mattie knew Renny so well, she didn't need to see Renny to know her thoughts or feelings.

Mattie lifted a hand to Renny's face. She stroked softly. "Your turn will come."

Renny's eyes widened as she searched her sister's features. The small smile made her shiver. She might respect and believe in her sister's gift of sight, but it still could sometimes startle her. Besides, the last thing she had time for at the moment was a man. Her eyes narrowed as she thought of one man in particular.

"I'm fine. Happy already." To prove it, she leaped into the fray, reaching down to tickle Kealan, who was on Reed's back. "Gotcha!"

Kealan fell off of Reed. He giggled and squirmed to get away from Renny.

Caitie squealed loudly and flung herself at Renny. Renny scooped up her baby sister, swung her around three times before burying her face in her Caitie's soft, silky curls.

"I love you, Caitie-girl," she whispered.

Caitie leaned back, framed her big sister's face between her small hands and grinned. "I love you too, Renny. Will you play dolls with me?"

"Dolls! Yuck!" Kealan picked himself up off the floor and stood in front of Renny.

Though he kept insisting that he was getting too old for hugs and such, Renny swooped down, yanked him off his feet and tossed him over her shoulder, much to Caitie's delight.

"What say we go dump him in the water trough, Caitie my girl?"

The O'Brien house once again erupted with laughter and good-natured shouts and teases. Finally, Renny set Caitie and Kealan back down so she could help Mattie finish preparing the evening meal.

Family was important to Renny. Her siblings were all she had in the world, all she held dear to her heart, yet throughout the evening, Renny felt lost and alone.

When the fire died out, Caitie and Kealan, who were both yawning sleepily, were ushered up the ladder into the loft with Reed. Hearing their eager pleas for bedtime stories, Renny once again felt deserted. Just as she had felt as a young child, abandoned by the father who'd preferred his military life to that of staying home with his young daughter. It hadn't been until her father remarried that Renny finally had the security and love she'd craved.

But murder had thrown her life into a crazy spin. It was bad enough to resent her parents for dying and then dealing with the guilt that came with those thoughts, but now she felt abandoned by her own brothers and sisters.

Her safe, comfortable existence had been shattered, and Renny was afraid that she'd never be able to pick up the pieces and glue them back together.

Chapter Two

Twilight settled around Sheriff Tyler like a comfortably worn flannel shirt. He stood beneath the spreading boughs of a lone oak, a dark figure in the purpling hues of dusk. The light of day faded. A hush settled over the land as though Mother Nature held her breath.

Dusk was a time of change, a shifting of activity. The energy of the day was collected, gathered as to a woman's bosom, then released back into the heavens to create a climax of shattered light.

Tyler embraced the change taking place around him, just as he did each morning when the sun peeked over the horizon and he had a few quiet moments to consider what that day would bring. He welcomed change. Change kept a man alert and on his toes. It made him stronger, smarter and vigilant, whereas a man who never varied his routine or took time out to embrace the new grew stale and old of heart and mind.

It was for this reason alone that he'd taken on

the responsibility and role of lawman over that of farmer. Though he dealt with his share of the mundane—drunks, fights between a man and his wife, petty thefts—he was never bored.

He smiled sadly. A year ago, he'd been deputy; his brother Grant had been sheriff. But Grant was gone now—a not-so-welcome change. Change wasn't always good, wasn't always what we wished for, but Tyler was of the belief that man must deal with the hand he was dealt. So he now embraced his new role as sheriff for the small town of Pheasant Gully.

Aside from his own outlook, and the need for law and order, he was also able to keep his brother alive in this way—by combining his brother's vision with his own to make a difference in their world.

Grant had been content with keeping things the same, enforcing the letter of the law while maintaining a distance between himself and others. Tyler, on the other hand, enjoyed the aspect of meeting both friend and stranger alike each day, seeing what life created and how each person played their hand.

Dealing with petty problems didn't aggravate him as it had Grant, yet all the paperwork required of his office drove him crazy, which was why they'd made a good team. Until his brother was shot and killed in the line of duty.

He drew in a deep breath. Change. He'd survived. Love and his belief in what he stood for had gotten him through the fog of grief. The very predictable nature of his town had restored his faith in mankind.

He scratched his chin. Yep, he could predict the daily routines of most, from the eldest to the youngest. He made it his duty to know the people of Pheasant Gully. Only by knowing them could he protect them.

His fingers stopped scratching. His nails dug into his jaw. Eyes straining, he peered across the dark meadow. He knew everyone well, could anticipate behavior and reactions with a high degree of certainty—with one exception.

Renait O'Brien.

Tyler shifted, his calm demeanor giving way to irritation as he shoved his hands into his pockets and turned to stare out into the darkening shadows.

He never knew what to expect from Renny, except trouble. And tonight was no different. She was late.

Again.

Which irritated the hell out of him. He strode off into the darkness, away from town. But after a few steps, he stopped and stared around him. Last night she hadn't taken the usual path home. He'd walked out to meet her and had been left to return to town, alone with his frustration and anger.

Kicking a clump of rock and grass, he returned to the proud oak tree that graced the small meadow. A small buzz near his ear made him swipe at the air to move the insect along.

Pulling his pipe from his shirt pocket, he struck a match. The flare of light revealed strong, rugged features and hard eyes that glittered for just a moment. He had to admit, if only to himself, that dealing with Renny O'Brien could never be considered boring.

He made a rude sound in the back of his throat. In this one matter, he'd prefer some semblance of routine and conformity. And hell, while he was wishing for the impossible, he'd gladly take some respect from the hot-headed O'Brien woman, who kept him dancing on his toes like a well-trained ballerina.

The image of a small figurine spinning slowly to a tune he couldn't remember flitted across his mind. His mother used to stare at the dancing figurine that her own mother had given her. As the ballerina went 'round and 'round, she'd sometimes sigh as though with regret.

Tyler knew she'd once been a dancer with dreams of dancing for a living but had given up that dream when she married and moved west with her new husband.

The sudden *rat-a-tat-tat* of a woodpecker shattered the peace. Tyler glanced up, but the thick boughs that held hundreds of oak leaves hid the bird. The irritating racket drove away the sadness that he still felt when he thought of his mother, who'd passed away when he'd been on the cusp between boy and man.

Bending down, he picked up a small pebble and tossed it into the branches, not to hit the bird but to drive it away. If he had to stand here and stew, he preferred to do it in silence.

Once again he scanned the darkening meadow. There was no doubt in his mind that Renny was deliberately provoking him by returning to town late.

Tyler folded his arms across his chest and drew deeply from the stem of his pipe. The burning tobacco glowed hot, like the anger welling from deep inside him. He narrowed his eyes as he searched the shadows for Renny.

No sign of her. He glared at the horizon, then paced. With each passing minute his anger grew. A sting on the side of his face made him smack himself to kill the mosquito that had bit him.

"Dammit! A man outta be able to relax in his chair in the evening and not be stuck out here fighting damn bugs." He thought of his meal waiting at home for him, likely stone-cold by now.

"Should just go." But he couldn't. He'd promised Mattie that he'd make sure Renny arrived home safely each evening, even though Renny insisted that she was a grown woman and didn't need looking after. Still, she'd agreed to return to the boardinghouse at the same time, via the same route, each evening, so he and Mattie wouldn't worry.

He gave a small bark of laughter. Worrying over Renny wasn't new. Neither was waiting for her. For the fourth night in a row, Renny had changed her routine. Last night she'd arrived south of his position. Night before, she'd slipped into town much earlier, leaving him waiting for hours before he went to the boardinghouse to find that she'd once again returned without him knowing. She was going out of her way to inconvenience him.

Tyler laughed shortly. Nothing new there. Renny went out of her way to inconvenience him whenever and however she could. The woman was bull-headed, unafraid to take on the world—or him. It was a trait he admired despite himself.

Renny was well liked by everyone, always polite, kind, and helpful, except to him. Tyler stared at the pipe, eyes fixed on the glowing embers. Him, she hated.

"Never meant to hurt her," he said. Hearing the words spoken out loud didn't ease the ache in his heart. He needed Renny to forgive him, or at least attempt to understand why he'd tried to take her three young siblings from her last year.

Staring up at the stars appearing in the night sky, Tyler knew that what was done was done. There was no changing the past and, it seemed, no getting through to Renny. The woman wouldn't give him the time of day let alone sit still in his presence long enough to allow him to explain that he had just been trying to help the O'Brien family, that he couldn't stand by and watch their pride cause them to make the same mistake he and Grant had made when they'd lost their parents.

Tyler leaned back against the lone oak in the meadow and inhaled the aromatic blend of tobacco and spice. He blew a ring of smoke upward, watched it waver, then fade into nothing. Memories of other nights, in another time, another place, rolled across his mind. . . .

Harsh hacking coughs shattered the stillness. Tyler closed his eyes tight against the tears trying to burst through the fragile control of a fourteen-year-old boy trying so hard to be a man.

The creaking of a rocker on the porch stilled for one moment. He held his breath. When the coughing inside the house stopped, the rhythmic rocking began. Opening his eyes, he stared at the climbing roses just beginning to bud after the harsh winter. He sprawled lower in the porch swing.

"Ma's sleeping." A young girl with dark, golden hair stepped onto the porch, shutting the door gently behind her.

Tyler saw the gleam of tears streaking her young face. He held out his arms and caught Gracie in an awkward but comforting hug meant as much for himself as her. Over her head, he met his older brother's somber gray gaze. Death wasn't far from claiming their mother. Over the harsh winter, the same illness had taken their father.

Staring at the nearly barren vines of the climbing roses that come spring would cover the tiny porch with bloom and scent, Tyler knew his ma wouldn't make it to spring—would never again sit here on her beloved porch swing and inhale the sweet scent of blooming roses.

Tyler tightened his arms around his much younger half-sister, his hand gently stroking hair a shade lighter than his own as her tears soaked his shirt. Across from him, Grant rocked and smoked the pipe that had been their father's. Soon, very soon, the Tilly children would be on their own.

A sharp, creaky squeak brought Tyler out of his bittersweet memories. Across the meadow he spotted the schoolmarm, Miss Marley, leaving the church that doubled as schoolhouse. She was on the plump side and laden with an armful of books and tablets. The wooden stairs protested her firm pounding steps.

Out of habit, Tyler pulled out his pocket watch. Yep, precisely six. Not a minute after, not a minute before. You could tell time by Miss Marley's schedule.

And that thought reminded him why he was still standing beneath the oak tree. His stomach rumbled, reminding him that it was well past suppertime. Tyler decided that enough was enough. It was time to put an end to Renny's petty games and make her listen to him.

The schoolmarm approached. "Evening, Miss Marley," he called out. He didn't want his presence in the shadows to startle her

Eugene Marley, prim and proper in gray, stopped crisply in front of him. "Good evening, Sheriff," she said, her voice stiff and formal. She sniffed and turned her head, her way of indicating her aversion to his pipe.

He lowered the pipe, holding it behind his back. "Lovely night." Tyler eyed the stack of books and knew she'd be putting in time this evening planning her lessons.

"How are your students these days? Enjoying their new classroom?"

When the townsmen had rebuilt the church, which had burned nearly to the ground a few weeks ago, they'd added on a separate room to be used as the schoolroom during the week, and for meetings and socials when school was not in session.

Eugene Marley shuffled her load. "Restless today, Sheriff."

"Blame the weather. Day was a beaut. I imagine most of the children are eager for school to be out." He paused, smiled wickedly. "Fishin's good these days."

He'd caught three boys playing hooky from school that morning and had taken them to the church, and their stiff-as-a-board teacher himself.

Another sniff. "The boys were given extra work as punishment, and I will personally speak to their parents."

He winced. Miss Marley tolerated no misbehaving, and no interference from parents. She ran her school tighter than a military unit. Tyler remembered his own anxious, restless school days when he couldn't wait for the summer months and appreciated the teacher he'd had who'd understood the need for children to be children.

Tyler tipped his hat back. He sure as hell couldn't blame the boys for trading a day inside with their noses stuck in their books for a day of warmth and freedom. He'd done the same too many days to count.

"They are good boys," he reminded her. He knew the homesteading parents of Albert, Johnny and Harold. The boys put in long hours both before school and after. Who could blame them for playing hooky?

"It is my job to see that they are educated," Miss

Marley said. She shifted her precariously balanced load then tipped her head.

"Good evening, Sheriff. I've lessons to ready."

Tyler rolled his eyes as he watched her tromp off. It was so very tempting to call out to her and ask her to give his greetings to Mr. Potts, the postmaster. But he kept silent. The entire town knew spinster Marley and the postmaster were having an affair, but no one said anything to the clandestine couple.

Funny, he mused as he went back to his smoking, how folk went about their private business thinking no one knew their secrets. In reality, most knew. Rolling his shoulders against the trunk of the tree, Tyler peered through the darkening dusk.

Across the creek, the saws at MacKinnley's Mill went blessedly silent, which meant Mac would soon be heading down to the Lucky Lady where he went each night for a meal, a couple pints and some flirting with Molly. How long before Molly Hansen became Molly MacKinnley?

Leaning into the tree, he gave the middle of his back a good, satisfying scratch. Things were always changing. Day into night, spring into summer. Life succumbing to death.

Gone. They were all gone. Illness had taken his parents and sister from him. The bullet from a gun had robbed him of his brother, leaving him alone in the world.

Tyler tried to shake the past from his mind. Why was he feeling so melancholy tonight? He grimaced. Because he was lonely. Potts had Marley.

Molly had Mac. And he had no one but a widowed woman who cooked and cleaned for him in exchange for a place to sleep.

It wasn't the same as family. Tyler wanted what he'd grown up with: a close-knit brood of siblings.

"Easy as pie," he muttered sarcastically. "Just find yourself a woman!" Unfortunately, the only woman he wanted refused to have anything to do with him, and everyone in Pheasant Gully knew it. Even now, most knew their sheriff waited out in the meadow every evening to be sure Renny arrived safe, just as they likely knew Renny wasn't cooperating.

Didn't matter that he told folks he was just looking out for her the same as he did for them. Didn't matter that everyone knew that the O'Briens had had a spot of trouble a short while back, that several of the O'Briens had nearly been killed.

Because trouble or no, he'd be standing here, waiting and worrying. Tyler didn't care that the entire town knew what was in his heart. It didn't bother him to know that the spats he and Renny got into provided a source of amusement to all. Deep down, he knew the townsfolk would love nothing better than to see their beloved sheriff settled with one of their own.

His jaw tightened. Unfortunately for him, he knew well enough what Miss O'Brien thought of him; she certainly told him every chance she got. "Glutton for punishment," he muttered, glaring down at the pipe in his hands.

Tyler glanced back up at the darkening sky, noting that stars were starting to twinkle overhead. What was taking her so long? He stared off toward the town. Chances were that she'd slipped past him again.

Normally, she and her family ate their evening supper early so that Renny could get back to town well before dark. So where was she? Was she safely tucked away in the room she rented at Jensens' Boardinghouse? Maybe staring out of her bedroom window to where she knew he waited, smirking at the thought of her latest triumph over him.

Tyler tapped the bowl of the now-cold pipe against the tree. After emptying the ashes, he shoved the pipe into his shirt pocket and left the dark shadows of the oak. Hell with this. He'd go by the Jensens', see if Renny was there.

If she was there, if she'd deliberately left him standing out here worrying and stewing again, there'd be hell to pay.

Renny left her family to return to town much later than normal. For an hour after supper she'd put off leaving until Mattie, finally realizing how late it was, started fretting that the sheriff would be worried.

Her horse stopped to lower his head to a patch of green grass. Renny let him have his snack. She wasn't in any hurry. What did she care if Sheriff Tyler waited up all night for her?

Renny let out a frustrated breath. She didn't care about him, but she did love her sister and had finally left to keep Mattie from worrying and Reed from insisting on riding back with her.

Dusk had settled over the land like a soft, furry blanket. All was silent around her except the jingle of harness. Tipping her head back, Renny let her mind wander and left the horse to walk his own pace. She wasn't in any hurry, didn't have anything waiting for her.

She made a face as she glanced up into the darkening sky. Not true. She had the Jensen sisters waiting for her. They always waited up for her, even when she told them they didn't need to.

The two sisters owned the boardinghouse where she rented a room. It was a nice room, the house cozy and clean, even if it was a bit cluttered with furniture and trinkets. She couldn't even find fault with the food. It just wasn't home.

Glancing over her shoulder, Renny stared at the still-visible glow of candles and lantern light from the log cabin windows. The sight beckoned, tempting her to change direction and return home.

Caitie and Kealan would love to have their eldest sister spend the night in the loft. Even Daire teased that things were too quiet at night without Renny and her silly stories.

The urge to return to her home, to her brothers and sisters, was so strong, it was all she could do not to tug the reins and turn the horse around. It was better this way, she reminded herself. The choice had been hers to move out of the cabin and into the boardinghouse. She'd wanted to give the newly wed Mattie and Reed time alone as man and wife. It wasn't like she didn't see her family each and every day. They were together all day. It was only nighttime that they were apart.

So why was she so unhappy?

Renny gripped the pommel on her saddle so hard, her knuckles turned white. Whatever the cause, her mood was fast turning from self-pity to something foul. She hated feeling like her life was caught between grass and hay.

Days were a plentiful harvest while nights made her feel like she was a weak blade of spring grass struggling to thrive and grow in hard, frozen ground.

Renny rubbed her eyes tiredly. She was exhausted. Each day seemed longer and harder to get through. Inside, she felt raw and empty. Though she went through the motions of living, she felt as though she was barely existing. Life was something she endured, not enjoyed. She hadn't for a year now.

Turning her head, Renny stared out into total darkness. She could no longer see the welcoming glow of light and warmth spilling from her family's home. Resentment slid through the growing crack in her heart. No one had followed her out to see her off or run after her to beg her to stay, not like when she'd first left her home.

Caitie and Kealan had been so upset at first, and though Renny was glad that they'd adjusted and accepted Reed as a father figure, she couldn't help feeling the tiniest bit hurt.

For the last year she'd been the authority figure: both mother and father. That she could be so easily replaced was a bitter pill to swallow.

"Snap out of it," she muttered. Her family still loved her. But need her? That was different. Her siblings had once relied heavily on her. It had been her strength and determination that had held them together.

"And they are still together," she whispered into the warm breeze. She felt more than heard the low hum of wind. Strands of hair floated around her face. She blinked rapidly.

After having to deal with the grief that consumed her siblings, she'd vowed to keep her family together. They'd desperately needed each other, and as much normalcy as she could provide. And that, she knew, was the crux of her unhappiness. She still needed her brothers and sisters, but they appeared to no longer need her. Not like before.

Renny hated herself for the resentment and feelings of betrayal. She hated what her life had become.

Empty.

Reaching two tall cottonwoods that seemed to be twisted together as though lovers, Renny veered to the right and fought the urge to sit on the riverbank and have a good cry.

Tears were useless, a waste of energy. Tears wouldn't bring back her parents, or give Mattie back her sight. Tears changed nothing and Renny, so much like her own father, didn't believe in wasting her time or energy.

Nothing could undo the past and make things go back to the way they had been. A sob fought its way up to the back of her throat, but Renny pushed it back down. It lodged in her throat, a hard ball that felt like it would burst through her skin.

Death gives birth to life. Birth is hope, and hope comes from despair.

Renny whipped her head around but saw no one. The voice seemed so real. Familiar even.

You are not alone. The comforting whisper came again, followed by a wave of warmth that seemed to encase her and chase away the chill in her soul. Once again, she felt the sensation of something brushing her cheek—something soft, gentle. Something loving.

A strange feeling swept over and through her. She felt calm. Loved. Comforted. Shaking her head vigorously, fearing that she was losing her mind, she spurred her horse into a trot.

"I am alone," she shouted into the night sky. "Nothing good comes from death." What was could never be as good as what should have been. Not for her.

Death brings change.

"No! No! No—"

A gust of wind came from nowhere. It whipped around her, shoved her shouted denial back down her throat.

Change brings growth. The voice slammed against her, through her, louder, demanding to be heard. It came from nowhere yet everywhere. Whirling around, clutching the reins tightly, Renny searched the area. Beneath her, the horse danced nervously with ears pricked forward, eyes wide and wild.

Dropping the reins, Renny covered her ears with her palms, pressing hard until all she heard was a muffled roar. She refused to hear words spoken in the wind. Refused to acknowledge their meaning and chose to turn her back on her once-held beliefs of spirits and the spirit world.

That part of her life had died with her Sioux stepmother. Once she'd believed. Once she'd embraced that world. But no longer. Now she relied only upon herself and what she could see. And control.

"I want no more change." She spat the words into the night, her voice low, fierce and defiant.

It is time for Weshawee *to grow!*

The command struck, loud and harsh, with power enough to make her gasp. For just a moment, Renny felt as though she'd been struck dead center by a jagged bolt of lightning. Heat filled her as the air around her seemed to crackle with energy.

Trembling, she hugged herself tightly as she stared up at the heavens. There were no clouds, no flashes of light. Fear turned the burning heat into ice and she shivered. For a moment she felt frozen, unable to move or think.

Believe.

The soft plea jerked Renny from her frozen state. Once, she'd believed in the unseen. She'd trusted in the gods and spirits of man and earth to care for her and her family but they'd failed to protect her parents or any of them from the horrors of the last year. Mattie was blind, the youngsters tormented by nightmares.

"Never! Never again will I believe." Renny jerked hard on the reins, startling her already spooked horse. The horse reared, then lunged forward. Caught unawares, Renny bounced up, came down hard and slid off the back of the gelding, landing flat on her back on the grassy ground.

Chapter Three

Glaring up into the glittering night sky, Renny calmed herself, drawing air back into her lungs. Beneath her, she felt the tremble of the earth as her horse galloped away. "Wonderful! A perfect ending to the day." Tired and disgusted with herself, Renny pushed herself up, got to her feet and started walking.

A short while later, she reached the meadow on the edge of town. Beneath the glow of the night sky, she saw the whitewashed church rising out of the darkness. Beyond that, the town lay bathed in soft glowing light. She stopped, and scanned the shadows.

He was there, waiting for her. Waiting to hear what had taken her so long. But what could she say? Who *had* she been fighting with? "Must have fallen asleep." It was the only acceptable explanation.

She shook her head and shoved her hands down hard onto her hips. Disgust weaseled through her. Not only had she fallen asleep and lost her seat upon her horse, but she'd forgotten to skirt around the meadow in order to avoid the one person guaranteed to worsen her mood.

Sighing, Renny considered her options. She was in no mood to see or speak to Sheriff Tyler if he was still lying in wait for her. She'd just sneak around to the other side of the church, follow the creek that ran around to the back of the boardinghouse and avoid Sheriff Tyler—pain in the ass, thorn in her side, slime stuck to her heel.

She heard the sound of a harness jiggling. Peering into the dark, she gave a soft whistle. Had her horse stopped to eat?

What luck. She took a step forward. "Come on, my sweet boy. You've had time enough to eat." She was relieved that her horse had not arrived at the stable without her. Now no one would be out looking for her, and it was a sure bet if her horse had shown up riderless, Frank, the boy in charge of caring for the horses each evening, would hightail it to the sheriff. She hurried forward, then stopped dead in her tracks when an amused voice addressed her.

"Figured it'd be a cold day in hell before you called me your sweet boy, Miss O'Brien."

The amused voice startled Renny. "Damn!" She kicked at some leaves in the dirt and glared at the heavens.

"Not a very ladylike greeting, Miss O'Brien." Anger booted the humor from his voice.

Renny eyed the shadows of the church. She'd

even taken one sidestep when Tyler emerged from the shadows. "Don't even think of it."

"Think of what?" Renny asked. When she came abreast of Tyler and his horse, she kept going, forcing him to wheel his mount around and follow. She grabbed the reins to her horse. Behind her, she heard Tyler dismount.

"Renny, you all right?"

"I'm fine," she snapped.

"Stop a minute. What happened? Why did your horse return without you?" Sheriff Tyler caught up with her.

Renny quickened her steps. "Nothing for you to be concerned about."

"Dammit, woman, stop for a minute!" Frustration fused with anger and worry. His voice was hard, edgy.

Renny ignored him, keeping her gaze trained on the soft glow of light coming from the town. The quiet, gentle bath of light eased some of the tightness coiling inside her. While not her home, it was her town. People she knew, cared about. Many whom she called friend. Not so the man dogging her heels.

"Not in the mood, *Troll.*" She grinned when she heard his sharp intake of breath.

"Dammit, Renny. I said stop." Tyler reached out and snagged her arm, swinging her around.

Just as quickly, as though this were a well-rehearsed dance movement, Renny whipped her own body into motion and twisted free from Tyler.

Glaring up at him, hands clenched into fists, he suddenly seemed like a good target for her pent-up resentments and frustrations.

"Missed your true calling in life, Sheriff. Should've been a nanny," she sneered. She gave a couple of clucks and heard him draw in a deep angry breath. He hated it when she clucked at him, reminding him that she thought him a bothersome mother hen. She stepped around him.

Tyler's long-legged stride easily kept pace with her shorter, stomping steps across the meadow. Once more, he reached out and took hold of her. "Dammit, Renny, answer me. Are you hurt?"

Tyler's large hands clamped over her shoulders. This time he was ready. He held her gently yet firmly, both hands cupping her shoulders to keep her from twisting away.

Renny stepped toward him. "Go away," she said quietly, her eyes as wild as a summer storm.

Tyler, ready for her move, pulled her hard against him to keep her from delivering a well-placed kick. "Why the hell do you have to be so damn stubborn? A simple answer is all I need from you!"

Renny opened her mouth to deliver another wrathy comment but a wave of warmth that rushed through her body made her mind go blank. She blinked. The top of her head was level with his broad shoulders. Out of nowhere came the urge to rest her head on those shoulders, to have those thick, strong arms close gently around her, holding her, keeping her warm and safe.

A long, heartfelt sigh escaped. What would it be like to feel safe and cherished instead of overworked, worried and insecure? So much weight rested on her narrow shoulders when his were so much wider, stronger.

She swayed slightly, felt his hands tighten gently, the back of his arm brushing against her cheek as he held on to her. "Renny?"

The soft, tender way he spoke her name broke Renny free from the trance she'd fallen into. In the starlight, Tyler's badge of office, pinned to his black leather vest, gleamed. That small silver star carried with it authority . . . and power.

Her gaze lifted to Tyler's. His eyes glittered in the dark. Stars twinkled above his head, in his eyes, on his chest.

"Renny . . ." He whispered her name, his lips relaxing, a warm breath of air fanning her forehead. His hands slid around to her back.

Renny heard the plea and responded. Her hands lifted, fingers gripping the edges of his leather vest as she swayed closer. "So tired," she murmured. She closed her eyes.

"I know, baby. I know." Tyler gathered her close.

The aroma of tobacco, and warm leather engulfed Renny. Her head dropped to his chest, her hands sliding up.

The sharp stab of a tin star at her chin made her jerk her head up. The loud oath as her head connected with Tyler's chin snapped Renny back to reality.

This man was her enemy. She stared at him

dumbly, wondering what had come over her. Sheriff Tyler was no friend; he had no shoulder to offer comfort or anything else. He was a liar; a betrayer.

"Get away from me," she ordered, all softness and tiredness gone from her voice. His gaze shone silvery-light in the darkness.

"Dammit, Renny. I worry about you. I just want to help." His voice sounded as tired as she felt. He let her go, dropping his hands to his sides, but he didn't step away or take his eyes from hers.

Unnerved by the genuine worry in his voice, Renny stepped back, blaming her own momentary weakness on the tide of loneliness sweeping though her.

Digging deep, she found the ragged edges of her anger and pulled them around her like a child snuggling in a favorite blanket. This man, she had to remember, had promised to be a friend.

After the murder of her parents, he'd promised to help her and her siblings. But he'd lied. He'd misused the power of his badge to try and take the little ones from her.

And even now, when she'd proven that she could take care of her own, even though her sister was married to Tyler's deputy, he still stuck his nose into their business.

Renny tipped her head back. "Just once I'd like to arrive back in town without having to see or speak to you, *Sheriff.*"

Tyler folded his arms across his chest and rocked back on his heels. "Seems you did just that yestereve when you snuck in without letting me know you were back." Anger whipped the tenderness from his voice. Fury, thick and mean, rained down on her head.

Renny's lips curled, anger and resentment her shield. She held up one hand and ticked off finger by finger. "You are not my father, nor are you my mother or brother or nanny."

She bent the last finger so her hand formed a tight fist. "Lastly, you are not my keeper."

Her nostrils flared as she struck both fists down onto her hips. "You are nothing to me, Sheriff. I come and go as I please."

Tyler let out a frustrated sound as he ran one hand through his thick hair.

"You know I promised both Reed and Mattie that I'd watch out for you now that you're living in town." His voice turned almost menacing.

Renny shrugged, not a bit afraid of him. For all his nagging, irritating and bossy ways, he was not a woman abuser. She could stand up to him and speak her mind.

"Your problem, not mine. Now leave me alone." Tyler's reminder that she no longer lived with her family deepened Renny's resentment, sharpened her pain and confusion.

Tyler fell into step with her once more, a shadow that refused to be banished. "Can't, Renny." His voice went soft with concern. "Let me help."

Something inside her longed to throw off the cloak of mistrust and share her fears with him. She wanted someone to hold her the way Reed held

Mattie. Part of her desperately needed to be sheltered and cared for.

More though, she needed someone to confide in, someone to share her concerns, fears and worries. Someone with whom to share the remnants of her dreams.

She slid a glare at Tyler, hating the way she eyed those shoulders and wide, welcoming chest. She'd fit nicely against him and knew that if she gave in, he'd protect her, warm her, comfort her. If she gave him the chance, he'd take the burden from her shoulders.

And how she wanted what he so willingly offered.

That realization shocked Renny to her core. Fighting the weakness creeping through her, Renny made herself remember the last time she'd listened to the man walking beside her.

Sighing beside her, Tyler stopped near the edge of the meadow. "One day you'll trust me."

Renny squared her shoulders. "Trust?" She spat on the ground then glared hard at the man beside her. "Did that once and look where it got me. No thanks, *Sheriff*."

Tyler threw his arms into the air and paced in front of her, oblivious to the volume of his voice and the fact that most homes and stores were now dark. "Renny, I was wrong! How many times do you want to hear me say it? I. Was. Wrong!"

Renny and Tyler stared at one another, each angry, each frustrated.

Tyler took off his hat and slapped his thigh. "I won't just go away, Renny. I made a promise."

Renny laughed without humor. "And we all know how you keep your promises. Well, guess what. I'll relieve you of that promise." She held up her right hand, palm out, as Tyler started to protest.

"Oh please. I insist.

"I, Renait O'Brien, do thereby relieve Sheriff Trowbrydge Tyler Thompkins Tilly of his nanny duties. You have my permission to go and find someone else to bother."

Renny took a deep breath, smirking at the look of fury darkening Tyler's face. The sheriff absolutely hated his full, legal name. She shot him a haughty glare. "For all that I care, you can go to hell. Just go. Away. Far, far away."

Renny hurried forward. Once before she'd foolishly shared her fears and worries with this man. She hadn't known how she was going to support and care for her family. Worried about harm coming to any of them, she'd asked Tyler for help on behalf of her siblings.

A hard ball of hate swelled inside her. Sheriff Tyler had listened to her, soothed her, then stabbed her in the back. She'd never forget the shock of having him turn those confessions and fears against her—against them all. She'd learned from Sheriff Tyler not to trust him, or anyone outside her family, ever again.

Her foot slid into a mushy pile. "Cow dung," she sneered, stopping to scrape the sole of her shoe along the grass. "Beneath me and beside me."

"Heard that, Renny. Someday that viper tongue

of yours is going to get you into a load of trouble a lot more smelly than what you stepped in."

Renny slid Tyler a hard glare. "I'd take trouble over having to deal with you, *Troll.*"

Tyler stepped close. His face dark and somber, eyes sad yet hot. "Someday you are going to push me too far, Renait."

Renny jabbed her finger into Tyler's chest. "Then get the hint, *Troll*. Don't need you, don't want you, just stay away from me. I know the way home." An ache of sadness slashed deep inside her. Home was back the way she'd come. She continued down the middle of Main Street.

Like a fly drawn to sweat, the constant pain in her backside ignored her bad temper. His smooth, silent stride contrasted sharply with her snapping steps, irritating her further.

In front of the now darkened mercantile, Tyler asked, "What will it take to prove to you that I care about you? All of you."

The scent of tobacco cloaking the man reminded her sharply of her father, of family and her own unhappiness. "There is nothing you can do," she whispered as the faint glow of lanterns in the second story windows above Tyler framed his tall, big-as-a-barn figure. The black-rimmed hat he wore cast his face in deep shadow.

Here was a man who rarely needed the guns strapped to his hips or the authority of the star pinned to his vest. His daunting size and looks were enough to keep both visitors and citizens of Pheasant Gully walking the straight and narrow.

But not her. Her breath came fast and furious. She saw through him, saw the controlling man no one else seemed to see. She was furious that he could so easily rile her and make her lose control. "Save your help and concern for the fools who want it."

Then she ran, from the man and the weakness within her that made her long to slide into his arms and accept the security he offered.

Frustrated beyond belief, Sheriff Tyler stalked up the boardwalk, shoved himself through the door to his office and threw himself down into his chair.

"Damn woman," he muttered, stacking his feet on top of the desk. "What will it take?" he asked as he snatched his hat off his head and tossed it onto his desk.

His encounters with Renait O'Brien were becoming increasingly frustrating. The more he tried to befriend her, help her and even apologize and admit that he'd been wrong, the more she ripped at him with her razor-sharp tongue.

"Is that you, Sheriff?" The clear, sweet voice came from the back hall that led to his private quarters.

"Yes, it's me, Maze."

Tyler pulled his feet off his desk when the woman who cooked and cleaned for room and board entered. Maze was a small, gently rounded woman. Her silvery hair was tucked loosely into a bun on top of her head with wisps of hair forming a halo around her face. She was the grandmother he'd never had.

She walked over to his desk and set down a tray. "You missed supper, Sheriff. I kept it warm for you."

He sighed. "Couldn't be helped."

"No, I suppose not," she said, her blue eyes twinkling at him.

"You wouldn't laugh at a man at his wit's end, would you, Maze?"

Maze pulled a large, cloth napkin from her pocket and handed it to Tyler. "That would be quite rude, Sheriff. Especially since you've been so very kind to me."

"Don't see how I got by without you," he said, watching as Maze scooped up his hat and hung it on the peg beside the door. The luckiest day of his life was when this woman showed up in town a few weeks ago, alone, having lost her family while heading west.

He'd felt sorry for her and had offered her a room until she figured out where to go. It hadn't taken him long to discover just what a jewel he had.

"She get back safely?" Maze's voice trembled ever so slightly with suppressed laughter.

Tyler eyed the heaped plate. His belly rumbled in response to the hunk of beef, the mound of creamy potatoes and carrots, all smothered in a rich brown gravy. Thick slabs of buttered bread completed the meal.

"She's home," he offered. He picked up the fork and stabbed a tender carrot. "Horse threw her, though. Came back on its own. Thought I was gonna have to go find her."

"Is she hurt?"

Tyler shook his head and attacked the meat next. "Just her pride," he said. "Woman's too hard-headed," he added, but that wasn't true. Just a month ago she'd been attacked, and suffered a hard blow to her head that could have killed her. Scared him nearly out of his mind.

"You going to eat that, or just stare at it?"

Maze's gentle voice washed over him, calming his pounding heart. "She's gonna be the death of me," he admitted as he popped the carrot into his mouth.

"Mmm, absolutely wonderful," he said. Hunger overrode frustration as he dug into the plate full of food.

"Don't know what I did to deserve you, Maze, but you are heaven-sent!"

Maze laughed softly. "Never know what life holds for us, Sheriff. Enjoy your meal." She left the room.

Tyler frowned at the truth of her words. He'd never imagined that he'd fall for such a stubborn, willful, vexing female.

Women were drawn to him; he'd never had trouble getting whatever woman he fancied. Until meeting Renny. There were plenty here in Pheasant Gully to choose from. But no, he had to go and pick the one woman in town who wanted nothing to do with him.

Suddenly, he wasn't so hungry. He shoved the plate away. Maybe he should just give up. Renny O'Brien would never forgive him. She'd never listen to him, and she'd never, ever fall in love with him.

A wave of despair engulfed him. He didn't want to spend his life alone. He had no family left. All he had was here, in Pheasant Gully.

From the kitchen in the back of the office, Tyler heard the clear, soothing voice of Maze singing.

Sighing, he pulled his plate back to him. He wasn't alone, he told himself. He had Maze.

What did he need with a stubborn woman who'd no doubt give him trouble every day of his life? Yet as he sat and finished eating, he knew that if given the chance, he could happily live with trouble if it was named Renait O'Brien.

Chapter Four

Renny didn't stop until she turned down an alley and stepped onto the worn path leading to Jensen's Boardinghouse. Candlelight in the front parlor window welcomed weary visitors needing a room and meal. Reaching the bottom of the steps, Renny paused to catch her breath and calm her emotions.

Slowly and quietly, she climbed the steps and turned the doorknob. The door squeaked loudly.

"Renny?"

Renny shut the door and looked longingly at the stairs. Though she was itching to go up and shut herself into her room, she didn't. Not for anything would she hurt or unduly worry the two women who tried hard to mother and befriend her.

"Yes, it's me, Miss Martha." Renny stepped into the parlor where the two sisters were sitting. Martha Jensen sat on one side of the moss green settee. Curled on her ample lap sat a large orange-striped cat, eying the strand of yarn being knitted into a shawl.

Sitting on the other side of the settee, Agatha Jensen, small and delicate, hunched over her lap quilt, straining to see as she stitched each of the tiny, precise stitches that went into all of her her quilts. "Welcome back, child."

Standing in the doorway, Renny smiled. "Thank you, Miss Agatha." The scene before her was nearly as familiar to her as evenings in her own home. But instead of being comforting, it made her miss her own family all the more.

"Well, don't just stand there, child. Come in and sit. Your family is well?"

Renny entered the room. "Yes, they are." To take her mind off her scattered and fragile thoughts, Renny stared around her. Soft light came from the two lamps sitting on the tables next to each Jensen sister; the room was bathed in shadows that hid the many treasures sprinkled lavishly throughout the parlor.

This room, as well as all the others, showcased the two women's talents with needle, thread, fabric and yarn. Added to their own creations were knickknacks of all sizes, materials and shapes, treasures the two women had collected over the past fifty years. Not a single surface was left bare.

"Sit, child. You must be exhausted. You work too hard, doesn't she, Sister? Was just telling Sister that you work too hard." She and Martha exchanged nods.

"Yes, indeed. We were just talking about you. It was getting so late."

There was no reprimand in the voice, just worry. Renny sighed. "I'm sorry, I left later than usual."

The two women clicked their tongues and shook their heads. "We understand, child. Hard road you've chosen, leaving your family. Very noble to give your sister and that gorgeous man she married time to become a family."

"Yes, very noble," Miss Martha parroted. Setting down her needles, she gently unhooked the cat's claw from the yarn. "How are your brothers and sisters? Been a while since they've come to see us."

Renny sat in an overstuffed chair and curled her legs beneath her. She longed to plead exhaustion or a headache so she could be alone but knew from experience that it would just send the sisters into a mothering frenzy.

"Everyone's fine. Spent the day with the boys—rode out to repair fences and herd some stray cattle back onto our land."

The O'Briens didn't have a large spread but had enough to be mostly self-supporting, which was all that her father had wanted. His riches, as he'd often bragged, were jewels in the form of his wife and children.

Staving off memories of her father and his love of the land, Renny launched into several tales of Kealan's exploits during the day, including putting a harmless snake in his older brother's water canteen when Daire declared Kealan too young to help with the fence repair.

Both women laughed. "Ah, boys will be boys," Miss Martha said, her voice a soft coo.

Renny smiled, her heart filling with love and pride. While they might not be the best behaved on all occasions, the children's indomitable spirits had helped them survive during the last year.

"Daire didn't think so. He tossed Kea into a mud puddle and sat on him. Then they had a mud fight until Kea promised never to pull another prank on Daire." She laughed softly. "I threw them both in the river to wash themselves and ended up getting pulled in. Spent most of the afternoon in the river."

The three women grinned. Kealan, being Kealan, would resume his prankster ways, and Daire knew it well.

"Kea is so determined to do whatever Daire does. Doesn't take much to set them off to arguing. They drive me nuts."

Miss Agatha smiled. "And you love every minute of it, dear."

Renny smiled softly. "Yeah, I do. I sure miss them." She couldn't help the soft sigh. It didn't matter that she spent all day, each day, with her family. She missed them at night, missed staying home and being part of the family.

Work kept them so busy during the day that evenings were typically the time when they were able to relax and enjoy all that came with being part of a loud and boisterous family.

Miss Martha ran her hands through her cat's thick fur. "Brave thing for you to have done,

Renny. Leaving your family like you did." She turned her head to smile at Miss Agatha. "Why, I don't know what Sister and I would do without each other."

Renny stared into the fireplace at the dying embers. Neither woman talked much about their past. She knew that Miss Martha had once been married yet still went by the single title of "Miss."

"Mattie and Reed don't need me underfoot," she said. "Better they be on their own while they get used to being married and all." She gave a helpless shrug. "Besides, I see them all day, every day."

"Not the same, though, dear. Not the same," Miss Martha said, echoing Renny's own thoughts as she placed her knitting into a woven basket. Her hand tightened on the cat's neck when he reached out a paw to snag the ball of yarn. The cat looked disgusted when his mistress put the lid on the basket. He jumped down and went to lie before the warm fireplace.

Catching Miss Agatha hiding a yawn behind her hand, Renny stood. "Well, guess I'll be turning in. Got a lot to do come morning."

"Goodnight, child," Agatha said, her voice trailing off as she yawned widely.

" 'Night, Miss Agatha. Miss Martha."

"Sweet dreams, child." Miss Martha stood, then bent down to blow out one lantern. "By the way, did the sheriff find you? Hate to think of the poor boy still waiting for you out in the meadow." She didn't bother hiding the humor in her voice.

Renny rolled her eyes. "Nanny Troll found me."

The barest hint of sulk escaped. Last person she wanted to talk or even think about was *Terrapin* Tyler. She smirked to herself. Childish to call the man names, even if only to herself, but "Dog Meat" Tyler was just one of many private names she had for the thorn in her life.

Miss Martha extinguished the last lamp. "Don't be too harsh on the poor soul, dear. He's just looking out for you."

With one foot on the steps, Renny glanced over her shoulder at the two white-haired women. "We don't need him. We have each other. Don't need his brand of help." Resentment thrummed through her.

Miss Martha smiled softly. "Sometimes the thing we think we don't need is exactly what we do need, child. Burdens were meant to be shared, and with your sister and Reed leaving soon to go visit his parents, you might need help. Don't let pride get the best of you."

Renny scowled as she tromped up the stairs while the two sisters went to their quarters on the ground floor. Miss Martha was off her rocker if she honestly thought Renny needed Tyler. If there was anything Renny did not need, it was a certain busybody sheriff.

Once in her room, Renny shut the door. She didn't bother lighting a candle. Undressing in the dark, leaving her longjohns on, she donned a large flannel shirt that had belonged to her father. Drawing it close, she sniffed.

Was there still the barest hint of the man she

loved, or was the scent of a father only in her in her mind? Wrapping her arms around herself, she sat on the window seat.

The window, open a few inches, let in the fresh, cool air. Staring up at the glittering sky, Renny could no longer ignore the truth. Mattie's leaving and taking the children with her to meet and visit with Reed's parents was the root of her unrest. They were travelling soon, and Renny would be left behind.

This was worse than her moving out. At least now, she got to see them every day, knew when she rose in the morning that it would only be a short time before she was with them once more.

But they were leaving soon. Renny had no idea when they would return.

Renny pushed her fingers hard against her closed eyes to stop the burning of tears. She would not cry. She'd be brave. She'd be supportive.

And she'd be alone.

She lifted her head and she shook it in denial. "No, they'll be back. Before winter sets in."

Her father had said he'd return soon in nearly ever letter he'd sent to her and her sister Emma. But he'd never kept those promises. Not even when she'd begged him to come home.

She'd gone the first nine years of her life without meeting the man who'd fathered her. He'd left when she was fresh from the womb and had continued to run from grief until she and Emma left home to find and join him.

That journey had been long, frightening and so

very exciting. The ending result had been a happy reunion, the marriage of her father to a Sioux woman, the wedding of her sister to a Sioux chief and the blending of two families and two cultures.

For a moment Renny retraced her steps into the past and relived some of those happy times when she, Mattie and Matthew had been much younger. The new family had returned to St. Louis. Back then, Renny had been so envious that her much older sister had gotten to stay behind and live with the Sioux.

But with an Indian mother, Renny spent the second part of her life immersed in that world so different from her own. Renny's finger dug into the buffalo robe she sat upon. Though she'd brought with her many treasures from home, it just wasn't the same. Nor did it bring the comfort she so badly needed.

The robe, quilts and dream catchers were reminders that everything was different now.

"Promised never to leave again, Pa," she whispered, fighting the urge to cry. It didn't matter that not one of them could have stopped the murders, that her parents would never have left their children willingly. All that mattered at that moment was that she hated what her life had become.

She hated it so much that she just wanted to weep and wail. Staring out into the dark, the tears remained frozen. Not once in the last year had she given in to that urge to cry. There was no time for tears, no energy to spare. Crying would not undo the past.

So she simply survived. And part of that survival meant letting her sister and Reed leave and hoping that they returned. No matter how many times she told herself it was fruitless to stew or worry over what she could not control, she couldn't help it. For the last year she'd been the one holding her family together. She felt responsible for the youngsters.

But they had Mattie and Reed now.

They didn't need her.

Renny couldn't hide from the stinging truth. Caitie, Kealan and Daire would now rely on Mattie and their new father figure, Reed. No matter how much Renny wanted the children to stay with her, she knew they belonged with Mattie and Reed. Especially as Reed was hoping to regain custody of his two children. Soon, they'd be a family.

Gazing out into the night and spotting shadows moving here and there as men returned to their homes from the saloon, Renny felt lost and alone. She hated the night. There was nothing to distract her from emotions and thoughts best left undisturbed, and there was no one to reassure her that all would be right with her world.

Fear of being alone and forgotten or discarded rushed at her like hail pounding at the earth. Her life felt as dark as a stormy night. She was a small, fragile bird huddled in a tree with the wind whipping branches and leaves around her. It was all she could do to keep her grip on her emotions.

Up in the sky, the pale moon had risen high. As she watched, a thick cloud cover slowly crept in front of the moon, slowly swallowing it from sight. One by one each star seemed to burn out until there was nothing to see but dark.

And as the storm that gathered outside, the storm of her life threatened to burst, seething through her and around her until Renny feared she'd lose control. She knew better than most how life could snap the controls away from a person so easily and gleefully.

Renny felt as though she stood on the edge of a cliff with no escape but down. Everything inside her screamed that it was wrong for the family to split. They belonged here, with her, together.

Renny buried her head between her knees and gripped her legs hard. Life as she'd known it was changing faster than she could handle it. She'd gone from being the one to hold her family together, overseeing all aspects of their lives, to—

—to nothing.

Needed by no one.

Everything inside Renny screamed for her to stop them, but it was too late. Matthew had left, Mattie would soon leave, taking the others. The family would be scattered with no reassurances that they'd all be together again any time soon.

How could they all just leave her? How could she let them?

A dark shadow flew past her window.

Weshawee!

It is time.

The voiced boomed in her head. Renny jumped

up and backed away from the window, glancing around wildly. She swallowed hard. There was no one in the room with her. Maybe she'd fallen asleep.

The pane of glass rattled. A gust of wind rushed into the room.

Listen to your heart.

Feeling behind her with one hand, Renny sat heavily on the foot of the bed. The voice reminded her of an old wise man she'd once met. For just a moment, she thought she saw the intensity of his dark gaze reflected in the window.

"It was long ago," she said, her voice a mere whisper of breath. She was young, and scared. She'd just been kidnapped, separated from her sister, and traded for fresh horses by a band of Indians.

A man in the village had found her crying one day when she'd been scared that she'd never see her sister again. She felt lost and alone and he'd come to her in the woods, a big man, with a big voice but gentle words. She'd never forgotten him, or the comfort he'd offered in his wise words.

Spirits are here. Everywhere. With us always.
They speak through the wind. They are the wind.
They are the trees, the birds, the animals.
They are the earth, the rocks and sky.
They exist. Hear them.
See them.
Listen and learn from the Spirits of the earth, for only then will you find peace within.

And she had, Renny thought bitterly, remembering how she'd learned the habits of every living thing, soaking up all that was told to her. Her understanding of the spiritual world had come as naturally to her as breathing—until the death of her parents tore from her her faith in anything not seen or touched.

"They were good people," she whispered. And good deserved the reward of life. Her mother had believed, and lived as one with the spiritual world of her people. And Mattie. Her sister with her unique gift of vision had had her eyesight ruthlessly taken from her.

Good people, living good lives, only to have them destroyed. The very spirits they'd prayed to, given thanks to, had turned on them. That was why Renny no longer believed. She believed only in what she could see, touch and control.

She would not be vulnerable ever again. She'd trust only in herself.

Turning to climb into bed, she startled at the sharp rap to her window. Spinning around, she grabbed the tall bedpost with one hand.

"Stupid," she cursed herself. "Just the wind. A storm brewing."

Outside, branches whipped back and forth. She relaxed slightly and felt foolish even as she ran to the window and closed it. Then she climbed into bed and stared at the shadows dancing on one wall. They seemed alive. Shapes grew and merged, blending and changing.

Believe!

The voice came again. This time it was a gentle nudge. The shape on the wall looked like the head of a horse for just a moment.

Renny flipped onto her belly, closed her eyes and pulled the pillow over her head, closing her senses to all sight and sound.

Chapter Five

Menacing tiers of clouds gathered overhead. For the second day in a row, summer storms brought temperatures down and stole the afternoon light, leaving shadows to merge into one mass.

Brenna Gilmore huddled beneath a small canvas lean-to erected between two narrow saplings. Ropes tied to stakes and the trunks held the small canopy firmly in place against the brewing storm. Shivering as tentacles of cold slid through her blouse and skirt, she longed for the comfort of home.

In her mind, she gave a bitter laugh. She had no home, no life, no family left except her brother Gil, who hated her. The loss of both of their parents within days of each other had been cruel, but what had pushed him over the edge was learning that their mother was responsible for the death of their eldest brother.

Brenna heaved out a long, silent sigh of regret.

Everything she'd once known had been destroyed in a single day.

Above her head, leaves and small branches skittered down the canvas roof. More blew inside. Brenna set her needlework down to pull her shawl more tightly around her shoulders. The cold air carried the promise of another wet, miserable afternoon.

Sitting across from her, Matthew O'Brien was engrossed in arrow-making. He didn't look up at her, or acknowledge her presence in any way. He was still very angry with her.

She didn't blame him. He had every right to hate her for using her knowledge of the Sioux against his family.

She'd been fascinated by the entirely different culture of the Sioux and had taken it upon herself to learn all she could. Matthew had also taught her how to use a knife, a stick and a rifle to defend herself.

So she'd used her knowledge against Renny; Renny, who'd so fiercely protected her family. All Brenna had wanted to do was stop her mother from killing Mattie. So she'd come up with a plan to scare Renny into taking her family back to the Sioux for the summer.

It had been such a simple plan and one that might have worked had it not been for Brenna's father—who had not been the man they'd all believed him to be.

He'd pushed Mattie and Gilbert into agreeing to marry. He'd claimed to want Mattie in the family—not as a widowed daughter-in-law but as the wife to his remaining son.

Mattie had agreed and Brenna had been afraid her mother would try once more to kill Mattie.

Brenna's suspicions had been right. But it had been the deceit and treachery of Patrick O'Leary that drove her mother to madness.

His actions, motivated by revenge and greed, had caused both Renny and Matthew to be hurt and Daire and little Caitie to be kidnapped.

He'd brought shame down on Katherine O'Leary's head, and she'd struck out at the one person she blamed: Mattie. In the end, Brenna had had no choice but to confess the truth to Matthew in order to save Mattie's life.

Now Matthew hated her.

Staring morosely outside, Brenna was in many ways thankful that it was all over. Keeping that secret, having to watch her mother closely, having to hide the fact that she knew in case her mother turned on her, had been hard.

The burden of guilt and truth had at times seemed far too heavy to bear.

Still, she'd carry her own burden of guilt for her part in the tragedy forever. She wasn't asking Matthew to forgive her, for she'd never forgive herself. But she longed for him to at least try to understand why she'd done what she'd done. He simply believed that she didn't know right from wrong.

Brenna jabbed the needle down through the fabric. That's where *he* was wrong. She'd known that what she was doing was wrong, but to do the right thing would have meant condemning her mother to death. She couldn't bring herself to do that.

Katherine O'Leary had tried to kill Mattie the day Mattie and Collin married. But instead of Mattie dying in the fire, Collin had perished.

Her mother had killed her own son and had suffered each and every day thereafter with the knowledge that she'd killed her firstborn child.

Her mother's death at the end of a noose would not have restored Mattie's eyesight or brought Collin back from the dead. So Brenna had kept silent. She'd been damned from the moment when she'd witnessed her mother trying to kill Mattie.

Another wave of leaves swirled in their shelter. She gently brushed the debris off her stitching then stared down glumly at her sampler. The stitches were uneven; the small deer she'd just finished sewing looked lopsided.

Sighing, she tucked the needle and thread back into the cloth. Later, she'd have to rip it all out and start over. Brenna shoved the cloth back into a beautifully beaded leather pouch.

She stared at the blue, black and red geometric pattern, then traced the white and blue medallion sewn into the center of the flap. Each bead had been sewn precisely and evenly. The workmanship was exquisite.

Brenna still couldn't believe that Mattie had given it to her the day she and Matthew had set out to join his tribe at their summer camp.

It held not only her needles, threads and material, but Mattie had also included a selection of feathers, beads, sinew and an awl—tools and supplies she'd need for her life in the Sioux village.

Glancing at the corner where her belongings were stashed, she eyed a second pouch. This one was plain, but, again, it was sewn with love and skill. It was old, soft as butter and filled with herbs and healing potions.

The two leather pouches had once belonged to Mattie. She'd been surprised when Mattie had given them to her, had tried to refuse the generous gifts as she hadn't deserved such kindness or consideration from Mattie.

But Mattie had insisted. They were things that she wouldn't be able to use and she'd wanted Brenna to have them. Brenna had felt so lost, alone and raw inside; she'd felt destroyed emotionally, that she'd gratefully accepted the gift. For with it, came the greatest gift of all: forgiveness.

Brenna's tears sparked hotly. Mattie, blinded by Katherine's hatred, had found it within herself to not only forgive but to understand.

Wiping the tears from her face, Brenna clutched her precious gift to her breast for a moment before putting it away. With nothing else to do, she gathered her shawl tightly around her, more for comfort than warmth.

Once again, Matthew drew her gaze. She felt chilled, both inside and out, and knew she'd never again feel warmth in her soul. But it was no less than she deserved.

She'd lost a cherished friend in Matthew, and something far more valuable: she'd lost all hope that one day Matthew would fall in love with her and make her his wife.

Brenna loved Matthew, and knowing she'd destroyed all hope of ever winning his love was her greatest punishment.

She watched him now, willed him to look at her, to see that she was sorry, and that she'd never meant to hurt anyone. But he would never look at her with those soft, brown eyes. No matter how long or how hard she stared at him, he ignored her.

She'd give anything to hear him speak to her as before, his deep voice warm as butter and often full of humor as he teased her. The man she'd known was gone, destroyed. Her actions had crushed something even more valuable and fragile: trust.

Brenna drew her knees up and wrapped her arms around her legs and swallowed the lump in her throat as she stared out into gloomy afternoon. It seemed that they'd been traveling across this frighteningly vast land forever. But she didn't mind.

She had nowhere else to go, and truthfully she was a bit afraid of facing his tribe. Right now, she didn't care if it took all summer to reach his tribe in the Black Hills.

A sharp clap of thunder startled her. The wind howled through their shelter. Brenna sighed. Before the day was done, she'd be wet, cold and miserable.

A hunk of dried jerky landed in her lap. She glanced up. So lost in her thoughts, she hadn't heard Matthew rise or go into the food supplies. He sat back down in silence.

Brenna couldn't eat. Her mind and stomach were in turmoil.

"Eat."

The sharp command slashed through the oppressive air like an ax splitting a log. Brenna glanced at Matthew, who was staring outside as he chewed a hunk of dried beef.

"I'm not hungry," she said softly.

"What game are you playing now, Brenna? Do you think to make my people feel sorry for you by starving yourself? You didn't eat this morning."

"What do you care, Matthew?" she asked. For nearly two weeks she'd endured his silent anger. She'd rather he yell at her. At least then they'd be talking.

"You agreed to spend a year with my people. It is not as harsh a punishment as you deserve. You're acting like a sulking child."

Brenna didn't really consider going to live with Matthew's people a punishment. She had nowhere else to go, and Matthew had promised both her and his sister that Brenna would be given a fair chance to regain her own self-respect and the respect of Mattie and Matthew's people.

But the loss of Matthew's friendship was punishment enough. Fat drops of rain splattered onto the ground. She figured they'd traveled a third of the distance, and were just a short way from the Missouri River.

From there, she knew they'd cross, and stop to see his uncle Wolf and aunt Jessie. Then they'd continue on, until they found his people's summer camp.

"I do not expect you to forgive me, Matthew, but can you not understand?" She wanted to ask him if he could have spoken words that might have cost his mother her life.

Matthew had every right to hate her. Brenna's mother and stepfather had caused them grief and heartache.

She stared at Matthew, willed him to look at her.

"I was afraid," she whispered. Matthew remained silent but she saw his jaw harden. She waited for him to speak, to give her the chance to explain. But he didn't.

Finally, Brenna jumped up, the chunk of pemmican falling onto the dirt ground.

"Where are you going?"

Brenna met his narrowed gaze. "Outside." She said it defiantly, daring him to stop her.

Matthew just shrugged and looked away. Brenna fled out into the storm. She ran through the tall grass, nearly tripping in the burrow of some animal.

She ran through the tall grass. At that moment, she didn't care if she lived or died.

She stopped at the stream that led to the Missouri. Panting and crying, her tears mingled with the heavy downfall of rain.

Blinded by the rain and deafened by her thoughts and the echo of Matt's rejection, she didn't see the dark figure moving closer to the shelter she'd just left.

But when the shot rang out, she whirled around. "Matt!" She screamed the word and ran back to the man she'd loved and lost.

* * *

Sunday suppers at the Jensen boardinghouse were loud, boisterous and chaotic. Food was passed around the table with dizzying speed, yet no one missed out on a single roll or scoop of dumplings or chunk of boiled chicken.

Forks clattered against good china, voices shouted for food or just to be heard over the din, and Renny loved every single loud, crazy moment.

Sundays were the one day she didn't make the trek from town to home. Instead, her family, dressed in their Sunday best, came to town for the weekly sermon in their newly built church.

It didn't matter the religion or belief, nearly everyone attended the service given by "Rev," a young pastor with a mild-mannered and often humorous style of preaching.

But the real draw was the socializing and gossiping that usually followed as those who lived in town often invited homesteaders to supper before they left to return to their farms.

Today, as on every Sunday, Martha and Agatha's long dining table was crowded with the O'Brien family. There were also two single men and another family staying for a few days. They were looking rather lost and intimidated by the spirited meal.

Chewing on a thick crust of bread slathered with butter, Renny conversed with the strangers, answering their questions. They were all part of a growing number of people moving westward.

Both men were heading farther west but the young family seemed interested in settling here in

Pheasant Gully. They'd heard about the land that belonged to Brenna and Gil.

Renny studied the shy young woman with dark blond hair, her towheaded youngsters and her blond giant of a husband. Noting that Caitie and Kealan seemed to have already made friends with the children, she hoped they bought the land.

Though Gil and Brenna were no longer in Pheasant Gully, the money from the sale would be safely banked. That much Renny and her family had agreed to do for Brenna before she'd left with Matthew.

Renny tried not to dwell on the heartache and pain of the past month. In many ways, Brenna and Gil were victims as much as Renny and her brothers and sisters.

Allowing the chatter, laughter and rumble of deep voices to wash over her, she contentedly watched each of her siblings. Only Matthew was missing. Sighing, Renny knew she was being selfish in wanting everyone here, with her.

It was long past time for Matthew to live his own life and she suspected that given a choice between their two worlds, he'd one day chose to live among their people.

"Renny, you're not eating?" Mattie's soft voice came from her left.

"I'm fine, Mattie." Renny scraped her fork around the plate but didn't fool Mattie.

"Stop playing if you are not going to eat. I know you well, sister of mine. You're sad."

Renny set her fork down. "How can I be sad

with all this happiness around us?" She tried to lighten her voice.

"Don't you dare try to hide what you feel from me." Mattie's voice was sharp enough to make her husband glance over at them.

Renny shook her head at him and then stood. Mattie stood as well. With a brief glance at their hostesses, Renny excused the two of them and led Mattie out to the porch and down the steps.

The warm air and bright sun warmed her face and felt good after what seemed like days of rain. "Don't worry about me, Mattie. I'll be fine. You just be happy and make those kids happy and make that husband of yours happy." Renny hugged Mattie to her.

"And you help him get his children back and make yourselves one big happy family. That's what our parents would have wanted." Enough of her own worries.

"And what of you, sister? You're worried that we won't return." Mattie squeezed Renny's arm.

"I'll be fine." Despite the full rays of sun beating down on them, Renny shivered.

She'd never been alone before—except for a short time after she and Emma had been taken captive and then separated. But even then, she'd been with a good family until she was reunited with her sister and father.

Still, she didn't want anything, even her own fears, to mar Mattie's happiness. She stopped at a grouping of chairs and benches and tables set beneath a spreading oak behind the Jensens' home.

A short distance away, another oak had a swing attached. As she watched, Kealan and Caitie ran down the steps toward the swing. The two tow-heads were right behind.

Renny and Mattie sat. "When are you and Reed leaving?"

Mattie folded her hands in her lap. Then she nervously pleated her skirt. "A week. Maybe two."

"So soon?" Shock rocketed through Renny. She'd figured that she had at least a month, maybe two, before the newly wedded couple left Pheasant Gully.

"Come with us, Renny." Mattie turned in her chair.

Renny stared into her sister's tear-filled eyes. She was tempted to shout out yes. But she bit her tongue instead and gave the same answer. "I can't." The last thing Mattie and Reed needed was her underfoot.

"Sell the house and land and come with us, Renny." Mattie paused.

"We've never been apart and I don't know how long we'll be gone." Her voice broke.

No matter how much she wanted to go, Renny knew it wasn't right. So where did that leave her?

Alone.

"Renny?"

"I'm sorry, Mattie. I won't go with you, but maybe it's time to think about selling."

"Where will you go?"

Renny thought for a moment, then shrugged. "No reason I can't stay here, in town. Must be something I can do," she said. "Could open my own business with the sale—that is, if it's all right with everyone."

Mattie smiled. "I think that's a wonderful idea, Renny."

"Won't be the same, living in town all the time," Renny murmured.

"No, I have a feeling nothing will be the same for you," Mattie said, her voice going soft.

Renny sent her sister a suspicious look. Mattie's eyes were glazed and unseeing and a small smile played around her lips, which usually meant she was having a vision. Whatever she was seeing, it seemed to please her.

A horrifying thought came to mind. Was Mattie seeing *her* future this time? She opened her mouth to ask her but before she could demand to know what Mattie saw, her sister's expression changed to one of horror.

Mattie doubled over as though she'd been punched in the stomach. She opened her mouth and started screaming.

"Matthew!"

Over and over she screamed her brother's name.

Renny grabbed Mattie by the shoulders. "Mattie! Snap out of it. Come back!"

Her mouth went dry and her hands shook when her sister kept screaming until her eyes rolled back in her head and she slumped in Renny's arms.

Chapter Six

From the spotlessly clean window, Tyler saw trouble coming. "Oh no," he groaned. He was just washing up, getting ready to sit down for Sunday supper.

Mrs. Burns, in a fit of temper, didn't bother to knock. The door flew open and crashed against the wall.

A formidable woman dressed in severe grays, she pointed a long-nailed finger at Tyler. "It's the Lord's day. A man belongs at home with his family, not out getting himself drunk."

"Now calm down, Mrs. Burns." Tyler kept a wary eye on the tall, thin woman. He also kept the wooden kitchen table between them.

"Don't you go telling me what to do, Sheriff. Your job is to serve and protect and uphold the law. I'm telling you it's a sin to have that place open, tempting our husbands into sinning on Sundays when they should be home reading their

Bibles and praying for forgiveness." She paused to take a deep breath.

Tyler ran his hand through his hair. "Now, you know I can't do anything about that. Don't have the authority."

Mrs. Burns slapped her palms down on the table, causing the silver and china to rattle. She leaned over, her eyes slits of fury. "Fetch him home," she demanded, her soul-searing, nails-on-a-chalkboard voice making him wince.

Tyler sighed. He couldn't blame Jake for trying to escape for a few hours. Two minutes around the man's wife gave *him* a pounding head.

"Not much I can do unless he's drunk and acting in a disorderly manner. Now, why don't you go back home. I'll make sure he gets home safely."

Still screeching about the sin of man, the woman left. Tyler let out a huge sigh of relief. Moments later, Maze hurried in.

"Did I hear voices?" She glanced around.

Tyler sat in one of the chairs. "Mrs. Burns was here."

Maze stirred a pot of boiling chicken then started dishing it out onto a platter. "Difficult woman," she commented.

"Difficult, hell. Woman's a snake. Swear she wears her hair pulled back so tight that someday her face is going to crack right down the middle." Except her mouth. Those thin, dry lips were puckered into a permanent frown.

The town was overrun with difficult women these days, none more so than a certain redhead who held the honor of being the most stubborn, prideful, difficult, and obstinate. And when riled, or threatened, she could be just plain nasty.

He remembered every word of last night's exchange. Damn woman lived to slash at him with her sharp tongue. Crossing his arms across his chest, he stared down at the gleaming china that he assumed belonged to Maze—all he had were a couple tin plates.

"You let her get under your skin, Sheriff." Maze was busy slicing steaming loaves of bread.

Tyler snorted. "Ticks get under a man's skin. Miss O'Brien is a burr beneath the saddle of a bucking horse. She'll be the cause of my death yet."

Hearing a muffled snicker, he narrowed his eyes. "Glad you find this so amusing." Renny's attitude and opinions of him shouldn't bother him—hell, he should be used to it. But Renny was like an itch that wouldn't go away.

Maze turned, her brilliantly blue eyes sparkling with laughter. "Oh, I do find this amusing," she said. "Heard she's kept you waiting four nights running. Before you know it, the entire town will come out to the meadow for a nighttime picnic. The two of you do provide a wealth of entertainment."

Maze nudged his booted foot with the tip of her shoe. Scowling, Tyler sat. He was surrounded by women intent on making his life difficult. "Don't start selling tickets yet, Maze. I'm going to end this."

Maze set the sliced bread on the table then stood back, hands on her hips. "I'll save my energy for helping you plan your wedding. That girl will make a fine wife."

"Wife?" Tyler choked on the word and stared at the woman in horror. "You been nipping at the sherry? Renny O'Brien isn't even a friend."

"Oh, it's there. Just need to be patient, Sheriff." Her eyes gleamed with determination. "She'll learn. And discover that all is not as hopeless as it seems."

Tyler stared at Maze, who seemed to have turned her thoughts and gaze inward. Then she shook her head as though returning from a trance. Passing behind him, she patted his shoulder. "Yes, it will all work out. We've seen to it," she said softly.

"Seen to what?" Tyler asked. "What are you up to, Maze?"

Maze tucked a loose strand of silvery hair back into her bun. "You just worry about yourself, dear boy, and leave the rest to us."

"Don't need more interfering women messing with my life, so just forget the matchmaking. You hear?" Tyler felt the urge to leave, get his horse and just ride off into the sunset.

Tyler watched Maze bustle around the kitchen, setting steaming bowls of potatoes and beans on the table. He opened his mouth to order her to stay out of his business but instead, he found himself voicing his greatest fear.

"She'll never forgive me for finding homes for the young'uns. Won't even try to understand that I was just doing my job." Something about Maze demanded the truth. Things he'd never told anyone seemed to just pour out of his mouth when he was around her.

"You tell her about Gracie?" Maze glanced out the window. "Supper's ready. You washed up?"

Tyler got to his feet. At the large sink, he washed his hands then used the towel she handed him to dry them off.

"Won't do no good to tell her. The stubborn woman won't let me explain that I did what I thought best. She should have trusted me."

Maze rolled her eyes. "Have you considered that she was doing what she thought best by refusing your help? They didn't know you back then, and had no reason to trust anyone." There was a hint of sadness in Maze's voice.

"Well, she knows me now. Should give a man a chance to have his say."

"Then go to her. Ask her for forgiveness. Then make her listen."

"Forgiveness? I did what I thought best, what I wish someone had done for me and Grant. Then maybe Gracie would still be alive."

He stared at the woman whom he was fast becoming fond of. So comfortable with her, he'd told her about Gracie and the guilt that still plagued him. He never talked about his family, but it had seemed so natural, so easy, compelling even, to talk to Maze.

A knock at the back door gave Tyler his much needed reprieve. He opened the door to a tall, rail-thin man with a full beard and hair down to his shoulder.

"Evening, Doc," Tyler said, holding out his hand.

"Evening, Sheriff. Maze." Casey Jameson took his usual seat at the table. "Smells awfully good in here."

After a short prayer of thanks for their meal, Tyler started passing platters.

Maze turned to the doc. "So nice that you were able to come, Dr. Jameson. Perhaps your presence will cheer our sheriff. He's a bit of a cross patch today."

"I am not cranky," Tyler said. "Just don't want to talk about women." Especially one woman in particular.

Casey grinned. "Saw you standing out in the meadow last night."

"Don't start, Casey," Tyler warned. Great, he thought, whole damn town was watching what went on between him and Renny O'Brien.

Before anyone could say more, there was a loud commotion outside. A breathless boy burst into the kitchen. "Doc, you're needed at the Jensens'. Quick."

Casey jumped up, his chair flying back and over. "I'll get my bag." He rushed out.

"What's wrong?" Tyler rounded the table and grabbed Renny's younger brother, Daire, by the shoulders.

The boy's eyes were a wide, bright blue. "It's Mattie. A vision. Started screaming then passed right out." Daire took a deep, gulping breath. "She's never done that before."

"Let's go." Tyler ran out the door with Daire at his heels.

* * *

Renny stared down at Mattie's white face. Her sister's dark eyes were big, black, unseeing. She didn't seem to be breathing yet Renny could feel the wild pounding of her sister's pulse.

Frightened, Renny shook Mattie gently. "Mattie! Mattie! Snap out of it," she demanded.

Mattie's pupils retracted. Her lashes fluttered, eyes closed then reopened as she moaned. Her eyes were full of pain and confusion, but Mattie was back from wherever this latest vision had taken her.

Renny sagged against her in relief. Never had a vision struck Mattie so violently. Renny tried to deny what this vision meant. Mattie had screamed Matthew's name. Over and over. Something had happened to him.

"No," Renny whispered. Nothing could have happened to Matt. The thought of losing her brother, another member of her family, made her tremble.

"Matthew," Mattie whimpered, tears streaming from her eyes.

"He's safe. He has to be," Renny said fiercely. She met Mattie's dark, fear-struck gaze and knew true terror. None of her sister's visions had ever been this sudden. Or violent. There were usually warnings, time to stop the vision. Somehow, Renny knew this one was different.

"Renny! Please no, not Matthew," she sobbed.

"God, Mattie, it can't—"

"Out of the way," a deep voice ordered.

Renny was grateful when Reed pushed his way through the growing crowd, but when he scooped up his wife into his arms, and strode off, Renny felt a wave of shock at the abrupt separation. The growing crowd swarmed after him.

Shakily getting to her feet, she was shoved to one side as more people from town swarmed onto the front lawn. Renny tried to run after Reed. Mattie needed her.

Hands tugging at her shirt stopped her. She was surrounded by concerned townfolk who'd heard the screaming. Questions were tossed at her like rocks in a pond.

"What happened?"

"Is she hurt?"

Then the questions turned into ripples of speculation.

"Maybe she's losing her baby."

"What baby—"

"Attacked. Broad daylight."

"What?" Several women screamed.

Renny covered her ears with her hands as gossip was passed from one person to another like a hot potato, each rumor more outlandish until the voices became an angry buzzing in her head. If she didn't get through the mob, she was liable to do some serious injury.

"Move it," she threatened, taking a woman by the arm to pull her out of the way.

"You heard the woman," a deep voice boomed. "Everyone back. *Now!* Return home. At once."

Tyler used one hand to clear a path, the other to push Renny ahead of him.

For once, Renny didn't mind his pushing her around. She ran up the steps and burst through the door, nearly colliding with Miss Martha as she hurried from the keeping room where Mattie sat on the couch.

"Mattie?" Breathless, Renny skidded to a stop.

Her sister was cradled in Reed's lap. She had her eyes closed. Reed was running his fingers through her hair, murmuring softly to her. Kealan sat on the arm of their chair. Behind them, Daire stood rigidly at their backs with Caitie in his arms. The O'Briens had formed a tight unit—one that didn't include her.

Renny tried to shove aside her own insecurities where her family was concerned. It was a new feeling, one that she'd ignored over the last couple weeks. But the truth was there for her to see and she couldn't dismiss it. They had formed a unit, and they didn't need her. Not like before. The realization frightened her far more than she cared to admit.

A low voice came from behind her. "She's okay, Renny. She's safe. Everything is okay." Tyler's hands were on her shoulders, rubbing gently.

Renny shook her head as she met Daire's gaze across the room. He looked years older than he actually was. His eyes were hard. Flat. Kealan and Caitie looked scared and ready to cry, and Mattie clung to Reed like moss to a tree.

No, none of them were the same, and never would be again after the events of the last year. The very foundation of their world had been cracked, starting with the deaths of their parents.

Renny went forward, dropped down onto one knee to take one of Mattie's hands in hers. Her sister glanced toward her and though she couldn't see her, she reached out a hand. "Renny?"

"I'm here, Mattie. I'm here."

Mattie closed her eyes, tears trickling down the side of her face. Renny wiped them with her finger. "Tell me, Mattie. We have to know. Is he alive?"

Mattie pulled her hand away to press her fingers to her mouth. "I don't know. It was fast. So sudden. Never been like that before." Her voice shook.

Reed spoke up. "She needs to rest. Ask questions later." He tightened his arms around his wife.

Renny shook her head as she stared into his worried gaze. "It can't wait," she said fiercely.

"Renny is right," Mattie said, struggling to sit. Reed shifted but didn't release his hold on his wife, keeping her safe within the circle of his arms.

Renny waited, as did all the others. They knew it often took Mattie time to put the thoughts and images of her vision into words.

"A storm. Rain, thunder, flashes of light," Mattie began. She closed her eyes as if willing the vision to return. Reed's arms tightened around her as she shook her head back and forth.

"The thunder. So loud." Her voice rose, trembled.

"Not from the sky. A gun. A gunshot."

She muffled a scream behind her hands but they all heard the horror of her next words.

"Blood. Rivers of blood."

Chapter Seven

Tyler wasn't sure what to do. He had no experience with visions. This was out of his realm. All he could do was watch. And wait.

His gaze settled on Renny as she talked softly to her sister. While she talked, her hand found Kealan's and she held on to the boy.

Something shifted inside him. The love she had for her family, the compassion she showed to those in need, had drawn him to her a year ago when he'd stepped into his brother's shoes to become sheriff.

And it was that bond that she shared with her family that had put the two of them at odds. Watching her with them, seeing Daire set Caitie down onto the chair so Renny could take her into his arms, made him think of his own family.

He and Grant had always doted on their baby sister. His mother had had several miscarriages, and death had claimed two brothers and a sister as babies. Then his mother had given birth to Gracie.

The joy that filled their house in the wee hours after two days of agonizing birthing was something he'd never forget.

Nor would he ever forget holding his tiny baby sister. His arms moved up to his chest as though cradling an infant. For just a moment he was back in a two-room cabin, holding the baby, staring into those squinting eyes and watching tiny rosebud lips tremble as she mewed weakly.

That sound, and the slight weight in his arms, had given birth to a deep, protective love. Gracie had always been fragile and they'd all lived in fear that sickness would take her from them as well.

But she'd survived infancy and had grown to be a fragile, but otherwise healthy child. Even the illness that claimed their parents had passed over her.

The room darkened as a cloud passed over the sun. He'd vowed to keep his sister safe. Alive. But he'd failed.

Remembering the day she'd died in his arms shattered his heart all over again. Watching this young family, the pain from losing his own felt as fresh and raw as the day he and Grant buried first their parents, then Gracie.

A gentle nudge from behind him startled Tyler back to the present. "Excuse me, Sheriff." Miss Martha sidestepped him. She carried a small tray with a steaming cup of tea over to the table next to where Reed sat with Mattie.

"Here, dear, I brought you some tea. Added some cool water and a splash of father's brandy."

"Thank you, Miss Martha," Reed said.

Tyler showed his respect by giving Mattie time to pull herself together. It also gave him time to observe the family who'd come to matter so much to him over the last year.

Reed took the cup, put it in his wife's trembling hands, and then cupped her hands with his. He murmured to her, encouraging her to sip. Slowly the color returned to her face.

Daire stood stiffly. Kealan was wide-eyed and quiet and Caitie slumped over Renny's shoulder, her thumb in her mouth.

For the first time since he'd met the O'Brien siblings, he had to admit that there were differences between these brothers and sisters and his own.

The kids, including Mattie and Renny, were all strong. Healthy. Each one possessed an inner strength, a core of courage that only enhanced their appeal and made them seem even stronger.

For the first time he realized just how much he truly admired them. Maybe it was that strength and courage that had drawn him to them, not just his fear of watching them make the same mistakes he and his brother made.

He shifted, growing restless and uneasy with his own private revelations. Perhaps Renny had been right to keep her family together. They were survivors. Their combined strength was formidable, and no doubt responsible for the courage shown in the last year.

The urge to approach Renny and do as Maze suggested burned hot in Tyler. He'd go to her, first chance, and ask for her forgiveness. He'd admit to being wrong. And maybe she'd give him a chance to explain that he'd reacted out of fear.

He'd learned the hard way the cost of pride and pure stubbornness and he hadn't been able to sit back and watch them make the same mistakes. Finally, he was ready to take the first step toward a truce.

But first, this situation needed to be dealt with. He stepped forward. "Reed, don't want to intrude, but I'd like to know what's going on."

Renny stood, handed Caitie back to Daire then faced Tyler with legs spread, hands on hips. "Mattie's fine."

"Not now, Renny. Something's wrong. With Matthew. Tell me," Tyler demanded.

"Go away, Troll. Not your concern." Renny took one step forward.

Tyler's patience plummeted. He stalked over to her slowly, then deliberately stubbed the toes of his boots into hers and leaned over her.

"Need to hear it again, Miss O'Brien? Let me repeat. Anything and everything that goes on in this town is my business. And if I understand correctly, Mattie had a vision and in that vision saw Matthew get himself shot."

He drew a deep breath. He didn't really know what to make of Mattie's statement, but he'd seen enough in the last month to not dismiss anything she said.

He pointed a finger at her. "Someone gets shot, that's a crime, and crimes fall under the jurisdiction of the law. And in case you've forgotten, around here, I am the law." He sidestepped Renny, dismissing her.

"Mattie—"

"She's told all she can. She needs to rest." Renny moved with him. Her blue eyes blazed with anger. And fear.

"Dammit, Renait." Tyler wanted to reach out, grab her by the shoulder and shake her senseless but she shoved past him. Snaking his hand out, he caught her by the arm

"Where are you going?"

"None—"

"So help me God, Renait O'Brien. One day you're gonna push me too far."

Renny jutted her chin out at him. "It is none of your concern. But just so the *law* is dutifully informed, I am going home. I am going to get some supplies, then I am going to go find Matthew." Renny stomped on his foot then strode out the door.

Tyler bit back an oath, but he didn't follow her. He needed to know more. "Mattie," he said gently, remembering that she couldn't see him looking at her. "Where is Matthew?"

Mattie pulled herself out of Reed's arms and stood. "I'm not sure. You know he left with Brenna to return to our people. He always goes by the same route: the James River, then smaller rivers and streams until he reaches the Missouri. He'll stop at the home of our aunt and uncle on his way." She drew in a deep breath.

"He won't have been in a hurry. The journey to our people is as important to Matt as reaching them, and I also made him promise not to make the journey hard on Brenna—so he'll be traveling slower than if he'd been alone."

Mattie took a deep breath and pushed herself out of her husband's arms. "We'll follow, and pray to both the God of your world, and the spirits of my world that we find him before it's too late."

"We?" Tyler and Reed asked the question at the same time. Both wore frowns.

Tyler shook his head, remembered that she couldn't see the gesture. "Tell me the route he took. I'll get some men and go after him."

Smiling sadly, Mattie shook her head. "Doesn't work that way. Many things could make Matthew change course. Weather, animals, other tribes."

"Then how do you propose to find him?" He didn't want to point out that she was blind and certainly couldn't track him.

Reed sighed. "She'll see more, know more the closer she gets to him. As much as I hate the idea, she is the one person who needs to go."

Mattie leaned back against her husband. "Reed is correct." She closed her eyes, looking young and vulnerable. "I'll see more. Much more." Her voice was soft, so soft he could barely hear her.

"I'm going with them." Daire moved to stand beside Mattie.

"And so am I." Kealan took his stand beside Reed. His hands were fisted and he looked like the fierce warrior he hoped to become.

"My Sioux name is *Matohoksila.* It means Bear Boy." Kealan pulled a leather pouch out from beneath his shirt. "And I have my own medicine bag, and that means I can go too."

Caitie just reached out to Mattie. Mattie took her into her arms. "We all go, Sheriff Tyler," she said softly. "My brother needs us. There is no more to be said."

Tyler ran his hands through his hair. He sent Reed a frustrated glare. "This is crazy."

Reed sighed. "Yep. That's what marriage does to your life," he said, not looking the least bit put out.

"Fine. Reed, find someone to take over the office of deputy. Mattie, get together a list of supplies we need from Hank. We'll send someone to fetch them for you."

"We need to return home, Tyler. We need clothing and—"

"I'll ride out now. I can go faster alone. You all come with Reed. I'll help Renny gather supplies."

Glancing at each of the three young siblings, he frowned. "Matthew has a long head start. If we are going to find him, we need to ride hard."

Daire nodded. "We can handle it."

For a moment, Tyler stared in his eyes then nodded before turning on his heel. Could things get any more complicated?

Renny arrived home shaken and scared. She moved as though a dream bogged her down and she had to force herself forward.

First, the house. What to take? Food, herbs, bandages, blankets, a change of clothing, two rifles and a pocket pistol that had belonged to her father.

She paused for a moment and let herself see the fun and happiness that had once been a part of her daily life: her mother at the stove, singing softly or telling stories to whomever was gathered at the table, teaching them their heritage in the way of her people—through stories.

Her pa, sitting in his chair each night with his children gathered around. The time with her father had been fun, for he'd loved to talk and listen to his children talk. They'd discuss everything from lessons to politics. Sometimes the mood was serious, other times, light and full of nonsense.

She'd had so much, but lost most of it and wasn't sure she could handle another loss. To keep from dwelling on it, she gathered the supplies piled on the wooden table and hurried out of the house.

With her heart aching, she hurried out to the barn. There wasn't time for her to waste. If there was one thing she knew, it was that Matt was in trouble.

A wave of nausea struck her hard. Renny dropped to the hay-strewn floor of the barn and put her head between her knees. She felt sick. What if she couldn't find him? What if she was too late?

Lifting her head, she stared bleakly around her. "Haven't we had enough?" she cried out. Hot, burning tears pricked the back of her eyes but she fought the urge to cry. For the first time in her life, she just wanted to lie down and ignore it all. She couldn't go through this again.

Death and tragedy had filled the last year. Worry and fear had become her way of life. But before, it had driven her, kept her going. Now it paralyzed her. Still she sat, her heart pounding, the pain in her stomach sharp.

"How will I find you, Matt?" What if she failed him? All of them? A small movement near her boot drew her gaze downward. A small, black beetle scuttled up and over the toe of her boot then stopped, its antennae moving back and forth.

It is time to leave the past behind.

The voice inside her mind startled her. It was her mother's voice. Star Dreamer had been the only mother Renny had ever known. She'd taken Renny into her heart and adopted her as her own. And she'd taught her, as a mother teaches her daughters.

One of Renny's first lessons among the Sioux had been learning to respect every living thing. The first time Renny had squashed a spider in the tipi had been her last. She'd learned quickly that the people who roamed and lived off the land revered all forms of life, taking life only when needed and always giving thanks for that life.

She'd also learned that the appearance of a brother or sister in the wheel of life—as all living things were considered—had meaning.

Staring at the insect that should have scuttled away, Renny found herself, for the first time in a year, questioning why the beetle had come to her.

Beetles were masters at change. They went from grub to winged. They had the ability to change.

Renny stared at the insect for another moment, then shook her head. Change was the last thing she needed. "No more change," she said harshly.

A shadow fell over her. She glanced up to see Tyler standing in the doorway. She jumped up. "Great. Just what I need. You." Renny couldn't face him. Not when she felt as though she'd crack and break into millions of pieces if she lost her grip on her emotions.

"I have something to say, Renny. Do me the courtesy of hearing me out."

Truthfully, Renny didn't think she'd be able to handle a verbal battle, so she folded her arms across her chest and leaned back on her heels. "Fine. Say what you want then leave. Got no time for you, Troll."

"Someday, Renny—"

"Gee, is that all you have to say?" She quirked a brow.

Tyler's lips tightened. "You are not going alone. Your family is on the way."

Renny felt her heart lighten. A huge measure of relief ran through her. The task of finding Matthew alone would have been a daunting one.

"Reed is going as well," Tyler added.

She nodded, feeling a soft glow of warmth overcome the coldness that seemed bone deep. She studied Tyler for a moment. "That leaves you off the hook, Sheriff. I won't be alone, and we will have the *law* with us. You can go back to town and nanny someone else for a while."

"Nope. I'm going with you. All of you."

Renny swung her arms out and up. "We don't need you, Troll. Get that through your thick head." She strode past him.

Chapter Eight

Tyler grabbed Renny by the arm as she passed. "I have something to say to you, Renny."

Renny froze and sent him her most haughty glare. "Save it for someone who wants to listen."

"Dammit, Renny!"

"You're the one damned, Troll. Now let me go."

"Not until you promise to listen to what I have to say." Tyler felt her shift and with fast reflexes, managed to avoid the heel of her boot.

To keep her from running, he slid his hands down her arms, pulled her close and held her arms behind her as he backed her up against the wall of the barn.

With his body close, his feet between hers so she couldn't knee him, he stared down at her. Her eyes flashed with green fire.

"Let me go, Troll."

"Not until you promise to listen."

"Never," she hissed. "You have nothing to say worth listening to."

Shaking his head, struggling with his own temper, he sighed. "Swallow that damn pride of yours, Renny."

Renny tipped her chin. "Pride kept my family together. You would have torn us apart."

"I wanted what was best."

"What you wanted was wrong." Renny's mouth firmed into a tight line.

"And I've admitted that to you," he shouted. "But there are reasons why I acted the way I did."

Renny snorted. "I don't care why."

"But I do," Tyler said softly.

Renny shot him a look of disgust. "Only thing you care about is Sheriff Trowbrydge Tyler Thompkins Tilly."

Frustrated, Tyler felt like shaking her senseless, or better, kissing her senseless.

"Now that we've had this little talk, get your hands off me, Troll—"

Tyler's mouth covered hers. All anger melted at the touch, and feel, and taste of her. She gasped and he drew her breath deep into him.

"I care, Renny," he whispered as he moved his lips over hers.

She shook her head. "No—"

"Yes. I care." He repeated the words and kissed her again. She didn't protest, didn't fight. He lifted her hands, threaded his fingers through hers.

He heard her groan. "Can't. You don't."

"Can. Do." He trailed his lips down the hard line of her jaw, then dipped his tongue into the small cleft in her chin. He returned to her mouth, drawn by her warm, sweet breath.

"Kiss me back, Renny. Kiss me like I'm kissing you," he begged. He'd waited so long for this moment, knew it couldn't last but was willing to take all that she offered. And he badly needed her to give him something—anything.

Renny moved her lips over Tyler's, letting him guide her, following his lead, giving as much as he gave to her. She tasted him, felt his tongue tracing the contours of her lips. It felt strange to kiss in this fashion. But it was also wickedly wonderful.

She filled her lungs with the scent of him. Her body felt weak, and fluid, like she just might melt into a puddle. When he released her hands, she wrapped her arms around him, drawing him hard against her.

Her skin burned. Her blood moved through her hot and heavy, leaving her with a growing restlessness and a need that made her bold enough to use her tongue in the same manner as he'd used his. She moaned, felt as though she would drown in the heady wonder of her first kiss.

His hands roamed up and down her back. Renny slid her palms down over his shoulders, her fingers gliding over the buttery softness of his leather vest.

Sliding her hands down the hard wall of his chest, she felt the pounding of his heart beneath her right hand. He groaned as she ran her palms over him, his voice a deep rumble in her ear.

"So good," he murmured. "Taste so good." Tyler bent his head, his lips and tongue tracing a fiery path down her throat.

Renny leaned her head back against the wall of the barn as Tyler planted kiss after kiss from her throat to the hollow of her neck.

Her hands left his chest, her fingers feathering softly along the hard, stubborn jaw. His skin was soft and smooth, hard and rough. The pads of her fingers moved over him, delighting in the texture and thrill of touching him.

Finally, needing to feel his mouth against hers once more, she cupped his face in her hands, forcing him to kiss her fully.

Tyler obliged her with a kiss that went deeper. He demanded more from her, then let her make the same demands. They were one, merged together by their mutual need.

Renny didn't think. She just let herself feel. And be. She was alive. There was nothing but this kiss, and her need.

She could have stood here all night and kissed. And might have had they not been interrupted by a voice filled with humor and delight.

"Well, this is a pleasant surprise."

Tyler pulled away, using his body to block Renny. He blinked at the woman standing in the doorway of the barn. It took him a long moment to recognize her as Maze. She looked nothing like the gentle, fragile woman he'd taken in.

Maze now resembled a pistol-packing grandmother. She wore a flannel shirt three sizes too big, baggy blue jeans that were fastened to her waist with a length of rope for a belt.

He glanced down at her feet and lifted a brow. She'd cut his jeans instead of rolling the excess length. On her feet she wore a pair of worn leather shoes.

He glanced at her. She smiled so sweetly, he couldn't protest the loss of a pair of pants.

Instead, he concentrated on the fact that she was here in the O'Brien barn at all. "Maze, what are you doing here?"

Maze adjusted her wide-brimmed hat complete with red ribbon tied beneath her jaw. Her eyes were alight with excitement. "Why, I'm going with you, Sheriff."

"But—" He glared down at Renny, who'd gone into a fit of coughing. Tyler tugged at her hair. "Not a word, Renny. Not a damn word," he warned.

Deciding he could only handle one difficult woman at a time, he shoved his hands down onto his hips. "Sure appreciate your willingness to go with us, Maze, but I don't know how long we'll be gone or what we'll find. It'd be best if you waited here for us to return."

Maze simply smiled, her eyes a clear, soft blue. She looked much younger. "My place is with you, and your young lady," she said. Her voice was soft, almost misty.

"Maze, this isn't a little jaunt into the countryside. It's going to be a rough trip, we're riding hard and fast. I'm sorry, I can't allow you to accompany us."

"Big mistake, Troll," Renny said, her voice low.

"Sheriff, I think I know the seriousness of the situation. I will not hamper you in any way." Maze was no longer amused but dead serious.

Tyler frowned. Had the world gone crazy? Since when did sweet little old ladies suddenly turn into rebels?

Beside him, Renny cleared her throat. "Um, as much as I hate to agree with anything the Troll—er, um, Tyler—has to say, he might be right this time." She refused to look at the man who'd just kissed her senseless.

Maze lifted a brow. "You have much to learn as well, Renny. Don't judge me by what you see. Judge me by what I am, and what I am to you."

With that cryptic remark, she turned and glided smoothly out of the barn with her long silvery braid swaying across her back.

Tyler threw up his hands. "Women! What have I done to deserve this!" He leaned down, gave Renny a hard kiss right on the mouth, then strode out after Maze.

Left alone in the barn, Renny stood rooted to the spot. Waves of heat washed over her. "Oh no," she moaned. Pressing her fingers to her lips she could still feel the warmth and moisture of Tyler's mouth moving over hers, could still remember her own heated and eager response.

Heat flooded her cheeks. How could she have kissed Tyler, the Troll? What had come over her? Why hadn't she slapped him, stomped on his foot, punched him in the gut? Anything!

He'd kissed her! Taken her into his arms, kissed

her, and to her mortification, she'd clung to him and kissed him back.

Renny shoved her hands onto her hips and looked around for something to kick. How had this happened? One minute they'd been yelling and fighting, the next moment, kissing like there was no tomorrow.

Renny groaned, horrified by the loss of control, the greedy need that had taken over. Then her eyes narrowed. Just why had he kissed her? What game was he playing now? The man was probably laughing at her, at how inept she'd been, how young and foolish.

A loud, booming voice made her whirl around. Tyler poked his head around the barn door. "Renait, don't got time for you to sulk. Get moving or we'll leave without you."

Renny picked up her loaded saddlebags. "Just try it," she yelled out.

She brushed past him, letting her bags smack against him and knock him off balance. "Don't be telling me what to do, Troll. And don't ever kiss me again. Don't know what game you're playing but it won't work."

Tyler grabbed her long braid, jerking her back. He leaned down, his breath warm against her ear. "One day you'll push me too far."

"Oh, I'm trying, Sheriff. I'm trying."

Without warning, Tyler laughed gruffly. "I'll say one thing, Miss O'Brien. Life is not dull around you. Come on, we'll finish this later. Got a few good hours of light left. We need to get going."

Renny followed. The sound of his genuine laughter along with his promise of more to come, unexpectedly warmed her from the inside out.

Rounding the side of the house, she grew sober at the sight of her brothers and sisters sitting uncharacteristically quiet on the porch steps.

They'd each changed into the clothing of their mother's people. Mattie wore a long buckskin dress and her moccasins. Caitie was dressed exactly like her sister, and looked more like a doll in Mattie's arms.

Kealan and Daire wore their breechclouts, leggings, moccasins and a fringed vest. Kealan had a long white feather tied to a strand of hair while Daire had just pulled his longer hair back and tied it with a beaded leather thong. She was the only one who had not changed into their travel-to-the-land-of-their-people clothing.

She didn't plan on it either. She'd renounced that world, or at least a big part of it. She would go as she was dressed: jeans and an old flannel shirt.

For the next hour, she helped saddle horses and pack supplies. Finally, everyone was mounted and ready to ride. Reed had Caitie in his arms; Kealan was riding with Renny, sulking that Daire got to ride by himself.

Glancing over at Tyler, their gazes locked. He rode up beside her, his horse prancing, eager to ride. "Ready?"

She nodded. "Thank you, Sheriff. We are truly grateful for your help."

And she was. Her mind was so overwrought she

couldn't think straight. But Tyler had stepped in, along with Reed, to get them organized quickly. Even the little ones had been given tasks so they felt useful and a part of what Renny hoped was a rescue mission.

Lifting a brow, Tyler smiled. "Well, if this isn't a first," he said.

Renny wrinkled her nose. "Just don't get too used to it, Sheriff," she warned.

"Only doing this for them," she gestured at her waiting siblings, "and Matthew."

Tyler inclined his head. "Understood."

"Then I guess we'd best get going," Renny suggested.

"I'll give the lead to you. You know the direction your brother would have taken."

Renny stared at Tyler in surprise. She'd figured he'd take command. "Thanks," she said.

He put his hand on her wrist before she could ride off. "There is just one thing I'd ask of you, Miss O'Brien."

Suspicious, Renny gripped the reins tight. "What?"

"Say my name," he asked, his voice low and soft.

"What?" Renny stared at him. She'd expected him to make demands, set conditions that she'd not be able to comply with—all in the name of protecting them and keeping them safe.

Tyler kept his gaze on her. "Just say it. Tyler. Just Tyler."

Renny felt like laughing. Her relief was so great. She didn't want to fight with him. Not now. Not after he'd kissed her senseless. Maybe later. A day or two. So she took a deep breath and said softly, "Tyler."

His mouth softened, and his eyes turned to gray liquid. "Thank you, Renny."

Renny nodded. "Tyler." It felt strange, this truce that seemed to have sprung up between them.

"Well, enough of this nonsense. Let's go. You might as well ride with me," she grumbled, nudging her horse gently.

Together, Renny and Tyler rode out of the yard with everyone falling in behind.

"Matt!" Brenna bent over Matt, frantic. Blood was everywhere. She took her shawl and tried to stop the flow of blood pouring from a wound on his side. She glanced over her shoulder at her brother. "Gilbert O'Leary, have you lost your mind?" Gil had shot Matt. She felt sick. "Why?" she sobbed. So much blood. It wouldn't stop.

"Get away from him," Gil ordered.

"No," Brenna said, tears coursing down her face.

"You left me, Bre. Like Collin. And our mother." Gil paused. "*He* took you from me." His voice was tortured, pain-filled as he pointed the rifle at Matthew. "Move."

Brenna turned to protect Matthew from Gil. "No. You cannot do this. You know that I agreed to go with him," she said. "You know he was taking me to his people."

"No right," Gil said. "No right to leave me alone."

"That is why you shot him? Because I went with him?" Brenna's heart sank. Matt was hurt, and hurt badly. It was her fault.

"He took you. You went. You left me." His voice rose.

"Gil, I didn't have any choice." Brenna tried to keep the fear and panic from her voice.

"Move away." He had the rifle ready, his finger poised to pull the trigger.

Realizing that Gil meant to make sure Matthew died, she stood, her body protectively in front of Matthew's.

"Please, Gil, what do you want?" She'd give him anything, including her own life, if he spared Matt's.

Gil's eyes were glazed with pain. "You left me, Bre. You all left me."

Brenna stepped toward her brother. "I'll come with you. I'll stay with you. I promise never to leave you if you promise not to shoot Matthew again." She feared her plea was too late. Without anyone to tend to him, Matthew wouldn't survive. But she had to do what she could.

Gil glanced from her to Matthew's bloodied body. He lowered the rifle. "You come. And you don't leave me. Ever." A quick flip had the gun pointing at her. "If you try to leave me, I'll kill you."

Brenna swallowed the bile in the back of her throat as she nodded. "All right. I promise." She bent back down beside Matthew. "Let me tend to Matt, first," she said, quickly pressing her shawl more firmly against the wound.

Gil grabbed her by her single braid and yanked. “No, the savage lives or dies on his own. Get the food and water.” He kept the gun trained on her.

Brenna scurried to do as he ordered. She grabbed the rations while Gil went through Matt’s things, taking what he wanted.

She watched her brother nervously. She’d go with Gil, but first, she had to try and do what she could for Matt. With her back to her brother, she pretended to be going through the food pouch. Leaning over Matt, she yanked a tiny medicine pouch from beneath her blouse and pressed it into Matt’s hand and closed his fingers over it.

“May the spirits watch over you,” she whispered. “Let them guide someone to you.” The Missouri River was so close. She hoped that someone would find Matthew before it was too late. She left her own water pouch, and some food, hidden beneath her shawl. She also left behind her pouch of healing herbs and medicines.

Standing, she followed her brother out of the lean-to, praying that she’d made the right choice. As she mounted her horse, she kept up her mantra of prayer. For herself, she asked for nothing.

Chapter Nine

The horse spirit, Silver Star, stood over Renny as she slept beneath the stars. The woman had a long journey ahead of her and not a lot of time. Silver sighed, her breath stirring the air near Renny's face.

Renny shifted slightly as though she felt Silver Star's presence in her sleep.

Silver lowered her muzzle and rubbed her nose against Renny's cheek.

Remember your friends.

We will help you.

Look for us.

See us!

"See you," came the murmured response. Renny stirred in her sleep and frowned, her lips moving silently.

Yes, see us. Listen to us. Believe. Remember.

Renny lifted a hand in sleep. Her fingers brushed over Silver's soft muzzle. "Believe. Soft."

Silver folded her legs beneath her and lay beside

Renny. There was a long journey ahead of them all. Tonight, Renny gave her hope.

Renny stood alone. They'd traveled hard for four days, following the James River to a smaller stream that headed west. Tomorrow, they'd cross a stretch of prairie land and come to the next stream, one that would take them to the Missouri River.

So far, they had not found any sign of Matthew or Brenna. Renny had climbed a small rise, hoping against hope to find some sign, while the others rested and the horses were watered. Once again she glanced upward.

Every time they saw buzzards circling, her heart started pounding for what they might discover. Thankfully, it was always an animal that lay dying or dead.

At the moment, a pair of golden eagles soared across the clear blue sky, circling lazily in the warmth of the afternoon. One bird glided down toward the earth on powerful, silent wings.

Without any warning, it seemed to stop, and suddenly swooped down with such speed and force that Renny heard the killing strike before the eagle rose triumphantly with a small rabbit dangling in its talons.

Renny held her breath and stared up as the majestic bird flew overhead. Her heart raced with excitement. The bird had struck so close to where she stood, she'd easily seen its bright eyes and sharp beak, the mantle of feathers on its head and neck.

A small dark feather drifted down in the bird's

wake. Renny followed it with her eyes, reaching up to grab it. Staring at the golden feather, she held it up to the sun and watched the colors shimmer.

For just a moment she forgot all her worries and allowed herself to remember her first summer living on the plains. Each day had been filled with the beauty and wonders of Mother Earth.

With all that had happened in the last year, she'd forgotten what it was like to travel across the earth and become one with this world.

Running her finger along the soft edge of the feather, she instinctively called forth the qualities of *Wambli,* Eagle.

Though her Sioux mother had continually taught all her children the ways of the Sioux, in the last few years Renny had been too busy helping her father with the land to really pay much attention to the stories and teachings she'd heard for more than half her life.

Closing her eyes, she called to mind the image of the graceful birds. Their ability to hunt and soar great heights still amazed and thrilled her. They spent most of their time in the sky, in the realm of the Spirit world, yet were a part of her world. The sacred birds maintained a balance between both worlds.

Leave the shadows of pain and despair and find within you the power to heal.

Renny stared at the dark speck as the eagle flew away. Eagles were sacred birds. Many thought they possessed the power to heal. What did the eagle mean to her? She wasn't hurt, it was Matt who suffered.

Tucking the feather in her pocket, Renny turned to join to her family. Movement near a stand of trees caught her eye. She held her breath at the sight of a beautiful horse.

Pale yellow, the horse stood out among the green grass. For a moment, two creatures of the earth stared at one another. Then the horse reared up, pawed the air, turned back and disappeared.

Renny started to follow. She had to see the magnificent animal again. Up close. Even just another glimpse would do. But Tyler's voice stopped her.

"Renny, where are you going? No one is to leave camp alone."

Whipping around, Renny scowled at him. "Correction, the children cannot leave camp without an adult. I am an adult and do not need you to play nanny."

Angry that he'd shattered the surreal spectacle that nature had put on for her, she stalked past him, purposely stomping her feet. When he quickly moved out of her way she couldn't help but grin. He was learning.

"I saw that," he grumbled. "We have a truce, remember?"

Renny wrinkled her nose. "An unspoken one," she said. One borne out of a kiss that haunted her dreams. She slid a glance at Tyler.

He wore his black leather vest over a plain white shirt. Dark pants and his dark hat made him look intimidating. The star pinned to his chest sparkled in the late-afternoon sunlight.

For once, the reminder of his authority didn't irritate her. She accepted, at least to herself, that on this trip she needed him. Matthew needed him. They all did.

He stopped and held out a large hand. "Shall we make it official?" The humor in his eyes was gone. "Truce."

Renny hesitated only a second before putting her hand in his. "Okay. Truce."

Then they each smiled. Renny averted her eyes and told herself not to get goofy about a stupid truce. Once they were back in Pheasant Gully, she had no doubt they'd resume their verbal sparring. He'd turn back into a mother hen, and she'd have to rebel.

She just hoped that somewhere along the way, they'd be able to share another one of those toe-tingling kisses. To cover any hint of awkwardness and embarrassment at the direction of her thoughts, she lengthened her stride.

At the edge of camp, Renny stopped to watch her family. They'd ridden as long and as hard as humanly possible, considering the size of their party and the wide range of ages.

She spotted Kealan lying down by the water's edge with a wooden pole dangling in the water. Given enough time, he'd probably fall asleep while trying to hook himself a fish or two for dinner.

Renny smiled proudly at the owl feather he wore in his hair. He'd also donned the clothing of their people. Kealan, her little warrior.

Across the river, birds soared, dipped, rose and dived through the air to catch a last meal of the day. Insects hummed, chirped and buzzed, and small creatures scurried through grass still wet from afternoon thundershowers. She turned to survey their small camp.

Sitting next to the fire, Daire sharpened his knife. He was quiet. Too quiet. She worried about him. He hadn't merely lost the innocence of childhood. It had been viciously taken from him.

Sighing, she spotted Mattie and Reed beneath a tree. Caitie lay asleep in Mattie's lap.

Maze was the only one moving about. The woman was a stranger to them yet seemed so familiar, almost as though they'd been friends all their lives. She had a kind smile, and always a kind word for all of them.

Maze had taken on the role of cook. It had only taken one sampling of her cooking for all of them to agree.

At first glance, Maze looked like an older woman with her silvery hair, her manner of dress and her gentle nature. But she moved like a much younger woman, and had more energy than the rest of them put together.

She glanced up from the fire and smiled at Renny. Renny smiled back, held in place by those wise, blue eyes. Whenever she was around the woman, her fears seemed to ease. She wasn't sure why. Turning away, Renny thought it might be the woman's eyes.

They seemed to reflect the day itself, going from a light pale blue in the mornings to a deep, dark blue each night with the twinkle of stars and so much more.

Restless, Renny glanced at the horizon and frowned. There was still daylight left, and they had far yet to go.

She, Mattie, Reed and Tyler had made a map, using the route Renny knew Matt would take. They estimated the number of miles and days Matthew had been gone. Using the day Mattie had her vision, they'd tried to estimate his location.

Of course, he could have veered off course for any number of reasons. Still, they had to start somewhere, had to have a goal in mind or they'd just wander aimlessly without ever finding Matthew.

She put her hands on her hips. They were so many days behind Matthew and Brenna. Renny pushed them all hard, needing to cover many miles each day. Once more she glanced at the sun, judged the amount of light left.

Tyler touched her gently on the shoulder. "They need rest. We all do."

Renny sighed. Tyler was right, though she'd never admit it to him. "We'll stop for the night."

"We'll find him, Renny." Tyler's voice was soft. Tender.

Renny shook it off. She needed her edge. Anger always drove her. But with their truce, she didn't have a ready target to keep that anger flowing. Still, she didn't have to sit back and do nothing.

"I'm going to go talk to Mattie. See if she's had

any more visions." She started forward but Tyler stopped her with a hand to her arm.

"Let her rest, Renny. Hounding her won't help. She'll tell you. You know she will."

Above their heads, large black-as-night crows squawked and fluttered from branch to branch of a tall cottonwood. Several flew off, their cries echoing around them.

"I know, but Matt—"

"We'll find him, Renny. Pushing yourself or the others won't speed it up. He's days ahead of us still."

Renny felt torn. She was very afraid that they wouldn't find Matthew in time. Often, Mattie's visions were of the future. Like her mother and grandmother's visions, fast action often stopped a vision from becoming real.

But this time she was pretty sure that it was too late to stop Matthew from being shot. That meant he was out here somewhere, hurt. Maybe dying. She could only hope that Brenna was still alive, and was caring for Matthew.

She glanced back over at Mattie. As frustrated and impatient as Renny was, she knew Mattie had it worse. Every moment was spent waiting for the next vision, knowing it would come and fearing what it would bring.

Tyler took her arm. "Take a walk with me," he suggested.

To his surprise, Renny fell in step with him. They walked, following a twisting, burbling stream. The land was flat and open. Still, Tyler kept an eye on their surroundings.

When minutes passed without any snide remarks, Tyler turned his head to study Renny. She seemed to have taken the truce between them to heart.

For the first time he could remember, she seemed relaxed. Her face wasn't tight with irritation or anger. Her mouth was soft-looking, not a firm, hard line. Even her eyes seemed softer, rounder.

As though she felt his eyes on her, she snapped her head around. "What?" Her eyes narrowed slightly.

"Nothing." He shrugged. "Just like looking at you, that's all." The words left his mouth. He winced to himself and waited.

Instead of jumping all over him, stabbing him verbally, or causing pain to his feet or shins, she ducked her head as though embarrassed.

"You're being foolish, Tr—er, Tyler." She coughed as though choking on his name.

Tyler laughed, low and soft. "Don't want to spoil things between us but it's true." He figured a truce between them was too good to be true and if he'd already blown it, he might as well go all the way.

"You're beautiful, Renny." He watched her, saw her shake her head in denial. She opened her mouth, her eyes flashing dangerously.

"What are you talking about, T—"

Tyler put a finger to her lips. "Please. Don't say it. Don't say anything to ruin this moment."

To his utter astonishment, Renny didn't say a word. Nor did she pull away from him. Once again, her face grew gentle.

"I mean it. Just gotta say it."

Renny rolled her eyes and shook his finger off. "Come on, Sheriff. Laying it on a bit thick, aren't you?"

Feeling her stiffen beneath his fingers, he ran his palms up and down her arm slowly, gently, as though calming a high-spirited horse.

"It's true." His gaze roamed over her short, slightly upturned nose, the smattering of freckles across the bridge of her nose, her golden-tipped lashes.

Staring down into her eyes, he saw the clear, clean splash of her innocence and felt himself fall into the deep, deep pool of crystalline green.

She tugged at him deep inside, had from the very first time that he'd met her. His hand lifted to her thick braid and slowly wound her dark, red hair around his fist, drawing her closer.

"I shouldn't, but I think I'm going to." His eyes dipped to her mouth. Her tongue snaked out to wet her lips.

"Going to what?" Her voice was husky, her breath sweet and tempting.

"Kiss you." His other hand slid around the back of her neck, his mouth inches from hers.

"Why?" Her question was low. Her lips barely moved.

"Because." He stared into her eyes, waiting for

them to harden, expecting her to shove him away, stomp on his foot.

To his surprise, she smiled, softly, the corners of her mouth tipping up in amusement. "Not much on words, are you, Sheriff?"

He grinned, felt his body jerk as a rush of heated desire slammed into him. "Tyler. Just Tyler. Say it."

Renny's gaze dropped to his mouth. She stared, then licked her own lips. "Tyler," she whispered.

Her eyelids fluttered, then she looked at him with longing in her gaze. "You talk too much, Just Tyler." Then she slid into his embrace.

Renny was ready this time. And eager. She closed her lips over his mouth and kissed the hell out of him. When he moaned, she grinned, well pleased.

Tyler's lips moved over hers. "Think this is funny?"

"Hmmm," she said. "It's wonderful." Her fingers were in his hair, threading through the golden silk.

A soft laugh rumbled from Tyler. He pulled her close and took control.

Renny hung on as she went for the ride of her life. The first kiss was gentle and tame compared to this one. Tyler held nothing back and demanded everything from Renny.

Renny gave. And gave. Then she took. And danced in a silent duel with his tongue. But in this, she found she was more than willing to share control.

Hanging onto Tyler, Renny finally broke off to

drag in a desperately needed breath of air. With her head against Tyler's chest, she heard him gulping deep breaths as well.

To think that just a few days ago she'd scorned the thought of locking lips with a man. Had anyone dared to suggest it would be Tyler, she'd have punched them out cold.

Ever since that first kiss, she'd dreamt of him, hungered for more even as she fought to keep him at arm's length. But today, the peace of the day, the worry in her heart, and the exhaustion of her soul, she wanted him close. She needed him close. At any time during their walk, she could have picked a fight to keep him at a distance. She was good at it—she'd had all year to hone that particular skill.

"What are you thinking, Renny?" Tyler ran a thumb over the small cleft in her chin. His cheek rested on her head.

"Thinking of all the things I could have said so you wouldn't kiss me." For once she answered honestly.

"Why didn't you?"

She shrugged. "Not sure." It was hard to think of him as the enemy when he was doing all he could to help her family.

Chuckling, Tyler wrapped his arms around her tightly. "Renny, you never fail to surprise me."

She clung to him for a long moment. "Don't expect it to last, Troll." For once, the name had a soft, almost loving sound to it.

Laughing softly in her ear, Tyler pulled gently on

her braid until they were staring at each other. He lowered his head, stealing a quick but just as potent kiss. Then he let her go and held out his hand. "Come on, let's head back before the truce is over."

Easy with each other, they fell into step, bumping shoulders as they retraced their path.

Chapter Ten

Bruised, tired and sick to her very soul, Brenna sat on the ground, her knees pulled up to her chest, her arms wrapped tightly around them. She was wet from the storm, cold to the bone and scared to death. She whispered her prayers, needing to hear the words aloud.

"Shut up, Brenna."

Lifting her head, she tried to see her brother but it was too dark. He was a shadow among shadows somewhere in front of her. She heard his harsh breathing, smelled the stink of too many days with no bath and the sour stench of drink. Gil never used to drink. Their mother wouldn't let him. She knew he'd found their stepfather's stash.

"Gil, please. Let's go back. I promise to stay with you. We need to help Matthew. I'll still go wherever you want me to go, but we have to go back. We can't let him die."

Her voice rose with hysteria. It might be too late. Every day she tried to talk to Gil, make him see that what he was doing was wrong. Part of her wished she'd just let him kill her. At least then she wouldn't be so tormented.

" 'Breed gets what's comin' to him."

Brenna heard her mother's voice in his words. Heard her mother's tone, her hatred. A sob rose in her throat. "God, Gil." How had she never seen just how much like their mother he was?

She couldn't believe that he'd been following them since they'd left Pheasant Gully. For two weeks he'd been somewhere near, watching, his hatred growing.

The first week, Matthew had set a slow pace, spending many of the days just walking. She hadn't minded. It had made her so tired at night, she'd slept soundly.

He hadn't talked, or told her why he wasn't making use of the horses. Or why he stopped in certain spots sometimes for a day or longer, or where he went when he ordered her to stay in camp while he was gone an entire day at a time.

She didn't really care whether they rode fast and furious or just picked their way across the land. It was time she had with Matthew, for she knew once they reached his people she'd not see much of him.

She rubbed her eyes with her palms. "None of this is his fault—"

Gil jumped up with a roar of rage. He landed a sharp blow to the side of her face. Brenna cried out.

"No. It's your fault. Yours and Ma's. Ruined everything, killed everyone I loved."

"That's not true!" Brenna bit her lower lip. Her

face was caked with dried tears and the dust of travel. Her throat ached, and her eyes felt raw from crying.

"Shut up," Gil shouted. "It's Ma's fault that Pa left."

Brenna shook her head, knowing he was talking about their real father.

"Pa was killed going west. He got sick. The letter Ma got said so. He would have sent for us had he made it."

"Liar!" Gil's hand shot out and grabbed her by the hair. He pulled hard, his hand going to her throat. "She drove him away. Told him to leave. I heard her. Then she got with that O'Leary bastard. She was probably having an affair."

Brenna tried not to whimper. She had no idea that Gil had always hated her mother for marrying Patrick O'Leary after their real father had died.

"You cannot blame me for what Ma did."

"You killed Collin," he said, breathing heavily in her face. "Could have stopped him. Or her."

"Tried," she sobbed. She'd never forget the horror of watching her mother attack Mattie with a shovel, and set the barn on fire, leaving Mattie to burn to death. She'd yelled for help. Everyone had come running at her frantic cries. Collin hadn't hesitated. He'd rushed in.

Things had seemed to happen in slow motion that day. Brenna had been in shock over all of it and unable to even comprehend all that had happened except that Mattie had survived, Collin had not, and her mother had truly lost her mind that day.

"Liar." Gil threw Brenna away from him. "They're gone. All of them and it's your fault. Yours and Ma's." He kicked her as he stalked away.

Brenna curled into a ball on the ground, hiding her face. With dried blood staining her shirt, skirt and soul, she prayed to whomever would listen.

Save Matthew. Keep him safe. Let him be found. Let him live.

Pain burned through Matthew, clawed at him from the inside out. Heat engulfed his body, and a coldness seeped into his heart and soul.

He was dying. Deep in his mind, he heard drums. His spirit song. The rhythmic chanting had no beginning, no end. It soothed his mind, allowed him to float high above the pain.

Shadows moved across the back of his eyes. *Wanagi. Ghosts, spirits.* The darkness of the world split in two. He stood among the dark, a spectator among the specters, those whose spirits were still tied to the earth.

Fear of death, of a joyless existence, made him force his eyes open. He blinked, could barely open them but managed to focus on the endless blue heavens high above him. The spirit world was there, high above him.

His body ached, his mind drifted, but he kept his eyes open, afraid to close them, afraid that darkness might claim him.

As he stared, colorful yet transparent tipis seemed to appear in the blue prairie sky. Off to his right, he spotted a glow of light. It moved across the sky, over him. He drew in a startled breath when he recognized that they were warriors riding proudly above him.

Off in the distance, he saw herds of buffalo. The spirit world was all that he'd been told it would be and he yearned for release from the pain racking his human body. The spirit world beckoned, faint wisps of clouds floated over him. Faces appeared.

He knew he was passing from one world to the next and though it hurt to look upon a world of light and beauty, of great mystery and sacredness, he fought to keep his eyes open.

I am ready.

Accept me.

He drifted off, no longer afraid of the darkness.

The next morning dawned crisp and clear. Renny rose rested and eager to be on the move. After a light meal, everyone was packed and ready to leave. Days of riding hard were paying off. It was time to slow down or they might risk riding past Matthew and Brenna.

Renny figured with the hard riding, they were only a few days from wherever Matthew and Brenna were, depending on how many stops Matthew had made. With Brenna along, she hoped he'd gone slower than normal.

"Mattie, which way?" There were two choices. The river split. One fork went west and led to another river. The second fork ran north. It would connect with the same river that led to the Missouri.

Matthew used both routes. Which one this

time? Renny tried hard to keep panic and fear from her voice. In her mind, she had envisioned her brother and Brenna making the trip. She knew his route, his traveling habits, and how long it would have taken him to reach every landmark.

The thought of failing her brother nearly paralyzed her, kept her from thinking and acting and leading the others. She paced. The sun had risen, they'd eaten. It was time to ride. She just wasn't sure which river to follow.

She took Mattie's hands into her own. "Mattie?" It was up to Mattie now. There were hundreds of spots where Matthew could be lying hurt, dying or—

No, she refused to believe him dead. She would not lose another member of her family. They wouldn't proceed without some clear idea of which direction Matt had gone.

"You have to help me, sister. You said you've had visions since."

"Yes, but nothing more of Matthew."

"Then seek a vision. Look for landmarks. A stream, the bent-man rock, the great hollow tree. Anything. Give me something so I know where to go."

"Renny," Mattie's voice was close to tears. "I don't know. I can't see him. I've tried to call the vision to me but there is nothing."

Hands on her shoulders made Renny stiffen. She shook her head, warning Tyler to keep silent. But she softened her voice, calmed her own fear of failing. "Okay, Mattie. It's okay."

Mattie shook her head. "No. He's hurt. I know

he's hurt. I feel his pain, see the darkness around him."

"But alive," Renny said, grasping onto that fact. Had he been dead, Mattie would have known. She'd have felt it even more violently than the first vision.

"Yes. But his spirit is weak."

"We won't let him die, Mattie. We'll find him, but you have to help me."

Sighing, Mattie turned and held out a hand. Reed came forward at once. "I will tell you all that I've seen but I fear none of it is enough. I can make no sense of it."

Renny held her breath and blocked out everything but Mattie. "Then tell me. Let me try to make sense of it."

Mattie nodded. "There is a man. A big man. He has white hair. I cannot see his face. Just the shape of him. When I try to see, he fades."

"He shot Matthew?"

Mattie shook her head. "No. Can't tell you why or how I know, but he's not evil. I feel safe when I see him."

"Okay. What about Brenna?" Though still angry at the girl she'd called her friend, Renny would never wish her harm. She understood better than anyone the pull of family, the need to protect, at all costs, those you loved.

"I'm not sure. There is something—feels like anger or hate." Her voice trailed off uncertainly.

"Then we go, but we go slow, and spread out." She turned away, ready to shout out the orders to mount up, but Tyler grabbed her by the shoulder and put a finger to his lips. He nodded toward Mattie and Reed.

Renny turned. Mattie had gone still, her eyes open but blank. Renny held her breath.

"A horse." Mattie whispered the words. "No, two horses. One is like a shimmering cloud. She follows you but you do not see. . . ." Her voice trailed off.

"The other—" She shook her head then opened her eyes.

Renny sagged with disappointment. "That's it? Me and two horses?"

Mattie reached out to run her hands up her sister's arms until her palms cupped Renny's face.

"Renny, all my visions but that first one concern you. I didn't understand. I was fighting my gift, trying to force it to tell me what I wanted."

Renny frowned. "There's nothing wrong with that, Mattie. What good is a gift like yours if you cannot use it?"

Mattie paused. She looked worried. "By trying to force what will not come, I am not paying attention to what the spirits *are* trying to tell me."

Renny was anxious and not in the mood for riddles. "Just tell me, Mattie."

Mattie sighed. "This is about you."

Renny frowned. Her hands covered Mattie's. "That makes no sense, Mattie. I don't have visions. I can't see what is around Matthew to guide us to him. I can't feel him. I can only help him if you help me."

Mattie leaned forward and rested her forehead against Renny's. "I understand now. Finally. Every day I see you leading us. Being strong. My visions say it is you who will lead us to Matthew."

"You're crazy," Renny whispered.

Her heart pounded. She'd never been so scared in all her life. The burdens she carried seemed heavier, harder to bear.

Mattie stepped back. "Listen to your heart, sister of my heart. It will guide you, and you will guide us."

Renny backed up against Tyler. His strong hands on her shoulders didn't warm the chill seeping through her.

"Mattie, please. Tell me which way to go. We are ready to go. Tell me which way."

Renny refused to be the one to decide. She didn't have Mattie's gifts. She had no idea how to find their brother.

Mattie sighed sadly. "Renny, I cannot tell you what I do not know. I have told you what I have seen. You must find him for us." With that, Mattie turned and let Reed lead her away.

Renny started to follow. To argue. To beg and plead even. Tyler stopped her, grabbed her arm.

"Renny, hounding her won't accomplish anything."

Rounding on him, their truce of the night before forgotten, Renny slashed out.

"And that nonsense she's spouting will? Stay out of this, Tyler. This is family. My family." She tried to tug her arm free but his grip tightened.

"Riling me up won't help, Renny." He let go of her arm.

Renny backed away. "No, nothing will help. He'll die. Because of me." Grief would once again tear her family apart. Renny felt sick to her stomach. She pressed her fist to her stomach, then turned and ran.

Tyler felt torn between comforting Renny and figuring out what to do next. He strode over to Mattie and Reed but didn't know what to say. How could he say anything when he didn't really understand.

Mattie gave him a half smile. Tyler knew Reed would have told her he approached.

"Sheriff Tyler, this is Renny's journey."

Tyler rubbed the back of his neck. "You willing to sacrifice your brother for this journey you speak of?"

"I have no choice, Sheriff. I cannot tell what I do not know. All I know is that somehow this is something Renny has to do. Without me."

Taking his own advice, Tyler knew he couldn't push Mattie. He turned. Renny would not be alone. She had him and he'd make sure she knew that.

He gave everyone brief orders to stay in camp and headed to where he'd found her the night before. A muffled sob stopped him short. Renny sat on the small rise with her head on her knees, her arms wrapped around her legs.

In the year that he'd known her, he'd never seen her cry. He hurried over, knelt behind her and pulled her against him. "God, don't cry, Renny."

She shrugged him off. "Not crying. Crying does a person no good," she said, her voice heating.

Preferring anger to tears, Tyler moved to her side, gripped her chin and forced her to face him. His heart cried for her. So much had happened during the last year and he felt ashamed for causing her pain and grief, even though his intentions had been honest and pure.

"Renny. We'll find him. I'll help you." Tyler would do everything in his power to help her. "Maybe you and I can ride out, see if we find any sign of him."

Renny stood and paced, her arms wrapped around herself, her steps slow, hesitant. "No. That will take too much time. And if Mattie has a vision, one that tells us which way, I want to be here."

"But she said—"

"She's wrong! She has to be." Her voice was low and fierce.

"Has she ever been wrong?"

"No," she whispered softly, her voice trembling.

Tyler sighed. "Then we wait." He tried to smile. "She said there were two horses. Maybe his and Brenna's horses will come and lead us to them." His eyes widened. "That could happen, right?"

Renny spun around. "What did you say?"

"Their horses—" He broke off when she waved him silent. He watched as she paced, each step deliberate, her hands on her hips, her brows drawn in deep concentration. She jerked her body around and stared down toward the stand of trees.

"What is it, Renny?"

"A horse. A pale yellow horse."

"Where?" He didn't see a horse.

"It was there. Last night. A real beauty. I was going to go after it, then you came." Her voice turned sulky.

"No one was to leave camp. Rules, Renny, that you made."

"Don't start splitting hairs on me now, Troll." There was no heat in her voice. She drew in a deep breath, closed her eyes and let her head fall back. After a few seconds, she opened her eyes and turned in a slow circle, her eyes scanning.

"What are you looking for?" His gaze traveled over the landscape, seeking danger.

"Signs."

"Like what?" Did she expect some arrow to magically appear?

"Come on, Renny. We need to talk to Reed and come up with a plan." He eyed a circling eagle. "Otherwise, we're just going to go in circles."

Renny was staring up at the sky. The eagle suddenly shot off to the north.

Renny jumped over to Tyler and hugged him.

"North," she said, her voice sharp, alert and confident.

"What?" The sweet scent of Renny had Tyler's mind suddenly blank.

"North. We follow the eagle."

Putting Renny from him, Tyler frowned. "Now that is just crazy, Renny O'Brien."

Renny shot him a haughty glare. "That is the

way we head out. You can come or you can wait." She took off, shouting for everyone to saddle up.

Tyler shook his head. What had just happened? Renny had gone from despondent to confident, all because some bird decided to fly north? He followed, and listened to her giving orders like a general in an army.

No one argued, or questioned. Watching, he had to admit that perhaps Mattie was right after all. Perhaps this was a journey that Renny had to make.

He just hoped that they found Matthew and Brenna alive. He wasn't sure what another death would do to her, or any of them.

Chapter Eleven

Late that afternoon, Renny wasn't feeling nearly as confident as she had that morning. In fact, she had to wonder what had come over her to even think that she could make such a decision based on so little.

She stared at the earth's endless expanse of greens and browns and fought the waves of panic rising inside her. Her body trembled with nerves. When they'd set out that morning, she'd been so sure that they'd find Matthew by the end of the day.

The eagle had been a sign; following it had felt right. Hadn't she followed Mattie's advice and let herself be guided? But after another long, weary day of riding, searching and finding not even a trace of her brother or Brenna, doubts were creeping into her mind like fog slipping beneath the crack in a door.

What if she'd been wrong? With miles of open land and hidden valleys, they could have ridden right by Matthew if he left the river for any reason.

Or worse, she could have led them in the wrong direction. He might have taken the other fork in the river. Her stomach burned.

Pressing a hand to her midriff, she let out a shaky breath. So many paths, so many choices, and if she made the wrong choice, Matthew would die. That was very clear. Somewhere out here, Matt lay injured. She didn't need the gift of sight to know that he'd been shot. She had Mattie. She knew her sister maybe better than she knew herself. Mattie said Matt had been shot. Renny accepted this.

What she could not accept was that it was up to her to find her brother. She turned her head slightly. Mattie rode beside her with Caitie cradled in her lap, sleeping.

"Mattie, what if I'm wrong?"

Renny had no wish to add to her sister's burden. But the weight of her brother's life seemed to be riding on her shoulders. It wasn't fair that the burden be hers alone.

Mattie didn't speak right away. Finally, she turned her head toward Renny and kept her voice low so she didn't wake Caitie.

"This morning you did not have doubts. You believed."

Renny's lips twisted in frustration. "Then where is he? Why have we had no sign since? We could be going the wrong way, or even have passed him." She swallowed the bitter taste of failure.

"Mattie, you've got to help. You can *see* him. Find him. Tell me where he is, then I can guide you to him. Please, Mattie," Renny begged. She was desperately worried. She needed Mattie more than ever.

Mattie shook her head. "I can't, Renny. There is nothing for me to see. What I have seen, and heard, I've already told you. You must find him. I am here with you, and I will help all I can."

"I can't do this." Renny's shoulders sagged.

"Of course you can," Mattie said, her tone sounding very much like their mother's.

"How?" Renny asked. She shifted in her saddle, then stood in her stirrups to stretch. "Tell me how. Give me a clue." She was tired, in body and spirit.

Mattie's voice softened. "You know the ways of our people as well as I. The answers lie within you. Trust your instincts, Renny. Stop doubting yourself."

Mattie drew a shaky breath. "Matthew needs you strong, sister of my heart. You must do this. For him. For all of us."

Renny plopped herself back down. The conversation was starting to make her mad and more than a bit afraid. "I can't, Mattie. Don't ask this of me!" Fear made her voice sharp.

Mattie's voice broke. In her arms, Caitie stirred. She calmed herself, her eyes filled with wisdom but her face lined with worry. "I'm sorry, sister. You must do this. As much for yourself as for us."

Mattie's voice was firm. Renny felt even more discouraged. Anger usually served her well, got her through whatever problems arose in her life, but she knew it would not help her this time.

Frustrated, Renny scowled. "Why, Mattie? Why must I do this?" She didn't want this responsibility. She couldn't do what Mattie asked of her, what they all seemed to expect. She needed help. Mattie's help.

Mattie closed her eyes. "Each of us must make a journey through life. Our paths are sometimes narrow and straight, but often they are wide and winding, with many forks and twists and turns. We are never alone. You have your animal totems, your spirit helpers. Call upon them to guide you."

Renny made a rude sound. The spirits had abandoned her family and she had renounced them the day she'd buried her parents. Why would they come to her now? Why would she waste time begging them to show themselves?

Mattie sent her a stern look. "Listen to your heart," she ordered. She sounded impatient. "Trust in yourself, Renny."

Renny's hands tightened on her reins. Her horse gave an impatient jerk until she relaxed her grip.

Mattie came to a halt. "I will tell you this," she began. "You are *Weshawee,* of the Miniconjou Sioux. You are the adopted daughter of my mother. Remember her teachings. Call upon them. Become *Weshawee* once more."

Mattie reached out, waited until Renny took her hand. "Believe as we did when we were children and roamed this land with a carefree heart. This is your journey. Take from it all that is offered and reap the rewards."

Renny held her sister's hand tightly. "And what

of Matt?" she asked, her voice rising. "Is it right to condemn him to death if I fail?" Her voice turned husky as she thought of what another loss would do to their family.

If Renny couldn't find Matthew, it would be like letting her stepmother down. Star Dreamer had taught Renny about The People. She had shown her the wonders of a strange and alien world. Star Dreamer had been the only mother she'd ever known and she'd taken Renny into her heart as though she'd given birth to her.

Renny's heart ached for her mother. She missed her so much. The pain was unbearable. When would it go away? "Mattie, what of Matthew?" Renny had to convince Mattie that she was wrong. For all their sakes.

Mattie shook her head. "I have not seen him in my visions since that first one. But he is alive, Renny. If my brother were dead, I'd know."

Renny believed Mattie and drew that tiny bit of comfort into her mind and heart. But she was not ready to accept her quest.

"He is your brother," Renny said. "Who better to save his life?"

Mattie smiled softly. "Is he not yours as well, my sister? You have it within you to do this. You must believe."

"And if I fail? What then?" She voiced her fear and found herself more afraid of Mattie's answer.

Mattie sighed. "I don't know, Renny. I don't know."

* * *

With Reed riding at his side, Tyler watched Renny ride off by herself. He shook his head. "You get the feeling that this is going to be an impossible mission?"

Reed frowned. "I feel sorry for both Renny and my wife. They are afraid and there is little I can do for either one of them."

Tyler felt the same way. He wanted to share Renny's burden but she refused to let him. He clenched his jaw. How could he help with something he didn't understand?

He kept his gaze on Renny as she left them all behind. She rode as though chased by demons. Taking off his hat, he ran his hands through his hair. Behind him, the rest of their party had fallen silent. He knew that they were all watching Renny.

Tyler glanced over at Reed. Reed was Tyler's trusted deputy and friend, whom Fate and past tragedies had brought back into his life. Like a tiny splash in a pond, the ripples of the past had flooded into the present.

One decision made by Reed's father so long ago was still causing ripples of pain. So much tragedy, so much loss. Tyler had never before really understood how one seemingly unimportant decision could have such grave consequences. One event triggering another, then another, then coming together in a sometimes not so nice and tidy package.

"What do you make of all this, Reed?"

Reed tipped his hat up with a finger. "I figure we are just along for the ride."

"Can't buy that." Tyler absently ran the reins

through his fingers. He kept his eyes on Renny. Her fear and loneliness called to him. He wanted to ride out and join her. He would not sit back and watch Renny torture herself like this.

Reed sighed. "Mattie speaks the truth. She has the gift of sight and you know it. What she sees or feels is real. You saw proof of that. Hell, I even had a vision myself."

"I remember," Tyler said. He'd never before believed in the supernatural, wasn't sure he believed now. All he could say was that things had happened that could not be easily explained. He had a feeling that before this rescue mission was over, he'd become a believer.

As though he could read his mind, Reed added, "Never would have believed it if I hadn't had a vision. Made a believer out of me, and I don't mind telling you, it is one experience that I could happily live without."

"Whether it's real or not doesn't help right now." Tamping down on the helpless frustration, Tyler narrowed his eyes, keeping Renny in sight. "Must be something we can do to help. Can't just stand by and watch her suffer like this. It's too much for her. She's going to break."

Reed kept pace with Tyler as he urged his horse to move faster. Renny was getting too far ahead of them.

He offered his friend what he could. "Keep her strong, Tyler. Either we'll find Matthew or we won't. He'll either be alive or he won't. It's out of our hands." Reed's voice was grim.

Tyler wasn't sure which he dreaded most—not finding Matthew and living with the unknown, or finding him and being too late. Every mile, every hour counted. And so did resting and eating.

Were it up to Renny and her siblings, they'd keep going long after dark. So far he'd been both surprised and impressed with the lot of them.

As young as Caitie and Kealan were, they'd not once complained or asked to stop. Like their older siblings, they endured.

Noting the position of the sun, Tyler made his decision. "Stop here for the night and set up camp."

Reed lifted a brow. "Renny won't want to stop yet. Couple hours of light left." Reed's eyes were scanning the area, always returning to rest on his wife.

Tyler drew in a deep breath. "Miss O'Brien can haul our butts out of bed a couple hours early. I'll deal with her."

Nodding, Reed tipped his head. "Fine. I'll take charge here. You go after her."

Tyler nodded. Nudging his horse, he galloped after Renny. Tyler knew more than most that often a person's own thoughts and fears were the hardest kind of fate to face. He kicked his horse into a gallop. No matter what anyone said about this being Renny's journey, Tyler refused to let her go through this alone.

Renny rode, the land blurring as tears of frustration burned the back of her eyes. She felt lost and alone in a world that was hostile and unforgiving.

Normally she loved it out here: the wide open space broken by rolling hills, ribbons of blue water that sliced the land into more manageable pieces.

Now she searched for any sign of her brother. There were many places where Matthew could be concealed: the tall grass, boulders, scrub brush. The task of finding him seemed impossible.

She was very much afraid that she was going to fail Matthew. And the others. She didn't care about herself. It was her brothers and sisters who mattered.

She tried to do as Mattie said. She kept her eyes trained on the land, searching for signs. But there was nothing. Just wild, intimidating wilderness.

For so many years she'd claimed this land as her own, not by birthright but by the love in her heart. This was the land of her mother's people; the life her mother had given up for love.

Her parents had been good people. They'd loved their children and each other and had given freely to those in need. They hadn't deserved to be shot and left for dead.

Where were the spirits her mother had believed in? They'd failed to protect her parents. They'd failed Mattie as well. Mattie, who was now blind because of hate and prejudice.

It's not so simple, Weshawee.

Startled, Renny glanced around. There was no one around but her. The others had fallen way behind. No, she admitted, fear had driven her into running far from them.

Listen.

With your heart.

Renny was too tired to deny that she was hearing the voice of a spirit. It was either that or she was truly so tired, or so discouraged, that she was losing her mind.

Either way, it didn't matter. She could not do this. Not alone. Nor could she be solely responsible for the outcome. If the spirits of her mother's world wanted her to find Matthew, then they were going to have to stop playing games and help her out.

"Show me the way," she demanded, challenging the voice in her head.

You are the way.

You must become, Weshawee.

Startled by an answer when she expected none, Renny came to an abrupt halt.

"How?" She whispered the question, very afraid of the answer.

Reclaim the world you once loved. Discover those who you've forgotten.

Renny's eyes misted for a moment as memories of talking to animals came to mind. She'd once found the study of her world fascinating and soothing. She'd felt alive, a part of a greater world.

She'd even imagined spirits where there were none. Her lips twisted. The childish dreams of a foolish girl who had once set great store by such beliefs.

But no longer. Blood shed in hate had dissolved that world.

"No," she shouted. "I am alone. There is nothing to speak of. No one to see or to believe in." Once more she turned her back on the voices that seemed to come from nowhere and everywhere.

Bending low over her horse, she rode hard and fast. Tears burned the back of her eyes but she refused to let them fall.

The thunder of hooves rumbled through her mind, reverberating through her body but not drowning out the argument in her head. Her fear and resentment blinded her to all.

A horse rode up alongside her. She glanced at the rider. Tyler. She saw his mouth moving. He was yelling at her but she couldn't hear him over the angry buzzing in her ears.

Renny ignored him and urged her horse to ride faster, as though she could outrun the voices in her head and the man at her side.

Once more, the voices slammed into her mind.

Trust us.

Hear us.

See us.

A gust of wind slapped at her face, blinding her as dust was blown into her eyes. She brushed a hand over her eyes and blinked rapidly as the air in front of her seemed to shimmer into a ghostly white shape.

Crying out in alarm, Renny yanked hard on the reins to stop. Her horse, caught unprepared, reared in protest.

Renny swore and flung her arms tightly around the horse's neck. The horse came down with a bone-jarring slam that had Renny sliding off sideways, landing hard on the ground. Winded, she lay there, stunned, her eyes searching for . . . ?

She shook her head in denial. She'd seen a ghost, one as large as a horse. Maybe a ghost horse.

Or a spirit horse.

She shivered and when Tyler's long shadow fell over her, she stared up at him wide-eyed with shock. "Did you see that?"

Her voice was a low, hoarse whisper as she pointed to the left of where she now sat. The shimmering image had been there but there was nothing there now. Her heart pounded and questions raced through her mind.

"See what?" Tyler bent down and ran his hands over her. His voice was low with fury.

When she opened her mouth to tell him, he cut her off with a furious glare.

"I'll tell you what I saw." His gaze latched hard onto hers. "I saw a foolish, stubborn woman risking her foolish and stubborn life. That's what I saw."

"No—"

"Yes," Tyler bit out. "You have no regard for your family. That was a stupid stunt you pulled. You know better than to ride off like that."

Renny stared up at Tyler, too shocked to speak as his tirade continued.

". . . horse could've fallen into a hole. You rode him hard. What if we'd been attacked? You wouldn't get far on an exhausted horse. Figured you'd have more consideration for your horse, even if you don't for your family."

He paused to take a deep breath. "Riding like that, you could have ridden into danger, gotten us all killed. And what of your family? What would happen to them if you'd broken your lovely neck in that fall? Or a leg? While we're out here, your actions affect everyone."

Renny forgot about what she'd seen or not seen. Tyler was right. Guilt made her squirm. She'd been upset and so driven by fear that she hadn't given her family or even her horse a thought. She'd let her own need to be alone wipe out her responsibilities.

She struggled to sit, pushing away Tyler's helping hand as she got to her feet. "I know—"

"No arguing, Renny." Tyler's hand shot out. He grabbed hold of her, interrupting her apology.

"You need to stop acting like a rash, spoiled child." His eyes were dark with fury. He held up a hand when she tried to interrupt.

"You just listen. It's time to stop feeling sorry for yourself and start thinking of others."

Renny froze mid-struggle. Everything she did was for her family. She always put their needs before her own, though she'd admit that messing with Tyler was for her own satisfaction. But then again, he so often deserved whatever she dished out.

"Let go," she said coldly.

"You're not going anywhere until we come to an understanding. Figured you were smarter than this, Renny."

"Go to hell, Troll." Renny was furious.

Forget explaining her actions to him, or admitting to him that he was right. She'd apologize to her sisters and brothers for acting rashly. And Maze and Reed as well. But not to Tyler.

"Dammit, Renny. You're a stubborn, willful thorn in my side."

"And you're a snake in the grass. Oh, wait. I forgot. You're a troll. A big, ugly, mean troll. Go back to your cave and hide your ugly face so you don't scare the children." So much for a truce, she thought sourly.

"Not until—"

Renny brought her foot down hard on his. He released her with a yelp of pain and hopped on one foot. Her grin turned to fear when he turned a furious gaze on her.

She backed away, for once very afraid that she had indeed pushed him too far. "Your own fault for not letting me go," she said, her voice wavering slightly.

"Warned you, Renny, that one day you were going to push me too far."

Deciding that self-preservation was far better than presenting a brave front, Renny turned and ran for her horse.

Chapter Twelve

Tyler's foot throbbed with pain as he hobbled after Renny. Damn woman knew right where to land a good stomp. He cursed heatedly beneath his breath. There was no doubt in his mind that Renny had perfected that little stunt on him over the last year.

He followed Renny as she ran toward her horse. The animal lifted its head, shook it and went back to eating. Tyler's horse munched grass nearby.

Neither animal seemed to care about the two humans, one seeking to save herself. "Renny, you get back here. We're not finished!" He wasn't sure what he was going to do when he caught up with her.

Ringing her neck sounded good. So did putting her over his knee or just hog-tying her so she'd be forced to listen to him once and for all.

It was time to clear things between them. Renait O'Brien had been a pain in his life for far too long. Noticing that she'd reached her horse, he pushed himself faster, ignoring the pain in his foot as he put on a spurt of speed.

Almost within arm's reach of Renny, his hand shot out. Renny shrieked, dodged him, and made a flying leap for her horse. The animal neatly side-stepped. Renny hit the ground belly first with a resounding thud.

Tyler tripped over her and stumbled. He caught himself, then whirled back to check on Renny, who lay motionless.

His heart flew up into his throat and he felt the blood draining from his face, taking the anger with it.

"Renny," he said hoarsely as he shoved her horse away from them. He fell to his knees. She still hadn't moved. Didn't even seem to be breathing.

He'd never met a woman who could play his emotions from one extreme to the other with so little effort.

Reaching down, he touched the side of her neck. "Renny? Dammit, Renny, answer me. Are you all right? Don't you dare be hurt, Renait. You hear?"

He reached down to touch her. She was trembling, shaking. He let his breath out. She was alive. Thank goodness.

"Renny, can you move? Please, tell me you are not hurt."

Renny continued to shake, which made Tyler's chest hurt. His heart seemed to be shrinking. "You are not going to die on me, Renny. You hear?"

His hands touched her shoulders gently. The trembling increased. Afraid to move her, yet needing to see how badly she was hurt, Tyler took a deep breath and turned Renny over slowly, his large hands gentle.

"Renny, please, talk to me—"

His plea broke off. To his shock, Renny's eyes were wide open. Her misty-blues were not only free from pain but filled with laughter.

Her lips twitched, then she giggled, her giggles birthing into a full fit of laughter.

Tyler sat back on his heels, stunned, at a loss for words. Had she lost her mind? "Renny, please stop. I'm sorry. This is my fault. Tell me where you hurt." From her struggle to breath and laugh, Tyler thought for sure she was seriously hurt and that hysteria was claiming her.

He tenderly brushed bits of grass and rock from her face. Her forehead and chin were scraped. He ran his hands down her arms and over her chest to feel for broken ribs. His face warmed when his hand skimmed over her soft breasts.

Renny's laughter hitched at the contact. "Sorry," he mumbled. "Got to check to see if you broke anything." He moved to stand. "I'll get some water, clean you up, then we'll see where you're hurt."

Renny shot out a hand and caught his arm. "Fine. I'm fine," she gasped.

Tyler sat back on his heels, looking and feeling both confused and worried. She'd hit the ground hard. He could see that she still had trouble drawing in air.

"You are not fine, Renny." He vowed to take

care of her. He'd never yell at her again. This was his fault. All he'd wanted was to help her, be a part of her life, and have her want to be a part of his.

After this, she'd probably never want to see him again. Deep inside, a loud, long cry rose. This was his fault.

"Winded," she said, getting his attention. "Just winded." She struggled to get up.

Tyler quickly helped her sit. Unconvinced, he watched her. She'd had an accident a month before. Had she reinjured her head? He watched her carefully.

After a few minutes of gathering her breath beneath his watchful stare, she sent him an amused grin then rolled her eyes. "Doing it again, Troll."

He frowned. "What?" He felt unbalanced.

"Playing nanny."

Warmth flowed back into him. She was all right. Had to be if she could sit there and tease him. His first thought was to yell at her for scaring the life out of him but he was too relieved that she hadn't hurt herself.

He lifted a brow. "Excuse me, but you're the one who went flying nose first into the dirt. Was a pretty stupid stunt," he said, jumping to his feet. She obviously had not done any harm to that hard head of hers.

Renny tipped her chin up at him. "And whose fault was that, I ask?"

Before he even opened his mouth, she'd hopped to her feet, proving she was perfectly fine.

"Yours," she said. She brushed herself off.

"How do you figure that one, Miss O'Brien?" He'd damned near died of heart failure while she'd been laughing. Laughing!

"You made me," she said defiantly. "You were chasing me." She shoved her hands onto her narrow hips and glared at him.

He glared right back, his stance matching hers right down to the hands on hips. "You stomped on my foot," he bellowed. "I warned you. By God, I warned you," he said, advancing on her, ready to pick up where they'd left off.

Renny stood her ground. "Don't you touch me."

Standing toe to toe with her, Tyler deliberately bumped against her, forcing her to stumble back just a little. He said nothing. Just towered over her, forcing her to tip her head back a bit more.

Truthfully, he wasn't sure he trusted himself to touch her. He was furious and at the same time, enamored, and so very relieved that she was standing there acting normal.

Tyler adored Renny and he was frustrated with her too. He wanted to hold her, love her, and he wanted to throttle her lovely neck.

Renny caused such contradictory feelings and emotions to rise up and choke him, he wasn't sure what he was going to do with her.

"Move back, *Troll*, or I'll stomp your other foot."

Her threat made his decision for him. Reaching out, he grabbed her chin, hard enough to keep her attention, but not hard enough to hurt or bruise.

"Do that and I'll turn you over my knee."

Her eyes went wide then darkened to blue-fire sparks. "Try it and you'll be sorry."

The thought of touching her made his fury give way to desire. "I think not, Renny. Lot of things I might be sorry for but spanking that sweet little behind of yours isn't one of them."

He felt the slight tremble in her jawline. Staring at him, watching his eyes latch onto her mouth, she licked her lower lip.

"Don't even try, Troll."

"Hmmm, no? Well maybe there is something better for us to do." He lowered his head.

"Don't think so. Don't think we have anything further to say." Renny chewed nervously on her bottom lip. She tried to pull away.

Tyler chuckled. "Wasn't thinking of talking," he said, drawing closer.

Renny glanced back the way they'd come. "Uh, we better catch up to the others. Going to get dark soon."

Tyler grinned at her obvious nervousness and discomfort. His fury didn't faze her, yet the thought of his kiss made her nervous. He tucked that bit of information away. A weakness. He might actually have found a chink in her hard armor.

Desire hummed through him as he moved in for the kill. "Reed's making camp. Lots of light left."

"Camp? We're not stopping yet!"

"Camp," he repeated softly. "We're stopping for the night." His lips brushed hers. His hands slid down her jaw to her shoulders then wrapped around her, holding her loosely in the circle of his arms.

Renny's eyes were locked onto his. "Says who?"

"I say," he murmured. "I need some time."

"Time for what?" Her voice was a low, husky temptation.

"A kiss."

She forced a laugh. "Why would I want to kiss an ugly tro—"

Tyler tightened his arms slightly, one hand giving a not-so-gentle tug to her long braid. "Never figured you for a coward, Renait."

Once more Renny tipped her chin. This time her nose brushed against his. "I'm no coward. And you know it."

His mouth moved closer until he was a mere breath away. "Prove it. Dare you to prove how brave you are."

"Fine." Refusing to give him anything to hold over her head, Renny slid her hands into his hair, tangled her fingers in the dark golden strands, then pulled him down.

She pressed her lips to his, intending to give him a single, hard smack and then step back. But the moment her lips touched his, she was a goner.

She went soft as butter in his arms. Her hands gripped him hard and her body fell forward, forcing him to tighten his hold on her.

The warmth of him, the taste of him, had her control snapping like a twig. She kissed him as though her life depended on it. She didn't give him the chance to lead or to control the intensity. She was in charge and like a starving man sitting down at a banquet, she devoured.

Her tongue demanded entry. No sweet, simple little kiss for her. She wanted everything he had. Demanded it. His breathing was as harsh and loud as her own.

"More," she said.

"Sweet heaven," he whispered.

And it was, Renny thought. It was sweet, and hot, and it demanded everything within her, more than she was willing to give. She tried to pull back.

"My turn," he said, his voice thick with desire.

"Too much," Renny said. Everything that had gone on between them in that short argument: the anger, the fear, the sheer silliness, the name-calling, and the kiss, were doing what nothing else had done up until that point.

The walls that held in her emotions and fears were slowly eroding and crumbling. She needed his anger, not his kindness. She didn't want his kisses or the sweet tenderness of his arms around her.

Everything she'd withheld, all those emotions that would make her seem weak and out of control, emotions that were buried deep inside her, were now rushing to the surface.

Her heart pounded as need coursed through her like a tide of floodwater sweeping over a bank.

She'd kept tight reins on her emotions for so long that she was afraid of letting them go. And the kiss she was sharing with this man demanded everything from her. If she lost control in a kiss, she'd lose control of everything. And that frightened her.

She whimpered. Tyler's fingers were in her hair, tearing her braid out, tugging the tightly woven strands free.

"So soft," he groaned as he ran his fingers through her silky red hair.

The wind whipped the loose strands around them. It formed a fiery veil. Heat rose, seemed to burst from her.

She was going to go up in flames. "Have to stay strong," she moaned. She had to stop, couldn't let passion, and the temptation of this man, take from her what had kept her steady and sane for so long.

"Baby, you're the strongest woman I've ever known." Tyler's breath was hot and sweet, his tongue gentle as he taught her a new dance, one that from that night onward belonged to only them.

"Nooo . . ."

"The strongest . . ."

Tyler tangled his hands in her hair, bunching it up so he could also cup her head in his big, gentle hands. "God, Renny!"

Renny felt her control slipping. Her hands were roaming over him, clinging to his hard shoulders, tracing the ridge of muscle, moving to his strong back before grasping his head, her fingers tangled in his hair.

When his mouth shifted down to her throat, she leaned her head back, giving him free access to caress and lick and suckle tenderly.

"Don't want to stop," she said, yet she fought to regain control.

"Not going to, baby," Tyler said. "Can't."

Renny let out a sob and found his mouth. She needed this. Wanted this. For just a little while she desperately needed to let herself go. She didn't want the worry, the responsibility. For just a little while, she wanted to be free.

"Want more," she moaned.

Tyler drew in a deep, shuddering breath. He pulled back and stared down at her. "Renny, we've got to stop."

Fear made Renny shake her head. "No," she cried. "Don't leave me. Don't let me go. Not now. It's too late. Can't stop it." Unexpected tears fell from her eyes.

"Let me feel. Please, Tyler, let me feel." Tears rolled down her face, a small but steady stream.

Tyler's heart gave an almighty wrench. "Don't cry. Don't you dare cry, Renny. That's not fair." He groaned and gathered her tightly to him. He kissed the tears from her face, then swallowed the sob that left her lips.

He'd rather she stomp his foot than shed tears. He knew how to handle a riled-up Renny but hadn't a clue what to do with a fragile, broken woman.

He swung her up in his arms and strode to the tall grass beneath a small grove of elm and cottonwood near the stream. Setting her down, letting her slide slowly down the length of him, he tipped her chin with one finger.

"I won't leave you, baby. I won't let you go. I'm here." Taking her hand into his, he placed her palm over his heart.

"Feel my heart beating for you. I want you, Renny. As a man wants a woman. If we kiss again, I'm not going to stop. I need you too much." He pulled her tight against him, letting her feel the extent of his need.

Melting against him, Renny slid her arms up, her fingers caressing the sides of his face, her fingertips soft against the shadow of his beard. "Show me how much you want me, Tyler."

Unable to resist, Tyler took them once more into that wonderful world of taste and touch. This time, he deepened the kiss, demanding more, and gave all that he had to give. He tried to go slow and gentle but she wouldn't let him hold back.

He sensed her need, was even a bit afraid of it, but could do no less than she asked.

"Feel what you do to me, Renny." This time he pushed her hand down until she touched him through his jeans. She moaned and stroked him until he thought he'd burst.

Turning her gently in his arms so her back was flush against him, he wrapped one arm around her waist. His other hand boldly cupped one breast.

Her head dropped onto his shoulder. He nuzzled her neck. "Feel what I can give you."

Slowly, he unbuttoned the buttons to her blouse and slid his hand inside. The thin shift she wore had been softened by time and washing. His fingers slid over her softly rounded flesh and found her nipples already hard.

Needing to feel her flesh against his palm, he unfastened her pants, pulled the shift from her trousers and slid both hands up over her abdomen.

He moaned when his fingers found her soft breasts. He caressed one breast until it was capped with a tiny, hard rosy peak. She was small, barely fit his palms, but perfectly formed.

He caressed both nipples, his hands covering her breasts, claiming her. "Feel me touching you," he whispered in her ear before lightly nipping her small, pink lobe.

Tyler's hands drifted down to her hips and pulled her hard against him. He dropped onto his knees, pulling her down with him.

"Feel me. Feel my need."

He held her to him for a brief moment before spinning her around and once again bringing their hips together. This time, his hands slid down to cup her buttocks, his fingers digging into her soft flesh.

Renny cried out and moved restlessly. "Tyler." She sounded afraid. Each breath was a short gasp and she trembled in his arms. She didn't push away. Instead, she clung to him.

"What do you feel, baby?"

"I don't know." She shook her head. "I—I just feel."

"Me too, baby." He lowered them both to the grassy mat. "Need to feel more. All of you." He pulled off her shirt, then her shift, and laid her down on her back.

Afraid that she'd protest or that maidenly shyness might take control, he lowered himself over her and kissed her breathless.

Driven by buried emotions, Renny gave herself to Tyler. Even if she didn't understand all the sensations racking her body, making her feel weak and out of control, she knew enough about mating to know what would happen.

So she took her turn at controlling the kiss, forcing his tongue back into his mouth, following. She nipped, tasted and claimed him as he'd claimed her.

Her fingers quickly unbuttoned his shirt and slid up beneath his undershirt. "Off," she moaned.

The clothing was yanked off, then his skin touched hers. Heat to heat. Hard to soft. Heartbeat to heartbeat. She moved restlessly beneath him as her hands roamed down his back.

Tyler broke the kiss and lifted himself up. Renny stared into his eyes, gray pools of heated desire. She ran her fingers through the thin mat of hair on his chest and over his tiny, hardened nipples. She felt a groan rumble up and out from deep inside him.

Tyler fell back onto her and rolled, bringing her above him. Before she knew what he was going to do, he was touching her, fondling her breasts, teasing her nipples.

She threw her head back and gave up all need

for control. For now all she wanted to do was feel, and give those feelings a place to go.

Once again they rolled. She tried to bring his mouth to hers but Tyler slid down her body.

He took one nipple into his mouth and suckled. Renny's back arched. She cried out. Over and over he kissed and suckled and caressed until she trembled with a terrible need.

"Tyler!"

"Feel, Renny. Feel what I do to you."

"Can't. Too much. Afraid," she whimpered as his lips trailed down the sensitive flesh of her belly.

She reached for him, silently begging him to let her hold him. She needed him, he was an anchor in a world where she was spinning out of control.

"Look at me, Renny."

She stared down into his smoky eyes as his hand slid down into her pants. He cupped her womanhood, felt her wet warmth slick his fingers as he touched her.

Her hips jerked. "Tyler!"

"Look at me. Feel me touching you."

Renny couldn't take her eyes off his. The feel of his fingers touching her so intimately should have embarrassed her, or made her hide her face in shame, but she drew in a deep breath and let her body react.

Her hips moved, circled, pressing harder and harder against his fingers. He caressed her, slid into her with the heel of his hand pressing hard against her as she set the rhythm.

Waves of need built. Her hands tore at the grass and she started to close her eyes.

"No." Tyler wanted to watch her, see inside her through her eyes as her body flew out of control. His fingers moved faster, harder. His breathing grew harsher with every gasp escaping her panting lips.

Her hips jerked out of control and his own body tightened painfully as he took her higher and higher toward her release.

With a suddenness that surprised him, her body jerked hard, stiffened and convulsed around his finger.

Renny felt as if her soul had just burst from the confines of her body. Color formed around her, within her. For just one magical moment in time she was freed from the bog of suffocating burdens.

She needed this moment. She needed to know she could feel wonderful, carefree once again—if even for a moment.

Everything she felt in that wondrous moment was drawn deep into her starved soul. She drank in the shudders coursing through her body, reached higher, fought to stay in that burst of sparkling light for as long as she could.

She so desperately needed everything she was feeling and the man who'd awakened her to the secrets of her own body. She needed him, his strength, his warmth, his touch. He, of all men, could give her this rare gift of self.

All too quickly, the moment passed, the lights

faded and she floated back to her spent and trembling body. Staring up into his eyes gone indigo with desire, Renny felt exhilarated. And very afraid that she'd set loose her own demons.

CHAPTER THIRTEEN

Tyler stared down into Renny's luminous gaze. Watching her coast back to awareness shook him to his very core.

He had shown her pleasure, and in return, she'd given him the most wondrous gift he could ever have imagined. She'd let herself go, had trusted him, put herself in his hands and had allowed him to take her to a place where no one had ever taken her before.

Watching Renny climb the peak and then soar made him want to send her up and over again and again.

"You're beautiful," he said, leaning his head down. His lips touched hers tenderly, a soft caress. He needed her more than he'd ever needed anything. As his lips settled more fully over hers, he covered her naked breasts with his hard chest.

He loved the feel of her soft breasts beneath him. She shuddered. "Baby," he moaned, braced for the heat of their passion to consume them both this time. His body melted onto her, a puddle of intense desire.

Beneath him, Renny trembled. His first instinct was to coax her to feel, to experience all that he could give her, but something felt wrong. Her lips were cold and her breath came in short gasps.

Tyler lifted his head. He'd expected to see many things lurking in her eyes: desire, embarrassment, maybe even anger. One never knew what to expect from Renny. He knew better than most that it was prudent to be on one's toes.

However, he'd never thought to see stark fear in her eyes. "Renny?" He felt like a dagger had been thrust into his heart.

He lowered himself protectively over her, sliding his arms along the ground until his palms cradled her face. "What is it, baby? What are you afraid of? I didn't hurt you, did I?"

Beneath him, Renny shook her head.

He brushed his thumbs over the soft, faded freckles that dusted her cheekbones. "I won't touch you, not unless you want me to," he promised.

No matter how much he ached for her, needed to touch her and be touched by her, Tyler would not add to her burdens.

Renny's hands lifted to grip his wrists. Her fingers dug into his flesh. "Tyler—"

Very afraid that she was going to reject him, or ruin what had been a moment of indescribable beauty, Tyler leaned down and kissed her gently.

His body throbbed. Just one kiss, even if he couldn't slide into her warmth, feel her body clench around him and take him to that wondrous place so far from the confines of their bodies.

Renny was all that mattered to him, all that he'd wanted and yearned for over the last year. He inhaled, drawing in her scent, then lifted his head.

"Don't be afraid," he repeated, his voice thick with desire. "We'll stop. I'd never force you, Renny." He pulled away from her.

"Not afraid!" Renny's fingers reached up and grabbed a fistful of hair, keeping him from retreating.

Tyler bumped her forehead gently with his. "Renny, Lord knows I'm no saint. But I don't want to hurt you and I don't want to frighten you."

He sighed, his body tight and coiled to the point of pain.

"I have to stop now or I won't be able to stop." He'd waited for her for so long, had imagined this moment on many hot, uncomfortable nights. So why was he hesitating?

Because one time wasn't good enough. He wanted more from Renny. He wanted forever and was afraid that once her mind cleared, and she had her emotions back under rigid control, she'd never forgive him.

Her lips brushed against the side of his neck. "Don't stop," she begged, pulling him down, her lips seeking his.

"God, Renny." He burrowed his nose in her neck. "Once done, it can't be undone, or forgotten. We live tomorrow by what we do now."

He was so used to her using her hatred to keep

him at arm's length that he expected the red-headed, sharp-tongued beast to rise and lash out at him.

When she went still on him, his body clenched in protest and braced for the attack. He could live with her anger, her stubborn pride and that unbending loyalty to those she loved, but he couldn't live with regrets. Or her hatred of him.

Renny trembled in his arms. Her pulse raced and he felt a wetness on his face and knew she was crying. He tried to pull away.

"You're frightened. It's okay. I understand."

"No. Not scared. Need you," she whispered so fiercely and so softly he froze. Her arms tightened around him to prevent him from looking at her.

He lifted his head, stared down into her eyes. They were wide and wild. He saw the fear mingling with desire.

"You're afraid," he said, his gaze searching hers, his voice demanding honesty.

Renny sighed. She traced the sides of his face with her fingertips. "Yes. But not of you. Not what you're going to do."

"Then what, baby? What are you afraid of?"

"That you'll stop. That you won't want me."

Stunned, Tyler stared down at her. "Not want—how?" Her fear was so off the mark, so ridiculous, he was speechless. But in that same moment, the truth struck.

Renny wasn't afraid of him. She was afraid of herself, of losing control. He saw it all so clearly now: the strength of her will, one she wielded relentlessly in order to control everyone and everything around her.

The temper that emerged whenever she lost control. Anger, he realized, helped her regain control and stay in control. Control to Renny was as essential as water to a fish.

Tyler did the only thing he could: he gave her the reins of his heart. He let her pull his mouth to his, let her set the pace, take charge.

He met each hard, almost bruising kiss with passion to match. He responded to her needs with the wants and desires of his body.

Finally, they broke the kiss and stared at one another with eyes blazing with desire. He slid his hands down her body, following the gentle curves. Grasping the waist of her pants, he hesitated a moment.

"I can't wait much longer—"

Renny didn't hesitate. "Then don't wait. I'm not afraid of you, of this."

Tyler shed their remaining clothing and slid back over her, his erection sliding over her soft, bare flesh.

Renny reveled in his touch, the feel of his naked skin sliding over hers, the gentle touch of his fingers gliding across her hip and that part of him that throbbed against her nest of curls.

She arched her hips, trying to bring them closer. She needed this. Him.

As he took her back along that wondrous path of love, a tiny part of her remained afraid. She'd lied. She was afraid. Very afraid.

Not of Tyler. Not anymore.

This man, who for most of their acquaintance had been her enemy. Now he was her lover. Her salvation, her anchor.

That's what scared her. She'd never be able to go back to relying only on herself. She needed him, and feared she wouldn't be able to survive without him. What if this was only a dream? What if she woke to find that no such place existed? Maybe she'd never find her way back into the warmth and light.

"Don't be afraid," he whispered in her mouth as he ran his hands all over her. "Trust me."

"I do," she groaned as his fingers slid into her.

Renny gave herself up and let herself feel. His touch made her feel beautiful, wanted. His moans made her feel needed and the sensations humming through her body took her far away from everything that tied her to the earth.

In Tyler's arms, she had no worries, no fears. Only this wondrous feeling of belonging. Of being.

"Might hurt," he gasped in her ear.

Renny pulled his mouth back to hers. "Already hurt. Need you. Need more." Her body felt on fire, and ached for release. She wanted to go where he'd sent her before. This time, though, she wanted him with her.

"Come with me," she begged.

"I will. Say my name, Renny. Say my name. Call me to you."

The small twinge of pain as he entered her,

stretched her, was swallowed by her crying out his name.

"Tyler," she moaned as she accepted him inside. He became a part of her. They were one, united, and that brief flash of pain was a small price to pay for such wondrous feelings.

She'd never felt this close to anyone. They were merged. She wanted it to last forever and yet she wanted that ending, that burst of light, the feeling of flying into forever.

"Again," he gasped.

Renny's breathing came hard and fast. She was climbing but he was holding back. She felt it. She moved hard against him.

"Say my name. Please," he urged her as he continued to kiss her lips, her face, the hollow of her neck.

Renny gripped his hair tight and pulled his head so she could see into his eyes. They mirrored hers: filled with a hunger that consumed.

"Shut up, Troll," she ordered, then kissed him hard.

He laughed, then moaned when her fingers dug into his backside and squeezed. He pumped himself furiously into her.

Renny rose to meet each thrust, held him tight to her with her legs wrapped around his waist and rode wave after wave of burning need.

"Now, Renny," Tyler gasped. "Let go now."

Renny let go and rose higher, faster and harder. This time, she didn't soar alone. And when the shudders subsided, she didn't fall back to earth by herself.

* * *

Matthew floated in a strange world that was a mixture of shadows and light. High above where he lay, a new and wonderful place beckoned him forward. Yes, he thought as he drifted closer yet. The place of his ancestors; a place where death became an everlasting life.

It was a good place. Peaceful, beautiful. All he had to do was lift his hands high and let his body soar upward where white buffalo roamed in herds so thick, the whiteness nearly blinded him.

His head fell back, his back bowed as he held out his arms. "Take me."

A roar filled his head. The herds of buffalo fled in a thundering mass. Shadows crept over the beauty and a gust of wind slammed him back to the shadowy world where his body writhed and twisted in pain.

"No," he cried out.

His eyes flew open. The world had turned white. He blinked but the whiteness blinded, like the sun shining down on a snow-blanketed prairie.

His breathing felt labored. His chest hurt with each short gasp as though he'd just been thrown roughly to the ground.

Pain assaulted him from head to toe. It radiated from his center outward and consumed him. He lay still, closed his eyes and struggled to hear his heat beating. The pain was so bad, so overwhelming, he couldn't hear his life's blood flowing in his veins.

Matthew knew he was hurt and hurt bad. He

vaguely recalled a sound like thunder before everything had gone black. He'd been shot.

He'd been shot once before, in the thigh, but this time was worse. He was dying, could feel his soul straining to leave his body. But a strange pressure on his chest kept him pinned to the earth.

He struggled to remember what had happened but his mind was fuzzy, filling with fog so thick, it was all he could do not to be pulled back down into unconsciousness.

He tried to move but felt as though he'd been bound tight. He was trapped. Struggling weakly, he cried out.

"Be still, child." The deep, gravelly voice should have made him feel threatened, but instead it calmed him. A wave of warmth brushed against him, stilling the trembling that had started deep inside.

Matthew's chest burned, each breath a struggle. He felt so weak. And tired. Keeping his eyes open was becoming harder and harder to do.

The pressure on his chest eased.

"Be still. You are safe."

The whiteness shimmered then came into focus. Matthew blinked as the apparition hovering close to him took on the features of an old man with a face as round as the moon. His skin—what Matthew could see between a white mustache and beard—appeared ancient, like the craggy side of a mountain.

Drawing in a deep, startled breath, Matthew choked against the deep waves of pain that followed each breath. He kept his breathing shallow.

Who was the stranger? Fighting the encroaching wall of gray, Matthew's gaze latched onto a pair of crystal bright eyes shining from the midst of the white. Old eyes. Kind eyes. Sad eyes.

Eyes that made him feel safe. "You are safe, child. She is on her way. You must fight the darkness and resist the temptation of the light. It is not time for you to depart this world for the next. You must be strong."

Matthew kept his eyes on the kind stranger. The man looked old as the hills. From him he felt a healing warmth seeping deep into his soul.

His eyes blurred for a moment. Once again he saw the blue and white spirit world, heard the victorious cries of warriors returning after battle. The translucent figures were so far and yet so close. Many of them seemed to be staring down at him.

He lifted a hand, as though begging them to come to him, to lead him up that path into a world with no pain.

"No," the command came harshly. "You will obey me in this. Here is where you must remain. Your time is not at hand." A strong gust of wind whipped over him, forcing him to close his eyes against the swirling dust.

Matthew's throat seized; he coughed and moaned in pain.

A hand slipped beneath his head and cradled him close. "Drink."

Matthew sipped water through his parched lips. He'd never tasted anything sweeter. He eagerly drank until the water flask was removed and he was once again lying on a soft bed.

"Enough," the voice ordered.

"What happened?" Matthew concentrated on the face above him, each breath a struggle.

"What happened?" he asked again. "Can't remember. Need to remember. Important . . ."

Everything was a hazy dream. A nightmare.

"Someone . . ." He started shivering.

A heavy fur was placed over him. "Sleep," the gruff voice ordered. "You will remember later."

Just as the heavy blanket of sleep claimed him, an image appeared: a dark-haired woman with big, green eyes.

"*Brenna,*" he said, his voice a weak sigh as he drifted away on a gentle cloud of warmth.

Chapter Fourteen

Renny stared up into the waning light. Soft, fluffy clouds skimmed across the darkening sky. Soon, golden-pink fingers would bathe the heavens in the elegant colors of the approaching night.

Funny, she thought. She'd never once figured that she'd like this mating stuff. What she'd just experienced had seemed incomprehensible to her. She'd figured it was just something women did to please their mates.

Living in close quarters with her parents either in her mother's tipi or the small cabin her father had built had clued her in that mating wasn't distasteful or painful. No matter how her parents had tried to hide it, mating was noisy and strange-sounding.

She grinned. And wonderful.

"What's so funny?" Tyler demanded, rising up onto his elbows to stare down at her. He trailed a long blade of grass between her breasts.

"Nothing," Renny said hastily. When he just

lifted a brow, she shrugged. "It was nice." Of course, it might not have been so wonderful with anyone else.

She hastily shook off the thought. She had enough pulling on her emotions. She didn't want to get into why this felt so right.

"Nice?" He lifted both brows. "Just nice?"

Now Renny grinned sheepishly. "Well, better than nice. It was wonderful. Thank you."

Tyler feigned a moment of shock. "Where is Renny? Who are you?"

Renny smacked him in the shoulder. "Don't ruin it," she warned.

"Ah, much better," Tyler said. The blade of grass snaked down over her belly.

Renny turned on her side so she could see into Tyler's eyes. He looked younger, and carefree. He looked happy, ridiculously so. She reached out to touch his mouth, loving the full softness. So often his mouth was tight and firm. Often because of her own behavior, she admitted. She frowned.

Tyler looked wary. "Uh-oh, do I need to move away, clothe my vulnerability, lest you decide to resume your stomping?" He looked serious, his hand going to cover his groin area.

Renny rolled her eyes. "I only stomp feet, Troll."

Exaggerating a huge sigh of relief, Tyler sat up. He held out his arms. Renny went to him, let him pull her across his lap. "Glad to hear that." He paused. "Why the frown?"

Renny stared at the slow-moving stream. Weeks ago, it would have been wider, full of melting snow, cold and gushing as it cut a swath through the earth.

Yet now, it seemed lazy. Sluggish, as though in no hurry as it meandered its way through the land. Once, not long ago, she'd seen streams as living entities.

They sustained life, and sometimes they took life. Each river, each stream or creek, had its own sound and personality. This one reminded her of an old woman enjoying her last days.

A nudge from Tyler brought her attention back to him. "I'm not sure. I feel good and that makes me afraid," she said honestly. "Too good to last." Afraid that this tiny bit of happiness would be taken from her, that the man holding her was now such a part of her that she'd not be able to survive without him.

The last year left her unable, and unwilling, to believe that anything good would last.

"Would it be so bad?" he asked.

Renny glanced away but Tyler turned her head back to face him.

"All I ever wanted was for you all to be safe. And happy," he said.

The moment of truth had come. Renny had a choice. She could accept what he had been telling her for a year or she could throw it back in his face and ruin the most wonderful moment in her life.

She took a step of faith. "I know." She said it quietly, and seriously.

"Can you accept that I still want that? And that I want more? Renny, I won't say the words. Not today, but I won't hide what I feel. Not now. Not ever."

"I know." And she did. They'd crossed a line that would never be erased. There were words in her, buried, caged. What if she could never say them?

"We'll save it for another day, baby. Just enjoy what we have right now."

Renny relaxed against Tyler, happy and content with the moment. Tomorrow would come soon enough.

Tyler tightened his hold. "Will you let me explain?"

Renny closed her eyes, afraid of destroying the mood with talk, but she nodded. "Guess I owe you that much."

Renny was afraid to hear the truth from his lips. What he said would probably make it impossible for her to continue hating him, and losing that emotion would make her vulnerable.

She scoffed at her own foolishness. Couldn't get more vulnerable than sitting naked out in the open. Reaching for her shirt, she pulled it on. "Can we get dressed first?" She stood and surveyed the area.

Tyler stood, pulled on his pants, then pulled her down before she even finished buttoning her shirt. "No one is coming."

Renny twisted in his arms. "That's right. You told them to stop and make camp. Lots of light left, we could've—"

Tyler put his finger over her lips. "You were riding off hell-bent for leather, your sister was upset, the kids tired. I made the decision, for their benefit—and yours."

Renny wanted to protest, to lash out, but didn't. He was right. She'd gone to pieces, then—and he'd put her back together.

She nipped his finger gently. "You're right." She bit her lower lip.

"Relax. They know you are with me and I suspect Mattie will know that we are fine."

"True." Renny still felt fragile and very vulnerable but she didn't feel so lost and alone. Scared of the future, and of failing, but for the first time in a long time, she felt as though she could share the burden—at least in part.

For now she wouldn't think about or dwell upon the fact that it was up to her to lead them to Matthew. She just couldn't face the thought of failing.

So she drew herself in, then gave herself back over to the man who'd managed to enter her barren, lonely heart after all this time.

Afraid of going beyond the moment, Renny pulled her shirt down over her drawn knees. "Talk." Better for him to talk than her. Her emotions were too volatile, too close to the surface.

"Okay." Slowly, he told her of his mother and father, how illness took them. Then he told her about his baby sister. His brother, Grant, she'd known as sheriff of Pheasant Gully while Tyler had been deputy.

"You would have loved Gracie," he said softly. "She was fragile, but so full of life. We had to be careful with her. She was so sickly, but that didn't stop her from demanding to go outside with me and Grant." He rubbed his chin on her head.

"She used to love to ride. . . ." His voice trailed off.

Renny tipped her head back so she could see him. "What happened to her?" It was clear from the sadness in his eyes that she was no longer alive.

"She died."

"Sickness?" Renny figured it had to be sickness if she was so frail of health.

Tyler shook his head, his eyes bleak. "No. She snuck out of the house one day while we were plowing the field. Fell, cut her leg." He fell silent.

Renny closed her eyes for a moment. She could guess the rest. She'd seen infection cause the loss of limb or life many times.

"Tyler, I'm sorry," she whispered, turning to look at him.

Tyler let out a long, shuddering breath. "Gracie didn't tell us, knew we'd be mad that she'd gone outside without us. She was eight. Not a baby, she'd say to us. But dammit, if she'd done as told, or confessed, she might still be alive. She didn't have to die!"

Tyler fell silent. Renny waited patiently.

Taking a deep breath, Tyler continued. "The cut turned nasty. She couldn't walk without us knowing, so she pretended to be sick so she could lay in bed. Then she got real sick. The doctor came, he found the cut and lanced it but—"

Renny took his hands in hers and kissed the rough knuckles. "You don't have to say it, Tyler."

"Yeah, I do. Still hurts, but you have to know." He threaded his fingers through hers. "She was too weak to fight the infection. She died. We blamed ourselves. We should have checked her, seen it."

Renny understood Tyler's fear now. He'd been genuinely afraid that the past would repeat itself. Remembering her meanness, some of the things she'd said, made Renny shudder.

She turned in his arms. "I'm so sorry I gave you such a hard time. But Tyler, you can't blame yourself."

Tyler refused to meet her gaze. "Why not? Don't you?" His pain-filled eyes held her gaze.

"Don't you blame yourself for what happened to Caitie and Daire and even Matthew?"

The truth of that statement struck home. Renny jumped up, her shirttails brushing against her thighs. She pulled on her pants then turned back to Tyler. He hadn't moved. He watched her silently.

"Yeah, I do." She paced. "Don't tell me it's stupid. If I'd been paying more attention, maybe we wouldn't have gotten ambushed."

She paced in front of him, her hands crossed. "If we'd gone cross-country instead of following the river, we'd have seen them coming." She glanced back in the direction where her family waited.

Tyler's voice dropped. "You go over and over it in your head, finding all the things that you should have done better, or differently, but no matter how many times you replay it, remember it, regret it, it never changes. Never fixes itself. Can't go back."

Renny didn't answer. There was nothing to say. He was right.

"Renny, you can't blame yourself."

"I know."

"But you do."

Sighing, Renny answered honestly. "Yes." She stared down at her feet. "Pa used to say that life was often unfair. He was right."

Tyler stood and came over to her. "Renny, O'Leary killed your parents and there was nothing you could have done to stop it."

Renny felt pierced by cold. She stared up at Tyler. "You're wrong."

Lifting her chin, Tyler forced her to meet his gaze. "Tell me, Renny. Why is it your fault?"

Pulling away, Renny paced. "I told them they had to go there, that I had a surprise for them. Waiting."

She smiled sadly. "I snuck some food out there, and flowers. Lots of flowers." She remembered how she'd walked for miles the previous day to gather the armful of blooms that she'd strewn everywhere.

"I wanted to give them a gift of time. Their time. Alone time." If they hadn't gone there, if she hadn't made them go, they wouldn't have been shot by Patrick O'Leary who'd gone there to bury his stolen gold.

"Renny." Tyler took a step closer.

"No." She held up a hand to ward him off. Her eyes stung with unshed tears. Not once in the past year had she cried over the death of her parents. She told everyone that she had to be strong, but the truth was, she denied herself that cleansing.

Grief and guilt were her burdens to bear. She turned away from Tyler.

Strong hands closed over her shoulders and drew her back. "You are not to blame. What you did was sweet. Thoughtful. We cannot say why tragedies happen, or if they could have been stopped. Some things just are, and you cannot blame yourself any more than I can blame Reed for Grant's murder or myself for Gracie's death." He pressed his lips to her head.

"Fate decides. Or God, or Spirits, whichever. Point is, there are some things out of our control." He fell silent.

Logically, Renny understood, but her heart bled with guilt.

"So much is within our control, but we make decisions, and oftentimes they are wrong and others end up paying the price for them." She knew this well.

Renny longed to turn in to his embrace. She so desperately wanted permission to grieve, to let the guilt flow out of her. But she tightened her lips for fear that Tyler would release the demons darkening her soul.

Tyler tried to guide her into his arms. She shrugged him off and stalked away.

Tyler finished dressing in silence. "That went well," he muttered as he watched Renny pace along the bank. He frowned as she kicked at some loose pebbles and sent them flying.

Tyler sighed. She was wound tight as a snake ready to strike. Everything inside him longed to go to her and beg her to let him help, but he hesitated to intrude.

He glanced at the horizon. There wasn't much daylight left and he didn't want Mattie and the others worrying about her.

After checking that the horses were fine, he strode after Renny. She hadn't gone far. He stopped a few feet away. She didn't move. She was lost in her thoughts.

"We'd better get back to the others," he said softly, not wanting to startle her.

Renny turned, her eyes filled with grief and sorrow. "Can't. Not yet. You go."

Tyler let out a harsh bark of laughter. "Not a chance in hell am I leaving you out here alone."

Renny jerked her head, indicating the distance behind him. "I can see the smoke from our camp from here."

"So?" He crossed his arms. He was not going to leave her.

"So, Nanny Troll, I'm a big girl. Don't need a mother hen clucking around me. Need to be alone for a while."

Tyler rocked back on his heels. He recognized the pattern: goad him, make him angry and push him away. "Not going to work anymore, Renait. Know you too well."

He glanced down at his booted toes. "And no

more stomping. If you don't want to talk, that's fine. But you will not be alone. Ever," he promised, determined to gain her trust and prove that she didn't have to do this by herself.

Renny looked surprised. Then she scowled. Tyler crossed his arms. "We do this together and nothing you can say will change that fact." He jutted out his jaw to match her own tipped-up chin. He could be just as stubborn and pig-headed if he needed to.

Renny looked as though she'd love to give him a good stomp or tongue lashing, but instead she sighed, turned her back and walked away. She didn't go far, just to the edge of his sight line. And he let her go.

Tyler figured his heart was truly ensnared when he found himself missing her arrow-sharp insults. At least when they argued and fought she didn't look so sad and lost.

And alone.

That bothered him the most. Surrounded by so much family, by so much love, she felt so very alone.

Tyler folded his arms across his chest and finally admitted to being in love with Renny O'Brien. She'd found the way to his heart.

No matter how much she frustrated him, she also fascinated him. He loved her, all of her. Stomping foot, lashing tongue, flashing blue eyes. She was full of life, had an indomitable spirit.

So Tyler did what did not come naturally. He sat and let her be without leaving her alone.

CHAPTER FIFTEEN

"Stubborn woman," Silver said as she stared down at Renny, who gazed out across the stream, unseeing. She shook her head. Her silvery mane flowed around her as she dipped her head, nose butting against Renny's shoulder.

Renny batted her away as though she were a bothersome insect.

Silver kicked up her heels in frustration. "What are we to do?"

As though in answer, a strong burst of wind caught the strands of her mane and kept them flying around Silver's strong, translucent head.

"We remain patient. She is strong. It is this trait that will see her through." The voice of *Tate* hummed through the air.

Silver shook her head. "Time is short. The journey must be made."

"You cannot make the journey for her. She must do this on her own."

Hiding her thoughts from *Tate*, she knew she'd do much to help this woman. Even break rules.

A low, rumbling laugh came from the wind as it ripped across the land. "You think to hide your thoughts, my friend."

"You do not know all," Silver said. Her tail swished back and forth and she pawed the ground.

Silence fell between them. Silver was nearly at her wit's end. What else could she do? She was pleased that Renny had let the other human close, but she had not let him into her heart. Renny refused to reach out and take what those around her offered. All Silver could do was to give Renny access to what she'd need to complete this particular journey.

"She needs help." Silver faced *Tate*, ready to challenge him.

"You are doing more than you should already." *Tate*, Spirit of the Wind, one of the four superior gods, sighed gently when Silver remained stubbornly quiet. He understood Silver. She cared much for this charge, this child of the land.

His breath calmed; the air blanketing the land grew still.

"Show her. Give her hope," he commanded in a gruff voice.

Silver bent her head as the wind swept over her before fading into warm, still air.

Once more she nudged Renny, whose focus was inward, reliving the past, dwelling on regrets and the hopelessness of that guilt that enveloped her.

Look.

See not with your eyes but with your heart and soul.

Let the spirits guide you. I give you the gift of hope.

Spirit breathed softly, letting her breath mingle with the air Renny drew in.

Around her, the air grew quiet and still. Renny sighed. Dusk was settling and there wasn't much light left. There was nothing more that could be done tonight except reassure her siblings that somehow, someway, they'd find Matthew.

But time was against her. Matthew's life, maybe Brenna's, depended on Renny finding them.

No matter how much she hated the idea, Renny knew it was up to her. Mattie was never wrong. And no matter how much she had tried to convince herself that the spirit world no longer existed, she had to admit the truth: one could not believe in Mattie, and her visions, and not believe in spirits.

All spirits. Including the voices she'd been hearing as of late, ones she'd rejected because it was easier to dismiss and reject that world rather than admit that she was no longer worthy of what she'd once taken for granted.

She rested her head on her knees. As a child she'd taken delight in studying life, finding the ties that bound her with the land. She'd found guidance, happiness and comfort in such simplistic yet complex living.

A long-distant memory stirred. It must have

been a dream, for it couldn't have been real. She'd been a child with a companion—a beautiful silvery-white horse that came to her in her dreams.

She ridden that horse, soared through the heavens. Once she'd also thought the magnificent animal had walked beside her during the day, as well as during the night. The images and feelings of comfort and friendship were still strong. She'd never told anyone, even though she'd been taught about animal helpmates.

As a young girl, she'd wanted to believe that she had a helpmate, a horse that walked beside her in her journey through life. She grimaced. The dreams were just that: dreams of a child who'd loved horses. Yet somewhere deep in her heart, she still believed in the ways of the Sioux. But after the death of her parents, she'd cut herself off from that world. She'd felt betrayed, and guilty. She no longer felt worthy of that world where pureness of the heart was revered.

Sitting there, alone, Renny tried to recapture that simple way of life, but the fear of failure kept her from concentrating. What would she do if they were too late to save Matthew? Could she be strong enough to sustain them all? Again?

Sighing, she stood and brushed off her pants. It was past time to return to the group. Mattie and the others would be worried and she would not put her needs ahead of theirs. She'd already deprived them of so much.

She'd try again in the morning. Mattie believed in her. She just had to believe in herself.

Yes. Believe.

The voice startled her, and excited her. She glanced around, spotted Tyler sitting patiently. His had not been the voice she'd heard.

Letting her instinct take over, she cleared her mind of all doubt and worry. She finally gave in and admitted to herself that the spirits had been trying to communicate with her many times. She'd just been too stubborn to listen.

Closing her eyes, she let the cooling breeze wash over her. She reached out with her mind and heart. "I believe," she whispered.

Open your eyes. Follow your heart.

Renny opened her eyes and gasped. Directly across from her stood the pale yellow horse. He stood silent and still. He watched. He seemed to be waiting for something. His tail swished back and forth and he bent his head and pawed the ground.

"You're back," Renny whispered. She stood.

The horse dipped his head then lifted it high, shaking his gloriously long yellow mane. His tail flicked back and forth as he pranced. Then he reared up, came back down onto all fours, and turned and faded back into the shadows.

Renny sprinted forward, splashed her way across the shallow stream, ignoring the shout behind her.

"Here we go again," Tyler said as he ran after Renny. He didn't bother with another shout.

Catching up with her, he grabbed a fistful of her shirt.

"Let go. We have to follow it." She broke free.

"Renny, get back here." He ran after her.

She turned her head and shouted over her shoulder. "It's the same horse I saw last night. Mattie said she saw horses in her vision. I think I understand. Come on. We have to follow it."

Tyler kept pace. "Dammit, Renait. You can't just go racing off alone. Especially after a horse that might have an owner nearby!"

Renny ignored him and ran between a stand of cottonwoods. She stopped. Her head turned from side to side as she searched her surroundings.

"Not alone. Got you." She slid him an innocent stare. "Got my Nanny Troll." She was distracted, her voice lacked heat.

Tyler frowned as he glanced around for a horse. All he saw were a few trees, some brush and tall grass spreading out all around them. Up ahead he spotted more cottonwoods. They lined the stream snaking through the rolling hills.

Renny bent down onto her hands and knees. She parted grass, moving slowly but methodically over the area. Suddenly she gave a triumphant cry and pointed.

"Look! It was here. The horse is real." She pointed to a set of hoofprints.

Giving her a strange look, Tyler asked, "What else would it be?"

Renny looked enchanted for a moment. "A spirit."

Tyler grunted.

"Don't pretend to understand," Renny said to Tyler.

"Good. I won't." He walked through the tall grass, every nerve on high alert as he noticed that the grass had been trampled in many places.

One hand rested on the butt of his revolver. He wished he'd thought to take the rifle from the scabbard on the back of his horse. Hell, he wished he'd brought the horses with him, but he hadn't been willing to let Renny go off by herself.

The appearance of this horse made him nervous. Too many places where they could be ambushed. He rounded a partially dead bush, then stopped. "Renny. Over here."

She ran through the knee-high grass over to him. "What is it?" Excitement and dread flowed through her.

He pointed to an area where the grass was flattened and cleared around a small fire pit. "Someone's been here."

Renny scanned the area then let out a long, relieved breath. "It's not Matt's," she said, her voice falling flat. She was also disappointed. She'd hoped to find some sign of Matthew.

Tyler glanced over at her. "How do you know?"

She indicated the rocks still forming a ring around the ash. "Matt would have erased all signs. He wouldn't have left a pit in the ground like this. Not only is it against all he believes in to destroy the land of his birth, but it makes it easier for the enemy to follow and attack."

She frowned as she watched Tyler pick up a discarded tin can. She wrinkled her nose in distaste and added, "We live off the land. We make our own food. He would never defile the land like this."

She felt let down. She'd been so sure that the appearance of the horse for the second time—and his interaction with her—meant that perhaps he was leading her to Matthew.

"Well, whoever was here is long gone," Tyler said.

Renny nodded. Then it hit her. "Wait." She let her idea play in her head while Tyler studied her.

"You think whoever was here might be the person who attacked Matthew?"

"Well? Could be. Gives us something. The eagle led me in this direction. The horse drew me across the stream, to this very spot."

Tyler's gaze narrowed as he searched the area. He pulled her out of the open and over to a thick cottonwood.

"Dammit, Renny! You did it again. Took off running without thinking. What if someone had been here?"

Renny stuffed her hands down into her pockets. "Well, you weren't exactly tiptoeing around." She hated that he was right.

"I was following you and you damn well know it!"

"Look, Troll—"

A sudden gust of wind slammed into both of them, knocking them sideways and into each other.

Instinctively, Tyler grabbed hold of Renny and steadied them both. "What the hell was that?"

Renny looked stunned. The gust of wind was gone. She laughed softly. "I think it was the spirits telling me that you, Nanny Troll, are, for once, right. I shouldn't have taken off like that, and if Matt were here, he'd have yelled at me worse than you."

Tyler looked slightly mollified. "Come on, let's get back before Reed comes looking for us."

Renny hesitated. "We have to follow. See if whoever was here leads us to Matt."

Tyler put his arms around Renny's shoulder. "Tomorrow. It's getting too late."

Renny wanted to argue. But she glanced over his shoulder at the nearly hidden camp and had to agree. She needed time to study the area, see if she could determine how many had been here and in which direction they had gone.

"Yeah, you're right," she said, wrinkling her nose. She stopped and glared at him.

Tyler held up a hand. "What?"

She scowled. "That makes twice that you've been right, Troll. Don't get used to it. You're just lucky today."

She walked off, leaving Tyler feeling slightly bemused. What a day.

"Hey! Get a move on it or I'm leaving you behind." Renny had stopped and was standing with her arms crossed, her foot tapping.

Tyler jogged to catch up to her.

"Women," he muttered, finding himself thoroughly disarmed.

Matt woke to the sound of birdsong. The chant in his head, the song that resided in his heart, was gone. He caught the flash of white from the wing of a mockingbird perched above him. The bird wasn't afraid, seemed to want company. He knew the mockingbird taught about the power of song and voice.

For a few minutes he closed his eyes, gathered inner strength, then tried to sit up.

"Do not." The voice was as rough as the bird's voice was smooth.

Matthew bit back a groan as his heart pounded. The voice came from a stranger. Not the soft, gentle voice of Brenna.

Brenna! Where was she? He tried to remember. He tried to move. Had to find her.

But he hurt all over. Felt so weak. His mind still felt fuzzy but he remembered Brenna, saw her face, and the hurt he'd put in her eyes.

What had he done? He'd put her life in danger. He needed to know where she was. *Please don't let her be hurt.*

"Brenna," he gasped. "Where is she?"

The stranger's strangely colorless eyes bore into him. "I found no one with you."

"Got to find her." Matthew struggled once more. This time the pain in his side was so intense he gasped, feeling sick to his stomach.

Sweat dripped down the sides of his face. The

sun was up, but it was still early morning. The stranger sat beside him, watching silently.

Matthew fisted his hands, hating the weakness. "Have to get up. Help me. Help me find Brenna." Desperation tore the words from him.

"You are in no condition to move." A thread of gentleness softened the rough voice.

"Have to. My fault."

What had he done? Matthew recalled the argument between them. He hadn't wanted to hear her excuses. There were none, so he'd refused to listen.

Brenna had destroyed more than his trust. So he'd lashed out, deliberately hurting her. And when she'd run out into the rain, he'd let her. She had nowhere else to go, so he knew she'd return eventually.

It didn't matter that deep inside he understood what had driven her to protect her mother at all costs. He even felt sorry for her. But loyalty to his brothers and sisters meant that Brenna needed to atone for frightening all of them.

But he'd never wanted her to be hurt or put in danger. So when she didn't return, when it started to rain even harder, he'd made up his mind to go after her. He was responsible for her, and he'd also been ashamed of himself for deliberately causing her sorrow and pain.

But then he'd heard a noise outside and had assumed that Brenna had returned. So he'd pretended to be engrossed in sharpening his knife. Unable to resist looking at her, he'd glanced up.

It hadn't been Brenna standing in the opening of

his canvas lean-to. It had been Gil. And to his shock, Brenna's brother had a shotgun trained on him.

Somewhere in the hazy recess of his mind, he recalled hearing a gun blast right before he'd fallen into a dark void.

Once more he tried to sit up. Stabbing pain made him gasp and fall back to the ground.

"You are not ready to move about." The stranger came over to him. He held a bowl in his hands. "You must eat."

Shaking his head, Matthew said, "No time. Got to find her. My fault. Have to be sure she is safe."

She was with her brother, surely she was safe. But why had Gil come after them? Why not just take Brenna and return home? It didn't make any sense to Matthew. He'd always gotten on well with the man.

"Open."

"No. Need—" He choked on the trickle of watery broth that was spooned into his mouth. Before he could protest, a hand slid behind his head and lifted. A bowl was put to his lips.

"Drink."

Matthew let the broth slide down his throat. He would eat. Then he'd get up and go after Brenna. Somehow he'd find her.

After a few minutes, the bowl was taken away. "Enough." The stranger stood and stared down at him. "She is not here," the stranger said.

Matt stared up at the old man. "Where is she? Take me to her. How do you know that she is alive?"

The old man drew in a deep breath. "Trust that I speak the truth." The white-haired man walked away.

"Can't wait. Must go after Brenna. Tell me, old man," he said. "How long have I been ill?"

The white-haired man shrugged. "What does it matter? You were near death and death still hovers around you."

Matthew groaned in both pain and frustration. "How much time has passed?" He immediately regretted shouting, for the pain that shot up his side left him gasping.

The old man looked him steady in the eyes. "We cannot always measure time. Days often feel like weeks, and weeks like minutes. For you, the time may pass quickly; for another, it may travel much slower."

Matthew closed his eyes for a moment. When he had the pain under partial control, he opened them. "I did not ask for a riddle, old man. I asked a simple question and require a simple answer in return."

The old man lifted a bushy white brow. "There are no simple questions. Each question asked is as complex as the man who asked it, as is the answer given to that man."

"She does not deserve this. I have to help her. Help me," Matthew begged.

"To help her, you must first help yourself."

Matthew stared at the man. He looked old as the hills with a shock of white hair like snow on a mountain. Still, the man moved as smoothly as a young lad.

"Who are you?" Matthew's voice ended on a croak.

Once more he found himself staring into wise, kind eyes.

"A friend."

Matthew frowned. His body craved sleep but his mind fought the fog closing in on him. This time he forced himself to sit up.

He was not going to lie here when Brenna was out there somewhere. He had to find her. Make sure that she was safe. Gil knew nothing about living or traveling in the wilderness. Once more the questions came at him. Why had Gil come after them? Did he now have Brenna with him?

The thought that Brenna might be alone out there, lost, cold or hungry, hurt worse than his injury. After much sweating, cursing and fighting the cold grip of nausea, he stood.

Hunched over, gripping the thick bandage covering his left side, he took an unsteady step, gasped at the pain, then felt the darkness closing in. "Brenna," he cried out as he fell.

A blanket of air caught him, cradled him, and set him down on his pallet with the gentleness of a mother putting her newborn to bed.

Beside Matthew, the stranger stood. "Rest." Then he faded from view, becoming wind and air.

CHAPTER SIXTEEN

Renny rode into camp just ahead of Tyler. She deliberately avoided looking at him. Now that she was back with the others and faced with what lay ahead, she wasn't sure how she felt about what had happened between them.

She wasn't totally shocked or surprised by their passion. She'd been attracted to him for a while, had fought against it by building a thick wall of anger and resentment to keep herself from caving in to the part of her that longed for love and friendship.

But his confession of how his sister had died, and his genuine need to see that none of them made the same mistake, had torn down the barrier she'd erected between them. It now left her vulnerable to the pull between them. She couldn't deny that something was there.

Renny figured that maybe he loved her, and had for a while. But she wasn't sure what she felt—

other than horrified and even a bit scared that she'd so easily given herself to him.

She grimaced. Given herself? She'd fallen apart and then begged him. That was something she didn't understand.

Her family always came first. They were smack in the middle of a rescue mission with a questionable outcome. It had been wrong of her to seek comfort in something so primal as lovemaking.

She should have spent the afternoon planning and thinking of her next step, not lost in some brilliantly colored world where there was just her and Tyler. But even as she felt guilty, she wanted to do it again.

Tyler had shown her a bit of heaven, and she didn't think she could live without it. Knowledge, she mused, could be frightening. Suddenly she wasn't quite sure that she could live without Sheriff Trowbrydge Tyler Thompkins Tilly clinging to her like the mother hen he was.

Sheriff Tyler.

Her Troll.

Renny chuckled a little. Who'd have thought the most insulting of names that she could come up with would turn into an endearment.

She sighed. It was done now, and there was no turning back. No one knew this better than she. Taking a deep breath, Renny decided to deal with Tyler and her own confusion later. Much, much later.

Clearing her jumbled mind, she took stock of

their camp. The spot Reed had chosen was near a small trickle of water. There were no trees.

No trees meant no wood, which meant no fire. Not that they always had a fire. If they had fresh meat, they made a fire. Otherwise, they ate dried meat, dried fruit, or hard biscuits. They had cornmeal with them to make cornmeal cakes when they cooked their evening meal.

They hadn't brought a lot in the way of supplies. They survived off the land. If they were lucky, they'd find some prairie chicken eggs for the morning meal or a bird or rabbit for lunch.

They didn't really go after anything bigger, as they didn't have the time to preserve the meat that they couldn't eat in one or two meals. It went against her upbringing to kill for sport or waste a life that had been given so they might live.

Renny sighed. She didn't mind going without meat or hot meals. She did, however, miss coffee. Nothing better than a mug of black-as-night, thick-as-mud coffee. The stronger the better.

Maze had brought some tea and sugar. But Renny had decided to forgo the coffee as it took time to roast the beans and grind them too.

Spotting Maze sitting on a blanket with Caitie, Renny watched as the woman helped Caitie with her sewing. Seeing that calm, simple domestic chore eased some of the tension from Renny's shoulders.

Renny found Kealan right where she expected: exploring the creek. The horses were nearby, munching on the abundant supply of grass with Daire watching over them.

Come nightfall, the horses would have to be tethered to stakes to keep the animals from running away. She gave the sky a quick glance. No summer thunderstorm today.

She was relieved. No matter how well trained, horses did not like the loud booms and bright flashes of lightning and tended to bolt in reaction.

Her horse needed no urging to go join the others. The mare knew the routine. Daire came striding up to her. He took the bridle in one hand while Renny dismounted. "Thanks," she said, gladly letting Daire care for her horse as he had since the start of their journey.

Mattie, she saw, sat off by herself. She was leaning back on her arms, face tilted up, hair loose and flowing in the breeze. For a moment Renny felt sorry for her sister. Being blind now, there wasn't much for Mattie to do. She couldn't even enjoy the beauty of the land, nor could she take a walk, not by herself.

It was one reason they hadn't gone back to their Sioux family after the death of their parents. Out here, in the open land, Mattie could not walk alone, tend a fire, or even go off by herself to relieve herself after a long day riding.

At home, she knew the feel of her house, the distance from house to outhouse. Everything was kept in its place, the yard clean and organized. Mattie didn't need her eyesight to live each day. But out here, there was nothing familiar but the scent of the air.

Renny walked over to join her. "I'm back," she called out softly so she didn't startle Mattie.

"I know." Mattie glanced toward her. She wore a big grin.

"What are you grinning at?" Renny eyed her suspiciously. When Mattie patted the ground next to her, Renny sat. She shifted her eyes away from Mattie as though afraid her sister could see the guilt of her stolen afternoon reflected in her eyes.

"Could I not just be happy and pleased to see you?" Mattie was still grinning.

Renny refused to look at her. She plucked a blade of ripening grass. "Well. Didn't want you to worry." She shifted then gnawed on her lower lip. "We were, um, gone for a long time." She spotted Tyler talking with Reed.

Remembering what she'd been doing made her flush. Renny slid an irritated glare at Mattie, who still wore a satisfied expression on her face. "What?" Her voice came out higher than she intended.

Mattie reached over and took Renny's hand in her own. "I approve of Tyler. Always have." Her eyes gleamed with amusement.

Renny scowled. Mattie might be blind, but her eyes still mirrored her thoughts, emotions and humor. Renny thought about pretending not to know what Mattie was talking about but knew that it was pointless. "Don't tell me that you *saw* us in your visions, Mattie."

Mattie chuckled. "No. Of course not. But I knew you were safe."

"Then how—"

"I just knew." Mattie smiled mistily as though remembering her own first time with Reed.

Once again Renny found herself watching Tyler and Reed. A horrible thought entered her mind. "You didn't tell Reed, did you?" She squeezed her sister's hand, a bit hard.

Mattie rolled her eyes and pulled her hand away. "Of course not."

Renny's relief was short-lived.

"Didn't have to tell him."

"He knows?" Renny groaned and plopped onto her back. She covered her eyes with her hands. "Great. How does he know?"

She bolted upright. "Don't tell me he had a vison?" Reed had only ever had one vision that she knew of.

There was no doubt from the way he and Tyler were acting that Reed knew or suspected. Renny squirmed on the ground.

Mattie sighed. "Renny, the two of you were gone too long just for one of your silly fights." She laughed and reached out and touched Renny. Her hand trailed up Renny's shoulder, past her ear, and skimmed over her hair.

"Thought so." She pulled bits of grass from her sister's hair.

Renny put her hands to her head and gave another groan. Her braided hair was a mess. She pulled out more bits of grass and leaves. She hadn't once given her hair a thought.

Quickly, she undid her braid, finger-combed her hair and braided it again.

"Well . . ." Renny decided not to pursue that topic any longer.

Before Mattie could tease her or make further comments, Renny rushed to tell her sister about the horse and the abandoned campsite.

"That's twice I've seen that horse." She leaned forward. "Mattie, he is gorgeous. He's yellow, a pale yellow with an almost white mane and tail. He's the sun and the moon in one," she said with a sigh. "I'd love to catch him."

Her chances, she knew, were slim to none because she didn't have the time to catch him and break him. Too bad, she thought. He'd be worth the work.

Mattie leaned toward her, her features intent. "You've seen this horse twice? Are you sure it's the same horse?" She pursed her lips. "My visions showed two horses."

"It's the same horse. I'm sure of it. Describe the horses you've seen," Renny demanded, hope rising slowly within her. This horse had to be one of the horses in her sister's visions. He'd led her and Tyler to the abandoned campsite.

Mattie closed her eyes. "The one you saw today is one of them. I see light, like the sun and moon," she said excitedly.

She frowned. "The other is pale. Maybe white. I'm not sure, as I could barely see it."

Renny jumped to her feet. She thought best when she moved about. "Okay, so I've seen the yellow horse not once, but twice, and each time he's pointed me in the right direction. That's good." It wasn't a question. A huge weight was lifted from her shoulders. She was on the right track. She had to be.

It was too much of a coincidence for that animal not to be important. But the second horse. Pale. Maybe white.

A distant memory flitted around the edges of her mind and shimmered into focus for only a moment. It was a horse. White? No, clear like crystal and bright like the diamonds her aunt had sometimes worn. A fairy-tale horse. But where had she seen it?

The memory hovered like a tiny hummingbird but refused to stay still and clarify. Renny shook her head and figured it must have been a picture in a book. Something she'd seen and read when they had lived in St. Louis.

Mattie folded her hands and rested them in her lap. "I know this is of no help to you, but in many ways this second horse doesn't seem real. More a ghost," she said softly.

Renny sat back down. She had too much on her mind to puzzle over something not real. "Well, we'll wait for it to show itself." She sat back on her hands and continued to mull things over until Maze stood to fetch the food bundles and called that it was time to eat.

Renny rose and helped pass out fruit and jerky and some leftover cornmeal bread. They ate gathered together as though the land was their table. But tonight they were all strangely quiet.

Everyone already knew about the campsite, and that it could belong to someone who'd shot

Matthew. Or it could just belong to a trapper or anyone else out traveling the land.

She just knew it wasn't Matt's. It somehow seemed to confirm Mattie's vision of Matt getting shot. It was a wild, untamed land with wild, untamed men roaming across it.

Kealan scooted over to Renny. He stared at his meal then set it down as though not hungry. "Will we find Matthew tomorrow?"

Renny pulled her seven-year-old brother close. "I don't know," she said honestly. She wasn't sure if Kealan understood the significance of the campsite—that whoever it was could be the one who'd shot Matthew.

Across from her, Daire gave her a hard, steady look. Renny knew Daire understood. He was only two years older than Kealan but his eyes seemed much older.

Renny was saddened that he'd had to grow up so much faster than any of them. She watched Daire take out a wooden flute from his shirt pocket and put it to his mouth.

A low, haunting melody flowed from the flute and wound around them. It was sad, yet there was a thread of hope in the notes that seemed to shimmer and hang in the air.

No one spoke until the last note died away. Then Tyler stood. "We'll want an early start. I'll take first watch."

Renny stood as well. "I'll take second," she said. Since leaving home, she, Reed and Tyler alternated standing watch at night.

She listened to Reed say he'd take the last shift. Everyone was moving away. Maze had already gone to bed, taking Caitie with her.

As Renny turned to go find her blankets, Daire blocked her way. "No," she said before he had a chance to speak.

"I want a turn," he said. He looked fierce. And determined.

"No," she said again. Every night he asked and every night she refused.

Kealan ran up to his brother. "Can't," he said, "too young." He looked quite pleased that there was something that Daire was not yet allowed to do.

Immediately, Daire began arguing and Kealan started saying if Daire got to, then so did he.

"Shut up, Kea. You're just a little boy." Daire glared at Renny. "I'm not."

"I'm nearly as big as you," Kealan shouted. His fisted hands were on his hips.

Renny held up her hand. "Stop," she ordered. "You've both been told no." Ready to order them to bed, she paused when Reed joined them. He cleared his throat. It was a soft sound but both boys heard and immediately subsided.

Reed glanced at Renny. "Can I have a minute?"

Frowning, Renny let him lead her a short distance from her bickering brothers. She crossed her arms in front of her chest and waited.

"Let Daire sit watch with me, sister." Reed used the formal way of speaking of her mother's people. And like her mother, his voice was gentle and respectful.

The moment Reed had asked for a word, she'd known he was going to give his permission. He was interfering with her authority. That didn't just make her mad, it also saddened her.

Once, her word had been law, but Reed was now the head of the house. Neither boy argued with him, not like they argued and rebelled against her.

Reed met her resentful glare. "Look, I know how hard this is for you, me stepping in like this—"

Renny felt small-minded and selfish. She held up her hand. "No. It's your right now." Surprisingly, she found she meant it.

Daire was old enough to sit with Reed. Had their father been alive, he wouldn't have hesitated to agree. Renny took a deep breath. It hurt to know that neither of her brothers would ever be able to share that kind of bonding with the man who'd sired them.

If she gave in, changed her mind, the time Daire spent with Reed would provide valuable time for the two men—one on the cusp of becoming a man, the other tossed into the role of father.

No matter her own fears and insecurities, the happiness of her siblings came first.

Reed held out his hands. "You are their sister. I just thought, well, never mind," he said. "I didn't have the right to step in like this."

Renny grabbed him by the arm before he walked off. "Wait, Reed. You are not just their brother by marriage, you are their father now. They look up to you," she said, without any trace of bitterness.

For the first time in a long time, Renny could admit that. Reed had a part in their lives and it was time she allowed him that right.

"As their father, you have the right to make decisions like this."

Reed smiled down at her. "You will always be very important to them, Renny." Reed put his hand on her shoulder. He didn't argue, which meant he was right, and she was wrong for trying to hold on to them.

Renny sighed. Life was so damn hard these days.

"Renny, thank you. Daire needs to be doing something while we search for Matthew. He needs to be a part of it, not a bystander." He grimaced. "Kealan—"

"Needs to do it because Daire is doing it." Renny laughed softly as she said it. She didn't want to let go but supposed she had to.

Reed put his arm around her and walked back to the two boys, who were pointedly ignoring each other.

Reed addressed Daire. "You will stand watch with me."

Daire nodded back seriously. "Then I will take myself off to bed."

Kealan stomped his foot. Renny, ready for his protest, held up her hand and waited for him to acknowledge her command for quiet. Then she nodded seriously to him. "You will sit with me. I have second watch so you'd better get to bed now."

Kealan gave a happy whoop and ran off to get his bedding. He set his roll beside his brother, talking excitedly to Daire. Reed walked over and ordered him to get to sleep. Kealan immediately buried his head beneath the covers.

Tyler came up behind her. "Nicely done," he said.

Renny shrugged her shoulders and shoved her hands down into her pockets. "Well, I suppose they are old enough."

Tyler leaned forward and kissed her quickly. "Yeah, they are, but I was referring to the way you and Reed worked this out."

Tyler had gotten out his smoking pipe and lit it. The woodsy scent drifted between them.

"Reed feels bad taking your place." Tyler let out several rings of smoke.

Renny watched them float on the breeze, the circles widening, distorting, then fading. Sighing, she let him put his arm around her for a moment. She needed his touch, his warmth, even if it meant letting everyone know that she was developing feelings for this man.

"Guess I have to let go." It was a scary, and hard, thing for her to do.

"Then hold on to me. I won't let you fall."

Renny rolled her eyes. "Better not, Troll, or I'll be doing some foot stomping." She shrugged away and went to her bed. She might as well try and get a couple hours of sleep.

Renny bedded down with everyone else. She tried to clear her mind of everything. She felt like she had a beehive of activity in her mind.

Memories of her afternoon with Tyler, fear for

Matthew, and even her own terror of failing, swirled through her head. So much going on, she figured she'd be awake all night.

High above, gleaming jewels of light welcomed the slowly rising moon. The light of the stars and moon turned everything a silvery white.

She listened to the rustle of blankets as her family and loved ones settled for the night. On the other side of the doused fire, she heard Mattie and Reed whispering. She imagined that Kealan would fall asleep fairly quickly despite his excitement.

Daire, on the other hand, would probably lie awake for a long time, thinking and worrying over what tomorrow would bring—as would she.

She was too restless to sleep: her body wound tight, her nerves on edge. So many worries crowded into her mind: Matt and Brenna. What had happened to them? Were they alive? What would she find in the morning?

She dreaded finding a body. Or two bodies. She only really knew that Matthew was still alive. No matter what she thought of Brenna, or what the girl had put them through, she didn't wish her harm.

That brought her around to what she would do if they couldn't find a trail to follow. The camp was not fresh, it was many days old, and the tracks could have been erased. She and Tyler had not explored the area for fear of treading on any visible tracks in the growing dusk.

Renny fidgeted. She resented having to waste these precious hours sleeping and doing nothing.

Yet there was nothing to be done until sunrise. She turned onto her side.

Unfortunately, patience was not her strong suit. She needed action, had to do something. Minutes later she flipped over onto her stomach. A stone beneath her blanket dug into her ribs. Moving, she removed it, then flopped onto her back.

Staring up into the star-studded sky, she tried thinking of something else. Tried to think of anything but Matthew or what she might or might not find come morning.

She stared up into the heavens. One of her favorite things to do when she slept outdoors was to play connect the stars. With her eyes, she'd draw invisible lines and create shapes and pictures. As a child, she'd always fallen asleep quickly while connecting the stars.

She tried it now. Her gaze traveled over the night sky but she couldn't concentrate on the task she'd once enjoyed. Her head fell to the side and she saw the dark shadow of Tyler sitting at the edge of camp.

Closing her eyes, she inhaled the aroma of his pipe. It so reminded her of him, the combination of tobacco, man and the sweat of the day.

And that once unfamiliar scent that hung in the air after lovemaking. It had clung to them both, combining their individual scents into one unique to them.

Her eyes flew open and she scowled up at the heavens. She didn't have time for distractions, and there was no doubt that Tyler was the biggest distraction of her life.

She needed to concentrate on Matthew, remember that Matthew needed her and she needed her mind sharp. Not muddled with mushy thoughts and wild yearnings.

She tried once more to empty her mind but it just kept filling with thoughts, images and those heady sensations. The way they'd kissed, touched, and joined as one, like a man and wife.

Renny drew in a sharp breath. She was a woman now. The thought stunned her. Up to that point, she'd just thought of how it had all felt. She hadn't looked deeper at what had happened between them.

She'd given herself to Tyler. Totally. Completely, body, mind and spirit. How had this happened? How could she have done that? She hated the man, cursed his presence in her life.

Trowbrydge Tyler Thompkins Tilly.

Sheriff Troll, her enemy, a sharp, irritating thorn in her side and the man she had a feeling she was going to fall in love with.

Maybe already had.

Renny groaned softly. She wasn't sure if she liked this or not. Much easier to just hate and resent him. A lot less complicated.

But that option had been taken from her along with her maidenhead. After today, she'd never be able to hate him. And she could never blame him for having her siblings' interest at heart. All that he'd done, he'd done out of concern. He cared.

Maybe even loved them all as a family loved each other.

Tyler might have been wrong, but his heart had been in the right place. Renny sighed. Maybe her heart had already been claimed and she had been too busy protecting what was hers to notice.

Renny sat up and ran her fingers over the top of her head. Normally, she slept with her hair unbound, but while traveling, it was easier to just brush it out in the morning, and braid it again. Tonight, she missed the calming effect of being able to run her hands through her hair and over her scalp.

She didn't want to be in love. Not yet. Her mind was too full of painful memories, her heart full of regrets and her soul dark with the blood of her parents. In her remote thoughts, she knew she wasn't to blame, but she wasn't thinking with her mind these days.

She dropped her head to her knees. The time had come to tell her family the truth of why her parents had been in that old adobe hut. She was afraid that they'd blame her, hate her even.

If that happened, then she knew she'd never be able to love. Her family was her life, the lifeblood that flowed in her veins. Without their love, she was incomplete.

Feeling very exposed and vulnerable, she stood, stepped around her sleeping family and paced on the other side of their camp.

First things first. Find Matthew. Then tell them all her secret and accept whatever came after that.

Tyler emerged from the shadows to block her way. "You can't pace all night, Renny. Go to bed. Get some rest."

Renny eyed the moon. There were many hours of nighttime left, too many for her peace of mind, so she skirted around Tyler.

Tyler reached out and snagged Renny around the waist. "Renny, don't do this to yourself. It hurts me to see you like this." He nuzzled her neck.

"I want you. Like before. More even." He leaned down, his breath teasing the corner of her mouth.

Renny went hot from head to toe. She burned where he held her, wanted nothing more than to lean into his embrace and kiss him until only he mattered. Because she wanted it so much, she denied herself that freedom.

She pulled away and elbowed him gently out of her way. "Go away, Troll."

Tyler laughed softly. "Woman of great words, Miss O'Brien." He gently took her by the elbow and led her to where he'd been sitting.

He pulled her down. Renny made a half-hearted gesture of refusal. "We can't."

Tyler huffed. "Give me credit, Renny. All I want to do is hold you. Maybe my presence will soothe you and you'll sleep."

Renny snorted. "Bore me to death, maybe, Troll." She glanced around. "What if someone wakes up and . . . and sees."

Wrapping his arms around Renny, Tyler pulled her in front of him. He immediately started undoing her braid. "Don't think it matters, baby. They know. Well, the adults know."

Renny's face flamed. She felt the heat creeping up her cheeks. "Not sure I like that," she muttered, closing her eyes as his hands threaded through her long hair.

She tipped her head back when he gently tugged. He kissed the side of her neck and she immediately felt her body relax. When he lifted his head, she sighed. Not with disappointment, she tried to tell herself.

Of course she was disappointed. It seemed natural, her and this man. Like they belonged—fit.

She grimaced. Just what she needed in her life: an overprotective nanny. When he pulled her into his arms, she let her head rest in the curve of his shoulder, closed her eyes and fell asleep.

CHAPTER SEVENTEEN

Renny's hair was soft. The strands curled around Tyler's fingers as he continued to stroke. He loved the feel of her hair spread out across his chest like a rich, red curtain.

Slowly, he lowered her until she lay with the side of her face pressed to his heart. With moonlight bathing her, she looked peaceful. And so unlike his Renny.

He smiled and just enjoyed the moment. Her body was relaxed in sleep, her lips soft and so very tempting. He ran a finger over her bottom lip. Her tongue darted out, touched his finger.

He pulled away but not before he'd felt the tug of desire grip his belly. It was torture to hold her, have her so close he could hear each and every quietly drawn breath.

As he continued to stroke her hair and her scalp gently, he was taken back in time.

"Brush my hair, Tyler," Gracie pleaded.

Tyler groaned. "Go ask Grant, Gracie. I'm busy."

Gracie, her hair in wild disarray, pouted. "He hurts me when he does my hair. And he doesn't braid so good either." She held out the ivory-handled brush that had belonged to their mother.

Staring into her soft, trusting gaze, Tyler knew he was sunk. Again. When it came to his baby sister, he'd do anything. Catching the gleam of triumph in her eyes, he pulled her close and gave her bottom a gentle tap with the back of the brush.

"Come on. You're going to be late for school." He started gently combing out the snarls, from the bottom up.

"I don't want to go," she said.

Tyler put the brush down, divided her hair into three sections and began braiding it. "Well, you have to."

"Why?"

Adding a dark blue ribbon to the end, he tied it in a big bow then turned her. "Because I want you to be smart when you grow up."

"Like you, Tyler?" Her eyes were wide, round, full of love.

Tyler tweaked her nose. "Yeah, like me. Now scoot. Grant will take you."

"I can walk by myself." Gracie's eyes turned rebellious.

"Yeah, I know." He got to his feet and walked his sister to the door.

She stopped. "Where's my books and my pail?"

"Grant has them. Get going. He's waiting."

Throwing him a haughty glare, she stomped on his foot as she stalked past. "I'm not a baby, you know. I'll prove it to you."

She had, he thought sadly. His and Grant's overprotectiveness had made her rebel. Fear of their anger and disappointment when she'd hurt herself had made her lie and deceive them. By the time he and Grant had learned the truth, it had been too late.

A soft murmur brought Tyler out of his thoughts. Like a mother waking at the smallest of sounds her baby makes while sleeping, he had heard Renny's soft moan. He let his memory of Gracie fade slowly, just as she'd faded from his life.

He tightened his hold on Renny. He loved this woman, and knew he'd never survive losing her. But he'd learned his lesson with Gracie.

Slowly, he relaxed his hold a bit. He would not smother Renny and give her reason to rebel and endanger herself just to prove something to him.

As he sat there with the woman of his heart, he wondered just when he'd fallen in love with her.

Then he grinned like a fool. "The first time you stomped my foot, I was a goner," he whispered to Renny.

Renny felt herself being shaken gently. She burrowed deeper in her blanket. She was warm and comfortable and didn't want to wake. "Go 'way," she mumbled.

"Wake up, Renny." Tyler's voice was a low caress.

His words penetrated the fog of sleep. She struggled to sit.

"What?" Sleep cleared immediately. It was time to take her watch. She glanced up at the night sky.

"I didn't let you sleep your watch away," Tyler grumbled.

"Better not," she said, yawning. She grinned to herself. The first night he'd let her sleep past her watch, claiming she needed the rest. She'd been furious, and had threatened him with bodily harm if he ever did that again. He hadn't.

Tyler stood. "I could sit with you," he offered.

Renny took the rifle from him and set it across her lap. She heard exhaustion in the low rumble of his voice, saw his attempts to stifle his yawns. Tyler had given them, her, so much and she'd rarely thanked him.

She reached out and stroked the side of his face. "No. Get some rest." She glanced over at her sleeping family. "Shoot, I have to wake Kealan," she said.

"I'll get him. And his bedding?" They grinned at each other, each knowing that Kealan would not be able to stay awake through Renny's watch. But she'd promised and maybe for the first time truly understood that, as young as he was, he needed to be a part of this.

Kealan stumbled over to her. He sat beside her, rubbing his eyes. Renny ruffled his soft, reddish curls. "Ready?"

Sitting up straight, Kealan nodded. "Do I get a gun?"

Renny and Tyler exchanged amused looks. "No," they both whispered.

"Aw—" The rest of his protest was cut off when he yawned.

"Go to bed, Tyler," Renny ordered when Tyler swayed. He looked as though he would just topple, he was so tired.

Tyler leaned forward and kissed her gently. "Call if you need me." He got to his feet and walked away, swaying with exhaustion.

At her side, Kealan made gagging noises. "That's gross," he said, giving his sister a disgusted look.

Renny chuckled and put a blanket across his shoulders. "Just wait. Day will come that you'll be doing your share of kissin'."

Kealan leaned against her. "Nope. No way."

Surprisingly, Kealan stayed awake for longer than Renny predicted. The two of them talked in low whispers. Then Kealan's voice drifted off as he fell asleep. He never stirred when Renny laid him back down onto his pallet. She drew her blanket around her shoulders to ward off the nighttime chill.

The moon drifted across the sky as minutes turned into an hour. Renny kept a close watch, peering into shadows, listening for anything that sounded out of place. She had no problem keeping her mind clear, as she had a duty to perform.

It was close to the end of her watch when without warning, Maze stood beside her. Renny gaped up at the woman. "What are you doing up?" she whispered, her heart pounding. Renny hadn't heard her or even seen her get up.

"Oh, I'm an early riser," she said softly.

Renny lifted a brow. "This isn't early," she said dryly.

Maze chuckled then sat beside Renny. Like the rest of them, she slept in her traveling clothing in case they had to move in the middle of the night.

"How are you doing, child?"

"Fine." She met the woman's steady gaze. Maze was a wonder. She was kind, could cook, traveled well—seemingly without ever growing tired—and had the patience of a saint.

Caitie, Kealan and Daire adored her, Mattie relied upon her and they all appreciated the way she took care of everything so that the adults could concentrate on finding Matthew.

Renny wasn't sure why Maze had jumped in to help them without really knowing any of them, but guessed that the woman felt indebted to Tyler for taking her in.

"I never thanked you for all your help—"

Maze cut her off with a wave of her hand and a level gaze. "I was asking about you."

"I'm fine," Renny repeated automatically.

"Hmm." Maze narrowed her eyes. "The truth, child. How are you are really doing?" Maze's voice was firm this time.

Renny felt almost compelled to tell Maze all her worries and fears. But over the last year, ever since Tyler's betrayal—or rather her perception of his betrayal—she'd been careful not to reveal the truth in case someone else used that against her.

But Renny found herself needing to confide in the motherly woman. After a moment, she gave in.

"I'm worried that we'll be too late to save Matthew and Brenna. I'm terrified that I'll never find either of them and so afraid that I won't be able to do this."

She glanced over her shoulder toward where Mattie slept in Reed's arms. Her only comfort lay in knowing that Mattie would know if Matthew's spirit had left this world.

"Why do you believe you cannot do this? From what I've seen of you, you are a very intelligent and capable young woman. You take charge and you lead." She waved a hand to indicate Renny's family. "It is only natural that the others would turn to you."

"But this is different," Renny said. She didn't know how to explain this to someone who didn't know her family or understand how different they were.

Mattie had the gift. She could use it and guide Renny to Matthew. That was how it had always worked with not only Mattie, but Star Dreamer, Mattie's mother, and Seeing Eyes, mother to Star Dreamer.

Maze stared out over the moon-bathed land. "You were very confident this morning. Why did you lead us in this direction?"

"It seemed right," Renny said slowly. She frowned. "The eagle, he was flying above me, moving in circles, then he just flew off. It was a sign. I thought," she finished. It sounded so foolish when she heard the words spoken aloud.

"You trusted yourself to know this?" The question was put to her gently.

Sighing, Renny nodded. "It felt right."

Maze nodded. "What about the horse?"

Renny glanced at Maze. The woman's eyes gleamed mistily in the night as though the stars shone through them.

Renny blinked and looked away. "Today was the second time I saw him," she said. "He too seemed to call to me." She paused. "I followed."

Renny had charged through the trees, expecting to find the horse, but the magnificent animal had disappeared, leaving her very disappointed until she'd found the campsite. Once again she'd gotten excited. Until learning it hadn't been Matt's camp.

But at least she had a lead now, one that hopefully would take them to Matthew. In her heart, Renny felt that tracking whoever had camped there was the key to finding Matt.

Her mind, the logical part of her, said that the camp could have been made by anyone. There were trappers, traders, and soldiers in the area. But some intuitive part of her knew better.

She just prayed that her hopes wouldn't be dashed, as they had been so many times before.

Maze nodded. "You are frustrated and worried because you haven't found your brother?"

"Well, wouldn't you be?" Renny asked, careful to keep her voice to a low, tight whisper.

Maze just smiled. "Mattie claims she'd know if Matthew was gone from all of you."

"Yeah, she would." Renny's voice was firm. Her gut twisted, though. "It's been so long since

Matthew was shot." She was sure he'd been shot the day Mattie had her vision.

"Have patience," Maze counseled. "He had a long head start on all of us. It will take time to catch up to him."

Renny snorted. "I'm not a patient person." She didn't add that she was afraid she'd never find him. She didn't want the older woman to worry.

Laughing softly, Maze rose gracefully to her feet. "No, *Weshawee,* you are not."

Renny whipped her head around. "What did you call me?" She narrowed her eyes at the woman. "How do you know my Sioux name?"

Chuckling softly, Maze tossed her head of silvery hair. "You'd be surprised at what I know." Her voice sobered before she continued. "Listen well. It is in your dreams that you will find the answers."

Maze walked back to her bedroll then lay back down, leaving Renny to ponder her words.

When Reed and Daire joined her shortly, she headed back to her bedding, figuring she'd never fall asleep. To her surprise, the moment she closed her eyes, she did just that.

At least she thought she was asleep as she saw herself walking over a lush, green prairie. Off a ways, she saw tipis, set in their circles. People of the earth, from the earth, went about their business as though there wasn't a white woman watching them.

Some of The People were elderly, most were women. Few men were present, which meant they were out hunting. She watched the children of the earth running and playing.

With a start, Renny realized she knew this place, these people. She'd spent time here, living among them. She walked along the outer edge of the village.

No one seemed to notice her but this was the place where she'd been brought, at age nine, by the kind man who'd traded his horses for her. Rubbing her arms hard, Renny wasn't sure she wanted to be here.

She'd been well treated, cared for and, she supposed, loved in a way that all children were loved. But she hadn't been happy. She'd been so homesick.

The sound of crying reached her ears. Her heart shrank a bit. She knew that cry, and as she followed the sound, she knew what she'd see.

Sure enough, Renny came upon a small girl with red hair. Stopping, with her heart beating furiously, Renny stared down at herself. At the scared, lonely child she'd been at nine when their coach had been attacked, everyone killed except for herself and her much older sister Emma.

She and Emma had been taken captive by the savages. Time shifted, the image blurred. Renny felt dizzy, as though falling, then everything went dark, as though in her dream it was now night.

Her heart hammered until she got her bearings. Embers from a fire drew her attention. Yes, it was night. She glanced around.

She recognized this place as well and knew just

where to look to find once more that nine-year-old version of herself.

Now, Renny the child was asleep. But she was restless, her face wet with tears. Renny covered her mouth with her fingers. She'd been so very scared of these people, and unnecessarily so. She'd been treated with the same love and patience as any other child. Praise and reprimands had been given as freely as their love and acceptance of her into their midst.

Renny smiled, her lips trembling. These people, the Cheyenne, she remembered, had been a lot nicer than the brutal, savage men who'd kidnapped her and Emma.

Renny turned to leave. She knew she was dreaming. She hadn't dreamed or remembered any of this for so long so she was confused as to why she'd do so now.

Before she could make the conscious thought to wake herself, her dream shifted around her. Now she was standing outside. Everything looked so big. Intimidating.

Renny glanced down at herself and to her shock, instead of watching herself as a child, she *was* the child.

And she wasn't alone. There before her stood the most beautiful and magical horse she'd ever seen. The animal was silver, and she seemed to glow. Renny figured anything this wondrous had to be female. She was like an angel with no wings.

Once more, the scene shifted like a kaleidoscope

shifting colors and patterns. This time, she was riding on the back of the horse. She felt small. Her legs didn't reach down to the middle of the horse's sides, and she couldn't grip hard, but she needn't have worried for the horse's gait was incredibly smooth.

Then, unexpectedly, the horse soared upward, taking them both high up into the starlit sky.

The woman inside the child let loose with a shriek of joy. Her happy voice echoed around them. Renny reached out to grab at stars that looked so close. So real. She felt alive. Safe with her angel who looked like a horse.

After what seemed like forever the horse descended. Renny slid off. Everything looked normal. She was the adult Renny once more.

The pale horse stood before her. "Do you remember me, *Weshawee?*"

Filled with wonder, forgetting that this was just a dream, Renny reached out to touch the horse who felt so incredibly soft. Long strands of silky mane brushed against her face like a caress.

Some part of Renny, that part of her that had lived so long ago, thought she did. But since Renny couldn't remember exactly, she shook her head no, being truthful. "No."

The horse looked sad and pawed the ground with one hoof that glittered as though encased in diamonds. Or stars. She started to fade. Renny could see right through her.

"Don't go," she pleaded as she reached out a

hand. "Tell me who you are." It was important that she know.

"Remember me."

Renny woke with those words. She lay very still, her eyes wide as she stared up at the still dark sky. It would start to lighten soon.

The dream had seemed so real. They *were* real, she thought, at least all but the ones of the horse. She frowned as she recalled the command the horse had given to her.

"Remember me."

And suddenly, she did. Renny smiled. The horse had been her friend. Renny had been so scared and alone that she'd created a friend that no one could take from her.

She'd called her friend to her each night. They would pass the time walking, flying and laughing. There were also tears and words of comfort.

Frowning, Renny recalled that she'd often pretended to see her make-believe friend during daylight hours. The animal had given her a lot of peace, appeared at her side whenever Renny needed her, like a guardian angel . . .

Renny bolted upright. "A spirit," she breathed. The word circled her mind. Over and over, round and round. Then she laughed softly, stunned at the revelation of her dream.

"Remember me."

Mazaska Wicahpi. The words popped into her mind.

Silver Star.

The horse had called herself Silver Star. She was a spirit—one sent to bring comfort to a frightened young girl.

She was the pale horse that Mattie had seen. Renny ran her hands through her hair as long-forgotten memories mixed with her thoughts. Questions rushed through her mind.

She closed her eyes, dizzy with all the images of her past that were spinning in her mind.

While she'd believed in spirits until her parents had died, she'd never seen one.

"Except in my dreams," she breathed. As a young child, she'd taken those dreams in stride. They hadn't seemed unusual. They had just been.

Now she started remembering those odd moments over the last week when she'd felt as though she were not alone.

"Oh," she said, her voice low.

"Oh." Renny closed her eyes. She could still see her, this beautiful, fairy-tale horse who used to come to her in the middle of the night to teach her how to control her fears so that they did not control her.

For a long time, the bad Indians had haunted her nights. Until Silver Star came and chased them away.

A shimmering mist appeared before her. "You have remembered. Now believe."

Renny stared at the horse for a long moment, then she reached out.

"I remember."

She drew in a deep breath.

"I believe."

Chapter Eighteen

Brenna lay awake, watching the approaching dawn with dread and a sick feeling in her stomach. She was so tired, so hungry and so very afraid. Wiping silent tears from her face, she kept telling herself she had to be braver. She had to be stronger, but it was so hard.

All she could think of was Matthew. The sight of him lying on the ground, bleeding, haunted her day and night. How many days had it been? She couldn't remember. Five? Six?

Oh God, he couldn't have survived alone for so long. Why had she left him? Closing her eyes, she made herself see the blood, feel its sticky warmth between her fingers. Her dress bore the stains and was a daily reminder that once more, she'd failed to do the right thing.

Yet if she'd refused to go with Gil, she had no doubt that he'd have shot them both. Killed them both. She'd done what she could to give Matt the best chance he had to survive. In her heart she knew this. But her mind couldn't bear the pain of not knowing Matt's fate.

Across from her, Gil slept as though he didn't have a care in the world. The rifle was in his arms and he slept lightly.

Brenna didn't dare try and leave. He'd wake. And he might make good on his threat to kill her if he caught her leaving him.

Staring at her brother, she wondered how he could do this to her. She'd thought they'd been close, that he'd loved her as much as she loved and adored him. His anger and shock over everything was understandable, but for him to react with the same violence as their mother frightened her.

He was crazy. Just like their mother. Brenna stifled a sob. She felt the cut on her lip and her bruised cheekbone where Gil had hit her.

Gil was so out of his mind with grief and anger, she wasn't sure that he wouldn't yet kill her. So she kept quiet and still, holding her fear, the hopelessness, deep inside her as she watched the birth of a new day.

What would today bring? More pain? Or maybe the end of it all. She was very much afraid that she'd welcome death if offered.

So much had happened. Her whole world had been torn into useless pieces that could never be mended and made whole again.

Drawing her knees to her chest, she rested her head on them as she struggled not to panic.

The days following the death of her stepfather

and her mother had been filled with confusion, anguish, and sorrow.

And guilt.

Waves of guilt and regrets.

Gil was one of her regrets. She'd been more worried about going to live with Matt's people and so ashamed of her own actions against a family she'd called friends, that she hadn't paid Gil much mind.

So wrapped up in her own world of sorrow and grief, she hadn't noticed that Gil was just as confused and grief-stricken.

He'd been forgotten in the aftermath of their stepfather's death. Devastated by their mother's attempt to kill Mattie for a second time. Katherine had died in a fire she'd set. Leaving Brenna and Gil alone, their entire family gone, just like that.

Brenna had been forced to tell her brother the truth, that it had been their mother who'd killed their older brother.

Gil had flown out of control. He'd blamed Brenna for Collin's death, for their mother's death. For all of it.

He'd said some hateful things, some unforgivable things, then left. He'd ridden away from his home and his only living relative.

Brenna should have gone after him. Or asked someone for help. He had no reason to leave. None of it had been his fault and no one had blamed him. But he'd left, angry and hurt, and not thinking clearly as he hadn't even taken any food or supplies with him.

And the next day she'd left with Matthew, trying to convince herself that Gil would come back to their home. She knew she herself would never return.

Her shame and guilt were too great for her to return to Pheasant Gully. It didn't matter that no one outside the O'Brien family and Tyler knew the truth.

She knew. Only now did she admit that the dispensing of justice had not been hers. In her mind, her mother had suffered terribly with the knowledge that she'd killed her firstborn. At the time, Brenna had thought it punishment enough.

Now Brenna had no life, no expectations of ever finding peace or happiness. She couldn't even cling to the hope that Gil would survive and be all right eventually.

Tears slid down Brenna's face. She cried silently, not over her own situation but how the taint of her parents, and her own actions, had rubbed off on her brother. Gil had been ignorant, caught in the middle.

He'd been innocent—until the day he'd shot Matthew. Brenna stifled a sob. Around her, the wind howled.

"Please," she whispered into the wind. "Take care of Matt. Keep him safe."

She repeated this prayer over and over as the sun stretched pink fingers over the sky as though embracing the world. She didn't care what happened to her; just let Matthew live.

A dark shape appeared in the sky above her. It

circled. At first she was afraid it was a vulture. As the shape drew nearer, she saw that it was an eagle, soaring gracefully.

It dipped lower, and with a gentle upward tilt to its wings landed in the scraggly bush a short distance from her.

Brenna held her breath. One of the things she'd loved about Matt and his family was their closeness to nature. She'd spent hours listening to Star spin her tales, to all of the children pointing out bits of nature and telling her what they meant to the humans of the world.

She'd never seen an eagle this close. Nor had one ever watched her so intently. Raised in cities all of her life, Brenna found the appearance of the eagle new and fascinating. And comforting.

What had Matt once told her about the eagle? She frowned. Something about facing hard days ahead. Discouragement slid through her and she chastised herself for hoping that the presence of the bird might have meant hope.

Not for herself but for Matthew. Matthew needed her. She had to get free so she could return to him. As though Matthew was there, she heard his voice in her head.

"Let the spirits guide you and you will succeed." Most everything in Matt's world had a moral, or lesson, tied to it.

What could the eagle be telling her? She wasn't sure that she really believed, but right then, she needed all the courage she could find.

"Let the spirits guide you," she whispered to

herself as she stared at the bird. But they wouldn't guide her. She didn't know how to talk to them. She was on her own, had only herself to rely upon.

The bird flapped its wings, drawing her attention back to the large eagle. The golden feathers seemed to reach out to her and encase her in their soft warmth. He opened his beak, as though about to impart great wisdom.

Brenna leaned forward, listening intently, but she only heard her own heart pounding in her ears.

Her heart.

Staring at the bird in awe, she knew she had the answer. She hadn't listened to her heart—her spirit—after the fire. She let fear take over. Had she told her stepfather, or the sheriff or Matthew, what she'd seen, much of the tragedy could have been avoided, maybe even Gil's feelings of betrayal.

It would not have changed what her mother had done, or what her father would have done. But it would have prevented Katherine from making a second attempt to kill Mattie. And Matthew would not despise her now.

In her heart, she'd known that protecting her mother had been wrong. But she'd convinced herself that no good would come from exposing the truth. She'd convinced herself that she'd been protecting herself, keeping what she most needed close: her family. And in the end, it hadn't mattered. She'd lost everything. They'd all lost. Including Gil.

Suddenly, she knew what she had to do. She had

to go back. She hadn't had a choice in leaving Matt. If she'd refused, they'd both be dead.

But she had a choice now. Going with Gil, letting him believe that what he was doing was right, was unacceptable. She had to take a stand and pray that she'd be able to fix things between them.

Doing right meant breaking the promise she'd made to Gil. He wasn't the brother she remembered, and what he had done, and was doing, was wrong. Just like what she'd done.

She had to make it right, even if it meant saying good-bye to her brother for good or risking her own life.

The eagle, as though agreeing, gave a shrill shriek and then flew higher.

Gil, startled awake, jumped to his feet. The bird had taken wing. Brenna expected to feel abandoned but strangely, she felt better than she had in a long time.

She had hope.

Renny rose before anyone else. Only Reed was awake. They nodded silently to one another as Renny walked past him. She smiled at the sight of Daire fast asleep. Her brothers, both warriors at heart, were still children.

For a while, she walked around the camp, staying within sight of Reed in order to not worry him. As she paced, she kept her eyes on the darkness surrounding them. But her mind was a beehive of thought.

She played her dream over and over, remembering those bits of her childhood where she'd been at peace with the world, and herself. Her sister, Emma, had fallen in love with Striking Thunder, Mattie and Matthew's uncle. For many years, Renny and her new family had returned for the summers to live off the land and become one with that world.

The primitive and untamed land was a place Renny felt very at home, at peace. The wild side of her nature found release in being free from society's constraints. The dream had acted like a door into that past. For many years the door had been closed. Over the last year, it had been locked. Now it was open, allowing images and memories to flood her mind.

How simple life had been. And how complex it was now. No matter how much she wanted to become that child once again, she knew it would never happen. But she had recovered a part of that child—the unwavering belief in spirits.

Renny paused to watch her family sleep. After those dreams she knew she could never deny or shun the reality of the spiritual world.

Life was a circle, she told herself. Man did not live alone. He lived and breathed the same air as the birds, animals, insects.

He walked upon the grass, relied on trees for fuel and homes to live in. She bent and picked up a rock. She cupped it in both hands. Even rocks were valued. They could be gathered to form fire pits, or fence lines.

So many uses and so much life attached, she thought as she watched a tiny insect crawling in a crevice in the rock. As a girl, if this insect had crossed her path, she'd have studied it, and tried to think what relation she had to that tiny bit of life.

Remembering the beetle who had climbed over her boot in the barn, she realized just how much she'd turned her back on. Setting the rock down, with the darker, moist part down as she found it, Renny resumed her pacing and focused her thoughts on the revelation of her dreams.

Silver Star. A horse who'd once been a child's companion. Her need of Silver had faded, and as she'd matured into womanhood, those fond memories had been boxed up and hidden away in her mind like her childhood toys that were even now stored in the attic of her aunt's home in St. Louis.

Like her childhood, there was so much forgotten. Things and events she'd left behind, figuring she'd never need them again.

But now, Renny realized that perhaps there was space to merge what had been with what was now. And somehow, it all tied to her finding Matthew. She had no doubt that remembering, the revelation of her dream, was for a purpose.

This time she smiled as she recalled her dream. As a young girl, she'd learned to speak with the animals and birds who shared the land with humans. She'd learned to listen to her world with animal ears and see her world with animal eyes.

The world around her was filled with teachers, friends and companions. The horse of her dream had been a companion. A spiritual companion. The golden horse she'd seen was one of her totem, or helpmate, animals. He had much to tell her, much to show her. She now trusted that he, and the other inhabitants of this world, would guide her to Matthew.

And guide her own inner-being along her life's path. She closed her eyes and gave herself over to that belief. She didn't know what she'd find, or how rocky the path, but she knew she would not make her journey alone.

She just had to find the key, and trust that the key would lead her to her brother. Walking softly over to the pile of supplies, she rummaged through the rolls of clothing and belongings.

Each person had their travel rolls. Clothes, combs, soaps, spare shoes, all rolled together in one neat bundle. She located hers. Sitting down, she untied the rope and spread out her belongings.

Spare pants, shirt, and shift were peeled away until Renny reached her goal: a soft buckskin dress. It had been a while since she'd worn the dress of her mother's people. It had been a gift from her mother during their last visit to the Sioux.

Renny fingered the fringe, rubbed the soft hide dress over her check, and held it close. Glancing down, she saw the knee-high leather moccasins. Inside one boot was a pouch.

Making up her mind, she stood and strode into the concealing shadows to change her clothing, replacing her jeans and shirt for her native dress.

The garment fell to her knees, and clung to her curves. Holding her hands out, she let the leather fringe dangle and flow in the wind.

Because she loved the feel of the dress, the fringe swinging against her calves, she unbound her hair.

Tipping her head back, she lifted her hands high, fingers reaching for the heavens. Her morning prayer came back to her, the chant that was hers alone, one used to greet the new day, and bless those around her.

So immersed in a world that had for a short while been lost to her, Renny didn't hear anyone approaching. Didn't see Tyler stare, his features both shocked and enthralled. She didn't hear him sit or feel his eyes on her as she turned in each direction, offering a blessing and prayer to the spirits of each direction, and to the heavens and sun.

When she was done, she took several deep, cleansing breaths, then opened her eyes to find Tyler watching her with a stunned look upon his face.

Tyler stood, utterly and totally in love. Until he'd seen this side to her, this almost primitive side, he hadn't known just how much. He went to her, put his arms on her shoulders.

"Renny, you are beautiful." He slid his hands into her hair and brought a strand to his face. He pulled her close, his hands sliding along the skin-soft dress, then he kissed her. He didn't care that Reed was there or that others might be waking soon. He had to hold her, kiss her, tell her what was in his heart.

"I love you, Renny. You are my heart and my soul," he breathed. "When we get back, I want to make you my wife."

Renny went still in his arms. Her mind raced. She pulled back and studied the man she had thought she had fallen in love with. No. She did love him. Period. But there was so much uncertainty in her life. She couldn't think of herself, not until she found Matthew.

"Renny?" There was a plea in Tyler's voice.

She stepped back, felt a cold wall rise between them. "I can't, Tyler." There was too much going on, too much uncertainty, and she was so afraid of where this journey would take her.

"You can. You do. I know you love me, Renny. Don't deny it." Tyler's voice was low and fierce but he kept his distance.

Renny didn't bother to deny the truth of his words. She'd spent many an hour last night thinking of him, remembering what they'd done. And that was the problem. She shouldn't have allowed anything—her frustration, his loving—to distract her from her goal of finding Matthew.

If she was making love with Tyler, she wasn't thinking and planning and seeking guidance from the spirits. Matthew was all that mattered. Coming through for her family was all that mattered.

Her own needs, wants and desires weren't to be considered. So she drew a deep breath and faced Tyler squarely. "There is too much that might happen, Tyler. Too much that already has. I can't let myself—"

"Let yourself love? Be loved?" Tyler ran his hand through his hair in frustration. He loved this woman with all his heart and soul.

"You're strong, Renny. Very strong. Look at you. You're the most fascinating woman I've ever met. You can do this. All of it. And together we can do more. Be more."

A part of Tyler was awed by what he saw in Renny. She looked formidable, like she didn't need anyone. And that frightened him, for he knew she needed him as much as he needed her.

"You're right, Tyler. I have to be strong. I have to do this. It is my journey. Something I have to do. Alone." She didn't tell him that if she failed, she wouldn't be worthy of his love or even that of her family. She could not fail in this task set before her.

"What the hell are you talking about?" Tyler indicated the rest of their party. "None of us are alone. We each have one another." He kicked at the ground. "You have me, Renny, whether you want me or not. You are not alone, and you will not do this alone."

Renny so wanted to lean on him, and let him share her burden. But if she failed Matthew, and the rest of them, then that burden would have to remain hers alone to carry. She sighed. Too much was at stake for her to lose sight of her goal.

"I'm sorry, Tyler," she said softly. Then she walked away, rousing her family as she went. The sun had not yet risen properly but she was ready to go. Ready to travel her path and brave whatever was hers to face.

Mounting her horse as everyone got up and ready, she searched the landscape. Golden grass stretched as far as the eye could see, except along the stream where cottonwoods dotted the winding path of water.

They'd camped near the slight curve of the stream. There were many streams, some wide and deep, others no more than a shallow trickling creek that would dry up before the end of summer and lay barren until winter's rain and snow returned.

Renny remembered the summers they'd returned for a few weeks to her mother's people. They'd cross the land, keeping to the streams, seldom going more than a day or two without fresh water.

Frowning as she waited on the others, she thought through their day. First, find the trail leading away from that abandoned campsite. She expected that the trail would follow the river until it ended in the Missouri River.

Thinking about that campsite reminded Renny why they'd been there yesterday. Had she not ridden off, she would not have been with Tyler, and would not have stopped at that stream, or learned the delicious secrets of womanhood.

And maybe, a small voice said, if she had not gone there, with Tyler, she might not have seen the horse or found that campsite.

Renny's insides twisted and churned. She'd hurt Tyler earlier, but she could not think of herself, and that meant she couldn't think of him.

But oh, she wanted to. She wanted nothing more than to go to Tyler right now, take him somewhere alone. As much as she wanted to kiss him, and make love with him, she also wanted to share her revelations.

But she couldn't. She was afraid of believing that he was hers, only to have him taken from her. So much could happen before this journey was complete.

Her emotions mirrored the streams. One minute her mind rushed and flowed with happiness, the next that happiness drained from her, replaced with a stagnant fear. Optimistic hope warred with the fear of failing.

She grew pensive. Last night, she'd been filled with contentment, and a false hope that everything would be all right. But in the cold light of morning she saw the bleakness that lay ahead.

She was afraid that she wouldn't find Matthew alive, afraid that her family would blame her—if not consciously, then subconsciously. And so afraid that she'd no longer feel worthy of Tyler's love.

No, better to wait. Hurt him now, save him from more pain later. No one knew more than her the feeling of being happy only to have that joy ripped from one's soul.

She clucked softly at her horse and moved through their camp. Everything had been packed, the horses almost ready. Mattie was mounted, Reed rolling their bedroll.

Tyler was doing the same, and as she watched,

Maze mounted her horse smoothly and gracefully as though twenty years younger. She sent Renny an encouraging smile.

They were nearly ready. They needed to get moving but Kealan and Daire seemed to be having problems. Kealan was in a bad mood, sulking because he'd been told to be ready to ride immediately. The morning meal would have to wait for just a little while.

She figured they could eat biscuits and jerky while riding. She and Tyler would go ahead, scout the campsite. Despite their earlier words, Renny knew Tyler would stick to her like glue. Part of her rejoiced in it, even though it would just make things harder if she failed.

Believe.

She nodded. She believed in the spirits. Believed that Tyler would be at her side. She even believed that her family would love her no matter what the outcome.

It wasn't the journey she feared. It was failing—not her family, but herself. Others would forgive her. She'd never forgive herself.

Renny grew restless. Antsy. The one thing she did not have, and never expected to have, was patience. Renny had waited all night to resume her journey. She was not waiting a moment longer.

Mattie and Reed were now ready but Daire and Kealan continued to argue.

Renny rode up to her brothers. Daire had just mounted and was waiting for Kealan, who was standing with arms folded across his narrow chest. He wore a stubborn, mutinous expression.

"Hurry up, Kea! Get on that horse," she ordered.

"I wanna ride in the front," he said. His lips quivered.

Renny glared down at her brother. There wasn't time for this. "If you can't get moving in the morning without sulking and causing problems, you're too young to take watch at night." Her voice came out harsher than she intended.

Kealan kicked at the ground with the toe of his boot. A single tear fell and his face turned red. "I got lots of sleep 'cause I fell asleep instead of doing the watch thing. I wasn't very good. I let you down." His voice quivered.

Renny let out a low growl and called upon some of that rare patience. She knew full well that Kealan seldom woke in a good mood, and that he always needed something to eat before he was human.

Normally when she growled at him in the morning, he growled right back. But she hadn't taken into consideration his young, tender ego or that he'd think he'd failed her because he'd fallen asleep.

She hadn't expected anything differently from a young boy of seven. But before she could think of a way to repair the damage to a very tender ego, Daire held down his hand.

"Fine, Kea. You can ride in front."

Kealan turned, rubbing his eyes. "Really?"

Daire grimaced as he helped his brother up.

"Yeah. And guess what?" He paused until Kea looked at him.

"What?"

"I didn't stay awake either." Daire sounded rather put out with himself.

Renny eyed her brothers with love. "I used to sit with Pa when we traveled and I fell asleep every time," she said.

Reaching into her pocket, she pulled out a couple strips of jerky and handed them to both boys. "Eat," she ordered, then rode away before she could be drawn into an argument.

She rode up to the rest. "I'm going on ahead. Might take a while to find a trail, if there is one."

"You're waiting for me," Tyler said as he walked around the horse.

She stared down at him, her gaze roaming over his face and settling on his mouth. He wore a dark shadow on his jaw that added to his rugged appearance. He looked grim and Renny felt guilty. She couldn't give him the words he wanted. Not yet.

Leaning down, she pulled his hat off his head and jammed it down onto her own. "Better get that ass of yours in the saddle then, Sheriff Troll, because I'm leaving."

As she'd hoped, a small smile lit his eyes as he mounted and rode after her. It felt good to know she wasn't alone.

Tyler caught up, reached over and took back his hat. "Lead the way, Miss O'Brien."

Chapter Nineteen

Tyler studied Renny as they rode. She seemed different this morning. And not just her clothing, though he had to admit, he loved the way she looked in the fringed dress and moccasins.

She looked wild, primitive and in total control. Her hair had been left unbound, and it flowed freely. She was, he realized, a free spirit, a part of this untamed land.

Her features were set and determined with that familiar aura of intensity that he knew so well. But there was something else. He studied her for a moment. Then it came to him.

She seemed at peace. Not in a relaxed, have-no-care-in-the-world manner, but as though she'd come to some decision or realization.

He glanced away when a pang of hurt rose inside him. Whatever had happened during the night to bring about this change was responsible for the new wall she'd built between them.

He'd thought he'd gotten through to her, proven

his loyalty and his love. He had believed that though she hadn't said the words, she felt the same.

Tyler wasn't a man to stew in silence long. "Going to tell me about it?" He easily kept pace with her.

She glanced over at him and frowned. "Tell you what?"

"You're different today." He indicated her clothing. "Not what you're wearing. Something more. Deeper."

Renny shrugged and trained her gaze ahead. "Same ol' me. Same ol' you, Nanny Troll."

Tyler laughed. Somehow, the insulting nicknames she had for him had taken on a loving caress. Who else could ever have called him Troll and lived?

He had flattened more than one boy growing up who had dared to shorten his given name in this manner. After countless fights, his mother had finally agreed to just call him Tyler.

"Okay. I'll take a guess."

She rolled her eyes. "Never get it in a hundred guesses," she said, her lips twitching.

"Hmm, I get a hundred. Should pass the time." He eyed her. "Guess one. Me." He didn't have long to wait for her reaction.

"You? What *are* you thinking, Troll?" She grinned. "Oh, gee, guess trolls aren't too good in the thinkin' department."

Tyler lifted a brow. He felt relieved. She was back to sounding like the woman he loved. Maybe he really didn't want to know what had happened, at least not until he had some idea of how to tear that particular wall back down.

"Okay, don't tell me," he said. He suspected that in time she'd share it with him. He just hoped it was something he could live with, and convince her that they belonged together. No matter what happened here or in the future.

Renny stopped, her eyes intent and serious. "I believe," she said simply.

Tyler moved closer. "In what, Miss O'Brien?"

Renny glanced around them and held out her hands. "In all this. In what I can see, and what I can't see but know is there."

She plucked at the fringe dangling from her native dress. "In this. In what it means."

Tyler mulled her words over. "What about me, Miss O'Brien? Do you believe in me? Do you believe that I will never let you be alone, that I'm here for you now, and will be there for you tomorrow? And the day after?"

Renny sighed but didn't look at him. "Yes," she said.

Tyler heard the unspoken "but" in her voice. He reached over and gently forced her to look at him. His thumb caressed the line of her jaw. "Say it, Renny."

Her eyes grew moist. "I believe you."

Reaching out, Tyler snagged her around the waist and pulled her as close as he could. It wasn't enough, but he had to kiss her, touch her, feel her in his arms. Their horses stood still as he kissed her long and soft, gently deepening the kiss. She moaned when he lifted his head. "Thank you for that, Renny.

"Who else do you believe in? Renny?" There was one person she had not included, one very important person: herself.

Tyler remembered vividly the desperateness coursing through her while they'd made love. He'd been stunned by the depth of her despair, her need for control. He'd always known that she was stubborn as a mule and as determined and strong-willed as they came but he had never before seen the fear and guilt inside her.

Settled back on her horse, she shook her head. "Let's get going," she said.

Tyler nodded sadly. Unless she believed in herself, that she was worthy of all he offered, there was little he could do or say. He'd watched her so closely over the last year, knew how she thought. Right now, he knew that Renny didn't believe that she had the right to succeed—or fail.

He followed her, staying silent. Now was not the time for him to force this issue. As she had said. Later. Later there would come a time when he'd make her see that she had every right to both succeed, and fail, and lose control, just like the rest of the human race.

Dismounting when they reached the abandoned campsite, they started searching for the single tracks of a shod horse. The fact that the horse had shoes told her that the person they were tracking was most likely white. Or a trapper.

She got back on her horse, feeling uneasy. By the time everyone else caught up with them, she was impatient to get going.

Renny and Tyler once again took the lead, following a trail of crushed grass made by the hooves of the single horse. The steady pace and straight line of travel told Renny that the horse had a rider guiding his direction and speed.

With every bit of distance she and her party covered, her hopes of finding her brother grew stronger. She just hoped they found him alive.

Minutes turned into hours. They followed the animal's droppings, saw where he'd munched at the grass, and even where the rider had stopped to rest, and maybe eat a quick meal.

And when the tracks left the stream, and headed out into open prairie, Renny spotted something else.

There were now two more sets of prints. In her gut, Renny knew that the other two sets of tracks, which were made by horses that were not shod, were Matt's and Brenna's.

It had to be them. They were on the right path after all. But she didn't stop. She shifted her horse over so that she was covering the tracks with the prints of her horse.

"Renny?" Tyler had noticed. He had one brow quirked in question.

"Kea and Daire. I don't want them to see."

Tyler nodded and they continued to ride at a fast clip, covering the ground rapidly. By mid-afternoon, they came upon another abandoned camp. This time, there was no fire pit. From the wetness of the ground, she judged that it had been raining hard in the area. One glance at the sky warned that it would probably rain on them before dark.

Tyler pointed to several sets of boot prints in the mud.

"Matt's?"

Renny shook her head. "No. Not Matt's."

"How do you know?" The question came from Tyler.

Renny squatted down to study the area. She glanced at Kealan. He answered at her nod.

"Tracks from a boot," he said. "Matt doesn't wear boots when he goes back home. He wears moccasins. Like mine." He held up one foot. "Like we all do."

Renny nodded to her brother. Dressed in their native clothing, he looked like a small warrior, especially with the feather in his hair. She turned to Daire, who was also dressed in breechclout, leggings and vest.

"Daire, what do you see?"

"One person. One horse." He'd walked around, stepping lightly, his moccasins leaving no prints. He held up his foot to one of the prints. "A grown man."

Kealan, who had wandered away, called out. "He goes this way." Renny walked over, spotted the deeper indents of a heel in the ground and ruffled her brother's hair. "You have good eyes," she praised.

Together, brother and sister followed the tracks

on foot. Then, to Renny's disappointment, the horse tracks faded into a sea of marshlike grass.

They were at the bottom of a rise of land. Water had collected, making tracking impossible.

"Spread out," she called to the others who'd followed on horseback. Everyone dismounted. "Kealan, you and Reed go north, Tyler and Daire east."

"You're not going off alone," Tyler said, daring her to argue.

Renny sighed, rolled her eyes at him then glanced at Maze. The woman didn't wait to be asked.

"She won't be alone. I'll be with her."

Renny grinned when she saw Tyler's disappointment. She and Maze headed west while Mattie and Caitie waited behind.

Renny climbed a slight hump of golden grass. Spread out below them, the land was open, they could see in all directions. It was mostly flat but for the brown humps and hills of prairie land.

She and Maze covered a large distance before admitting defeat. All they'd found was evidence of a herd of antelope, which meant there was water in close range.

"Nothing," she said with a sigh of disappointment.

"Do not give up hope, child." Maze's voice was gentle.

When they returned, Reed and Kealan were waiting with Mattie and Caitie on top of the small hill where the ground was drier.

They were looking at her. To her. Even Mattie

seemed to be staring at her, though Renny knew it was because her sister heard them approaching.

From her vantage point, she could see Tyler and Daire still searching. It wasn't looking very promising.

She glanced skyward. "Now what?" she whispered to herself. If Tyler and Daire came back empty-handed, she'd have to admit defeat.

"What would the child do?" Maze's voice drifted around her, through her, inside her, warming her from the inside out, calming the nervous pounding of her heart.

Renny glanced at the woman. "Kealan or Caitie?"

Maze laughed softly. "No, *child*." She stared intently at Renny for a moment before slowly closing her eyes, then reopening them.

Renny gasped. Maze's eyes had turned a rich, dark blue, like that of a glass-smooth lake. In those eyes, she saw herself reflected there. Or rather, a much younger version—the child she'd once been. Renny, the woman, stared at Renny, the child.

"Who are you?" she asked Maze, her voice hoarse with fear and excitement. She blinked, and her reflection was gone.

For a moment, Maze seemed to shimmer. "I am one who wishes to help you," came the simple reply.

"Trust yourself. Find that child within and let her guide you." Maze turned and walked away.

Renny stared down at her, and for just a fleeting moment, the woman's single, silvery braid seemed to swish and flow like the tail of a horse.

"I know you," she whispered.

Maze glanced over her shoulder. She was smiling. "Yes, child. We know each other well. Trust yourself. Do what the child would do."

Stunned, confused and a bit unnerved, Renny watched as Maze joined Mattie. Caitie went right into her arms. Renny had the feeling she knew just how Caitie felt around the woman: safe, loved, and secure. Exactly how Renny had felt in her dream so long ago. Silver Star, her companion during both day and night, had always made her feel warm and safe. And very loved.

It seemed too much to take in. First her dream last night, the return of her beliefs, and now this. Renny shook her head. This was much more powerful. And scary. For it meant that if she was right, Maze was none other than Silver Star.

Once more, the spirit horse had entered her life.

Renny wanted to go to her, beg her to guide her, teach her what she needed to know. Even more, she wanted comfort and forgiveness for having doubted.

But she didn't chase after the woman. The spirit had given her the answers or else she would not have walked off. Renny turned back to the view.

Already another storm was gathering. The clouds scuttling together, forming huge thunderheads. Before the day was over, they'd be wet.

But how did this knowledge help her? Below, Tyler and Daire were still searching. Kealan had run down to join them.

What would the child do?

Renny frowned. As a child, she'd tended to act first, think later. She'd gotten into many a scrape with her impulsive, impatient nature.

Slowly she turned in a circle.

What would the child do?

She wouldn't have given up. That much she knew. She'd keep searching, too stubborn to stop until she found what she wanted. Maybe she needed to go back down there, retrace her steps. Perhaps she'd overlooked something.

A shout drew her attention. Tyler and Kealan were on the next rise. Kealan was jumping up and down.

Renny didn't hesitate. "Stay here," she told Mattie, Reed and Maze. She jumped onto the back of her horse and rode over to join them. "What is it?" She jumped off before the horse stopped.

"We found some tracks. They go that way." Kealan was pointing northeast.

"Let's get back to the others. The rain is starting." A few fat drops had just begun to fall.

She'd just mounted when the first rumble of thunder rolled across the land.

"Renny, we need to wait out the storm." Tyler had grabbed her by the arm.

Renny shook her head. "Can't. We'll lose the trail." She signaled the others with a loud call and the waving of her hands.

When the rest of them arrived, they once again mounted. Renny was ready to give the order to ride when Tyler called her name.

"What?" She didn't have time to talk, or fight.

"Look." Tyler was pointing.

The heavens had just opened in a burst of water. She peered through the sheet of rain. "What—"

"Look," he said urgently. "A horse."

A flash of lightning illuminated the land below her. And she saw it. Her magnificent horse. The golden one who seemed to be her helpmate in this journey.

He stood watching them, then turned and ran east.

"It's him," Renny breathed. Far in the distance, she saw the yellow-gold of the horse, the high flick of a pale tail. She held her breath.

What would the child do?

Renny firmed her lips. The child. She, Renny, would follow that horse. No matter where it led her or what anyone said, she'd follow the horse. She'd follow her heart and trust in the wisdom of the spirits that were guiding her.

Renny glanced at Maze. Maze just met her gaze, leaving it up to Renny. Drawing in a deep, shaky breath, the child within her demanded that they follow that horse. But the woman the child had become was wiser now.

More cautious.

Finally, Renny made her decision based on a combination of what she once had been and what she'd become.

She nodded to the horse that everyone was now watching. He rose up on his hind feet and pawed the air. Then he turned and galloped away.

Renny's heart was with the horse. Something

drew her to him. She made up her mind. "I'm following the horse to the east. Reed, take everyone else and follow the tracks."

Tyler moved beside her. "Are you sure? The horse is going in the opposite direction of the trail we found."

Before Renny could answer him, another flash of light lit the heavens. Several bolts of lightning raced across the sky like rivers of molten silver. And there in the center, Renny saw something she'd never forget: the silvery image of a horse rearing high into the sky, mouth open.

Silence fell over the group. Even Tyler was struck dumb.

With tears in her eyes, she nudged Tyler. "You're with me."

Tyler nodded, his gaze glued to the now rain-laden clouds. "Without a doubt, Miss O'Brien. Without a doubt."

Brenna hid with Gil in the trees. Out on the prairie, a band of Indians was hunting. Antelope fled in every direction, the flash of their white tails a signal that could be seen for a great distance.

"Maybe I should give you to them," Gil said. "You want to go live with them, don't you?" he asked, his voice filled with contempt.

Brenna didn't respond. It wasn't the first time Gil had made the threat. She knew he was trying to frighten her. He got perverse pleasure in frightening her, and making her beg.

She pressed her fingers to her lips to keep them

from trembling. "They're gone," she said, getting to her feet. She went to where their horses waited.

"Then let's go," Gil ordered, shoving her out of his way.

Leaning against her horse, Brenna knew she couldn't take much more. Her nerves were shot. She was hungry, tired and getting discouraged, losing heart.

Listen to your heart.

She recalled the eagle she'd seen that morning and her decision to follow her heart. She glanced up at her brother on his horse, the rifle cradled in his arms. His eyes were glazed with grief, anger and exhaustion.

Brenna got onto her horse. When Gil turned away, she remained where she was.

He glanced at her over his shoulder. "Get moving, Bre."

"No, Gil," she said. "I'm sorry." Her voice dropped to a whisper.

"What do you mean, no?" His voice rose with fury. "You promised."

Brenna's eyes filled with tears. "I know. And I'm sorry. So sorry."

She took a deep breath and gathered her shreds of courage around her. "It was wrong. All of this. It's all wrong."

Gil's lips twisted in a sneer. "Yeah, you started it. It's all your fault."

Brenna felt the familiar cloak of guilt slide over her. "No," she shouted. "Not all of this is my fault. I made a choice. It was wrong. But you made a choice too, Gil. You chose to shoot Matthew. You shot him in cold blood." She covered her mouth with her hands. *God, don't let him have killed Matthew.*

It was time for her to take a stand. The right stand. She couldn't change the past, couldn't change what Gil had done, but she could end it now. She'd return to Matthew.

If he was dead, she'd take his body home and she'd live with the guilt of leaving him forever.

It didn't matter that Gil had left her little choice. If Matthew was dead, then it didn't matter that she'd tried to bargain for his life. But if Matthew was alive, somehow, someway, then maybe she had done the right thing.

But it was time to go back.

"I'm leaving, Gil."

Gil spun his horse around. "You can't," he screamed. "You promised."

"Then let me go, Gil. I'm your sister. *Your sister,*" she cried, tears streaming down her face.

"You're all I have," he said fiercely. "I won't let you go."

"Then I'm sorry, Gil. I'm so very sorry." She turned her horse.

"I'll shoot you," he screamed at her.

Brenna looked at him one last time. "Then you will have killed all that you have left, Gil."

She held out a hand. "Gil, it isn't too late. Come with me."

Gil fingered the trigger. "Never. I'll never go back and I won't let you go either."

"Then we have no more to say, Gil."

She turned once more. Her heart pounded painfully loud in her ears, and her chest felt ready to explode. One moment turned into two. Silence stretched taut between them.

"Good-bye, Gil," she whispered, not turning to look at her brother.

Crying, she urged her horse forward. She felt Gil's eyes on her, felt the rifle aimed at the center of her back. She broke out in a sweat of sheer terror.

Would he kill her? With each step, she wondered. Would he call her name? Would he run after her, try to stop her? Would he threaten her again or would he just make good on his promise to kill her if she ever left him again?

Nothing happened. She urged her horse a bit faster, holding her breath the whole time. She let the air out of her lungs and kept going, sobbing loudly, hoping one day Gil would forgive her.

Suddenly a shot rang out.

Chapter Twenty

Matthew woke as though from a long sleep. He glanced around. He had no idea how long it had been since Gil had shot him.

He also had trouble distinguishing dreams from reality. But he thought he remembered hearing Brenna crying, her lips so close to his own, telling him she was sorry, that she had to go, right before the veil of darkness descended.

But was it reality or dreams? Had she known that Gil would come for her? Had they planned this? His heart immediately rejected that Brenna would do anything to hurt him. But, he'd never have suspected that Gil would shoot him either.

He struggled to sit up, gasping in pain. He'd thought it hurt when he'd gotten shot in the thigh nearly a month ago. But this was worse. Much worse.

His side burned, as though on fire. He felt the bulky bandage, felt the strips of torn cloth that bound the bandage to him biting into his waist.

As he sat, a small object fell from his bare chest. He was clothed only in his loincloth.

It was a tiny leather pouch with no markings. But as he held it, felt the warmth of it, he knew it was Brenna's medicine bag.

He brought it up to his nose. Her scent clung to it. "Brenna," whispered. The need to find her rose in him. If she'd left this with him—for him—then she was not part of this treachery.

She'd asked him once what was in his medicine bag. It was larger than hers, usually worn on his belt. He'd told her that the contents were only known to the owner, and then he'd taught her the value and uses of a medicine bag.

He'd had no idea that she'd made her own. Though he longed to see what she considered to be her medicine, he didn't open it. But the fact that she'd left it gave his heart hope. The canvas above his head sagged, as though the wind had loosened it, and there was a long, narrow strip missing from one side. He glanced at the bandage around his waist. It had come from the shelter. Someone had been here tending him.

An old man. He remembered the gruff yet gentle voice, the firm and tender hands. He frowned. He also recalled chanting. And prayers.

Reaching over cautiously, Matthew picked up the flask of water that the old man had kept filled and within easy reach. Matthew drank deeply.

Shifting, he managed to scoot his body over to the trunk of the tree where he'd tied one corner of the canvas cloth.

He leaned back and took stock of his injuries. With every breath in and out, his side hurt as though dozens of spears were being jabbed into him. He pulled the bandage away, saw the raw and red wound, and the seepage of blood.

His side looked as though it had been torn from him.

Blinking, struggling not to give in to the urge to lie back down and drift along in a pain-free world, he peered outside. He couldn't see anything.

"Old Man," he called, his voice weak as a newborn's. He couldn't remember the man's name. A small heap on his other side drew his attention. He reached out and picked up Brenna's shawl.

His heart nearly burst through his chest when he saw the blood on it. "No. No," he said over and over. She couldn't be hurt. He didn't remember her being hurt.

A shadow moved outside. Matt clutched the shawl. "Old Man," he shouted. Unable to help himself, Matthew shook the shawl out, ignoring the pain. He studied the blood. It was hard, dried and all in one spot, as though used to soak up blood.

Matt felt his side. Had Brenna tried to help him? Did that mean she was alive? With Gil?

He closed his eyes, pulling from the haze of pain, and remembered Gil shouting at him.

"You took her from me. You left me alone."

A rush of wind whipped into the shelter with a low whistle. Matthew's eyes flew open. He searched the shelter, and found the food pouch gone, along with her personal things.

"She's alive. She has to be." He twisted again to look outside. The old man must be off hunting. He struggled to his feet with a goodly amount of sweating and cursing.

"Can't wait. Must find Brenna." He waited until he got his breath back before taking his first step. While he walked on legs that trembled like a newborn fawn's, he wondered how much time had passed. He had a vague memory of asking the old man that same question but had only gotten riddles instead.

When he was sure he could walk without toppling over, he left the shelter. It was as he remembered—a small clearing with many saplings crowded together along with some thick brush.

It had made a good shelter. It had not been a safe one, however. The shelter he'd sought had also provided cover for Gil and had allowed the man to sneak up on them.

Matt would never forgive himself for being so careless. Though he hadn't been speaking to Brenna, he hadn't been able to make himself travel faster to get rid of her.

So he'd decided to go slow. Make her walk much of the way. They'd lived off the land—she found them berries and roots, he hunted in the way of his parents and grandparents.

They'd been alone, he'd kept them out of sight of other bands of Indians and trappers. He'd wanted to be alone with her.

It had been torture, but he thought the only way to get Brenna out of his mind and heart was to be with her, and convince himself that she was not worthy of his thoughts or feelings.

Then, when he no longer cared, he'd take her to his people and leave her there, returning only in one year's time, as promised. But his plan had backfired. Each day made it harder for him to hold on to his anger, and he found he didn't want her to be without him.

What if he took her to his people and another warrior tried to claim her? His gut had burned at the thought. Until he could rid himself of those feelings, bring himself to the point where he did not care, he'd keep her to himself.

He clenched his hands into fists. His resentment of her had cost him dearly. And her as well. He wouldn't be able to live with himself if anything happened to Brenna.

Using the thin saplings for support to help keep him from falling, he walked around the shelter. There was no sign of anyone. Not the old man, not Gil, not Brenna. Not even his horse.

Where was the old man? The one who'd fed him, kept him abed and tended to his wounds. He appeared to have left without a word. Even more strange, there was no sign that anyone had been here with him.

No fire pit, yet Matthew remembered warm, rich broth being spooned into his mouth and warm water being used to bathe his wound.

Puzzled, he returned to the shelter and packed what he needed: weapons, food, water. Everything else was left behind. With all that he needed on his back, he began the search for Brenna and Gil's trail.

Among the horse tracks, he found what he was searching for—a set of shod prints. His horse and Brenna's were not shod. He followed to be sure that there were two sets of tracks leading away from where he'd been shot.

The trail was easy to follow. No attempts had been made to hide it or erase it. It led out into the open, endless prairie. For a moment, the task before him seemed daunting. Impossible.

Gil was on horseback. Matthew was on foot. How was he going to catch up?

Tipping his head up and back, Matthew sent a prayer heavenward. "*Cetan,* Hawk Spirit, lend me endurance and make me swift of foot." Though he thought he was shouting, his voice was a weak croak.

The snap of a twig made Matthew spin around. The wrenching pain sent him to his knees and the sight of the horse coming around the back of his shelter made him cry out.

Over and over in his mind, he thanked the spirits for sending the horse to him. It wasn't his. This one was a warm, golden yellow with a mane of liquid moonlight.

He stood absolutely still and willed the animal to come to him. To help him.

How long he waited, he didn't know. Finally, the horse moved toward him. With a twisting shake of its head, it started running right at him.

Matthew didn't move. He didn't try to grab the

horse as it ran past, not touching but close enough that Matt felt the warmth of the animal.

He turned. The horse repeated this several times, as though wanting to be sure Matt was brave and worthy of such a magnificent animal.

When the horse stopped and dropped his head, Matthew limped forward. With a gentle hand and soft breath, he chanted a song of praise to the horse, and thanked the animal for coming to him.

With great difficulty, he mounted, and urged the horse in the direction Gil had taken Brenna.

Across the sodden grass, Tyler and Renny gave chase to the golden-yellow horse. It moved with the swiftness of the wind and stayed well ahead of them, becoming a streak of gold in the distance.

The rain slowed them; they could not push the horses. Finally, heading westward, they outran the afternoon storm and urged their horses faster.

But it was too late. The golden-yellow horse had disappeared behind the distant line of trees.

"No!" Renny shouted the word, her voice echoing. "Faster, we need to catch up."

"The horses need to rest," Tyler shouted back. He figured they'd be all right until they reached the trees, and the stream he knew would be on the other side.

Renny glanced at him for a brief moment. "Not yet."

Tyler fell back half a pace so he could watch his warrior-woman. God, he loved her even if she oftentimes scared him stupid. Like now. She was so intent, so focused and determined to fulfill her destiny, he worried what would happen if she failed.

Her jaw was set, her eyes nearly unblinking as she stared at the spot where they'd last seen the horse. She was so stiff and unyielding in her goal, yet her body was fluid, her spirit one with the animal beneath her.

Her hair streamed out behind her, and the long fringe of buckskin along the underside of her arms moved in a smooth swing. She was wild, primitive and part of the land they rode across.

And she was his.

But only if she found Matthew. The thought made him feel sick. She hadn't said the words, but he knew her well. Renny kept herself under tight, rigid control. And she expected more from herself than all of them together.

Tyler knew that if she failed, she'd blame herself, and hold it in until it ate at her from the inside out. He'd already seen it happening, had been waiting for her to crack so he could be there to hold her.

If not for Mattie's vision of Matthew, he might have gotten through to her. But she'd closed herself off again, and was expecting too much of herself.

Of course, it didn't help to have Mattie telling her that it was her journey, or for them to keep seeing a horse that sure as hell appeared to be leading them across the prairie. Not to mention spirits in the sky.

Until he'd seen that image of a horse in the sky,

he wasn't sure just how much stock he put into the whole vision and spirit thing.

But he couldn't deny seeing the silvery-white horse. The moment had been powerful and incredible, unlike anything he'd ever experienced. It filled him with awe. And maybe, just maybe, he, too, believed.

They reached a line of trees along the river. The growth was thick and the horse tracks were gone.

Tyler felt Renny's disappointment, saw her shoulders sag with a bone-deep weariness. The life seemed to go out of her, as though she were giving up. "He's gone," she whispered as she frantically eyed the ground near the stream.

"We keep looking. He went through here." They both had noted the position of the trees: two on the left, two on the right, as though standing guard.

As they searched, he yearned to go to her and pull her into his arms. He needed to hold her and assure her that everything would be all right. But he couldn't make promises that he had no control over.

Control. With Renny it all boiled down to control: of herself, of those around her. She kept herself so tightly reined in that it drew out his own need to protect her, and shield her.

But he'd learned, finally, that there was a time and place to be protective and a time to let go so that the woman he loved could grow.

Renny needed support right now. Not coddling. She needed him to be here, and to prove that she would never be alone.

"I can't do this," she cried out, jumping down from her horse. She kicked at the rocks then sank down onto the ground.

"He's gone. We lost him." Her voice ended on a strangled choke.

"We'll find the horse, Renny." Tyler stood behind her. He knelt down but didn't touch her.

"And if we don't?" Her voice rose. "What if I'm too late? What if I was too slow? I should have stuck to the trail. But I listened to the—"

"Listened to what, Renny?"

"The child," she whispered, looking over her shoulder at him in stark horror. "What have I done?"

Tyler wasn't sure he understood what she was talking about. However, he knew Renny well. "You've followed your heart," he said. "Every day, you've gone by your instincts. Don't doubt yourself now."

Her eyes were wide with fear. "And if I'm wrong?"

Tyler turned her to face him. "What if you are?"

Her face went bone-white and she doubled over. "Then I will have failed."

Tyler forced himself to not touch her even though he wanted nothing more than to pull her into his arms and keep her warm and safe. But he didn't.

"What happens if you fail, Renny? What is the worst that can happen?"

Renny jumped up and backed away from him,

her eyes glittering, her lips moving soundlessly. She just shook her head at him.

Tyler rose and followed her retreating steps. "Answer me, Renny. What if you fail?"

"I can't," she whispered. "I just can't."

"Renny, there are two things to consider." He held up one finger. "We find Matthew, and he is still alive. That means you didn't fail." She bit her lower lip but didn't speak.

"Two." He lifted a second finger. "We find him but he didn't survive." He held up his hand when she cried out in protest. "That is the worst and if it happens, it will not have been your fault."

"Mattie would know," Renny said, her voice trembling.

"Okay, if we find him—not alive—then there are two things to ask yourself. One: What is the worst that will happen? Will everyone hate you? Will I hate you?" He answered for her. "No one will blame you. Not for this, not for the deaths of your parents."

Renny turned her back on him. "And two?"

"Can you accept whatever we find? Whether he is alive or not, can you let it go?"

Renny didn't move or speak. He went to her and put his hands on her shoulders. "Don't answer. Just think about it. Maybe the purpose of this journey isn't about Matthew, but about you."

Renny put her hands to her face. "I couldn't live with myself," she said. "I can't let everyone down," she said, her voice shuddering.

"Everyone. Meaning your brothers and sisters?"

She nodded. He pressed on before she could break in.

"And me? Will you have failed me as well, Renny?"

She nodded again. "Yes." Her voice was a faint whisper of sound.

Tyler rubbed at the knots in her shoulders. "And what of you, baby?"

Renny turned and looked up at him. "Me?"

Tyler gave in to his need to touch her by caressing the side of her face. "You're not just afraid of letting us all down," he said. "I think you are more afraid that you'll let yourself down."

At that, Renny pulled away. "This isn't the time." Her voice was tight.

Tyler rocked back on his heels. Everything inside him urged him to gather her close. But he didn't, for there was also a time for a good swift kick in the behind.

This was one of those butt-kicking times. Renny was too close to the surface, ready to give up—not on him or any of them, but on herself. He refused to allow her to do so.

"Yeah, well, maybe it is. Hell, you're not the only one who has a stake in this."

Renny turned wide eyes to him. "I never said—"

"No, you never considered anyone else. You are so afraid of failing that you aren't thinking of what the outcome of this mission will mean to all of us. Including me."

Tyler softened his tone. "Think I don't see that

you feel you aren't worthy of happiness, that if you fail you will deny us both that chance?"

He trailed his fingers over her jaw. "You aren't to blame for any of it, Renny, and if you think you are, then you're not as smart as I thought you were."

Tyler leaned down and kissed her gently. "Ask yourself one more question, Renny. Ask yourself what you most fear."

Seeing that she was off-center, unsure whether to be angry or hurt, Tyler took charge. His voice was firm, authoritative.

"That horse you're intent on chasing had to have crossed the stream here. We'll do the same and search the other side."

He didn't wait for her but mounted his horse and urged the animal across the shallow bed of water. A glance over his shoulder showed that she was just standing there, confused over his abrupt dismissal.

"Renait, get moving," he ordered. "You can feel sorry for yourself later."

Renny started. Then her eyes narrowed. "Watch it, Troll," she shot back, "or you'll be the one feeling sorry for yourself after I've stomped a foot or two."

She rode past him, sending water spraying over him. He smiled. "Never one to disappoint, are you?" he said softly.

Renny stewed with anger while she searched up and down the stream. How dare Tyler speak to her that way! He didn't understand.

Up and down the stream she rode, searching, looking for any sign of Matt, or the horse. Anything. So far, nothing.

She'd thought they'd been so close to finding Matt and Brenna because of the dreams last night, the return of the golden horse, the light show in the sky. All of it had built her hopes up. Now they were dust on the ground.

"Where are you?" she called out. "Show yourself to me." But no horse appeared from between the trees. No spirit horse materialized in the sky. She didn't see any birds or other animals to gain direction from.

She was alone. No Maze, no Mattie. Just her.

And Tyler.

Renny glared at him when she caught sight of him moving through the trees. She was furious with him. "Terrapin Tyler," she muttered. Dog Meat Tyler.

As she searched, she seethed. How could he say those things after just that morning telling her that he loved her. That he wanted her to be his wife.

"Ha!" Over her dead body.

The thought sobered her as she considered what Tyler had said. His words made sense. So far, this entire trip seemed to be about her, not Matthew. He was the driving force, but what if they were too late? What if Matthew was dead?

Would her brothers and sisters blame her? Tears welled in her eyes. No. She'd blame herself, and in doing so she'd unintentionally strike out at those she loved—especially Tyler—as she'd done over the last year.

On some level, she knew she could not have known there was danger to her parents, that they'd ride out in the morning and never return. She frowned. It had been her intention to confess her guilt to her siblings, to beg their forgiveness, but there was nothing for them to forgive. It was time to let the past go, time to concentrate on her future with Tyler, as long as she wasn't fool enough to let him go. She smiled a little. The Troll really did know her, and he knew just how to get under her skin and keep her off balance.

With the sunlight filtering between the trees, Renny admitted not only that she loved Tyler, but that her greatest fear was losing him.

Renny knew he loved her. His had been an unselfish love all this time and she'd been too blind, too stubborn and too wrapped up in her own worries and fears to see or admit the truth to herself.

What do you most want?

The question seemed to float on the wind. Her hair was lifted, teased. She closed her eyes and sought the answer deep in her heart.

She wanted Tyler. She wanted to be happy, she wanted what Mattie had found with Reed.

"So why are you just standing here like an idiot?" she asked herself. She was grinning now. She wanted to be Tyler's wife. She wanted Tyler. She loved Tyler.

For a moment the wonder of that bloomed deep

inside her. Love shone as bright as the sun, warming her from the inside out.

Mattie had said this was her journey. She drew herself up. Maybe this was her test. Something she had to pass to prove herself worthy. No, she was worthy of Tyler's love already.

She laughed softly. She'd just passed her test. She was worthy. That was the answer. What she most wanted was to believe herself worthy of love.

Tyler had made her worthy. He was the other half of her soul. He filled her heart, and he cleared the fear from her mind. She felt free. Free to confess her love to Tyler.

The thought made her feel gooey inside, all soft and mushy. Warm and hot and all jittery. With a start she realized that she was indeed in love with Tyler. Her Nanny Troll, her clucking mother hen.

She remembered how he'd just taken charge and turned her despair into anger, which had gotten her thinking. He'd known just what to say to rile her, and get her hopes back up.

Spurring her horse over to where he searched, she yelled out, "Trowbrydge Tyler Thompkins Tilly, I want a word with you!"

CHAPTER TWENTY-ONE

"Now you've done it," he muttered to himself. He'd been watching her and waiting for it. The play of emotions on her face made him dizzy.

The anger, the puzzled frowns, then a small smile. He'd have given much to know what prompted that smile. But she wasn't smiling now as she sat on top of her horse with her arms crossed. As he neared, she lifted one leg over the top of the horse's head then slid off.

Her eyes glittered, and he figured he'd be safer up on his horse. But she walked over and stared at him until he slid down the side of the horse. He tipped his hat back.

"You called?" His voice was neutral. Cautious.

She tipped her chin up at him. "You owe me, Troll."

He lifted a brow. "Ah, Miss O'Brien, what do I owe you?" His mind was racing and he just wished he knew what was going on in hers.

Without warning, she threw herself into his arms. "A kiss," she said. "Lots of them."

Then she was kissing him. Hard. His insides turned into a hot puddle of desire. But before he could kiss her back, she pulled back, a very satisfied expression on her face.

"What was that about?" Tyler held his breath.

"It's about you," Renny said, her eyes shining with tears. "I want you, more than anything."

Tyler reached out and pulled her close. "Are you sure, Renny?" He needed her to say it.

"Yes," she said. Renny pulled away from him, but didn't release him. "I love you, Tyler. I really, really love you and don't want you to ever leave me." A single tear ran down her cheek.

Tyler's thumb brushed it away. His heart felt full to bursting. Renny was on her way to healing. There wasn't time now to talk, but he just needed to hold her for a moment more.

"I love you, Renny. You'll marry me?"

She laughed low in her throat. "Yep. Gotta make an honest man out of you now."

Tyler swung her around. "You never fail to surprise me, Miss O'Brien."

"Good. Keep you from getting bored." She buried her head in his shoulders.

"Say it again, Renny."

"I love you." She tipped her head back to look at him.

"My name, too."

An impish grin lit her face. "Sheriff Troll?"

Tyler growled low in his throat. "Baby, you're

going to push me too far one of these days." In truth, he loved hearing her call him that.

"Yeah. Get used to it, Troll." She sighed. "We best get back to searching."

They strode over to their horses. The pair of animals had wandered a short distance away where the prairie land stretched out on this side of the river.

They were almost there when Renny grabbed Tyler's arm. "Look." She pointed to a tiny grove of saplings and brush. Something white was dangling from the trees and blowing in the wind.

Brenna rode, away from what was left of her brother. There were no more tears. Gil was gone. He'd made the choice to end his life instead of hers.

She wanted to cry but she was numb with shock.

Gil had shot himself with their father's revolver. She didn't even know he'd had it with him. A sob rose but lodged itself in her throat. He'd let her go.

"Why, Gil?" She couldn't believe that he'd shoot himself.

Immediately she wanted to start blaming herself. But that wouldn't help Matthew. Blame got a person nowhere. She couldn't have saved Gil. But maybe it wasn't too late to save Matthew.

She rode until the sun started going down. She was so tired but she couldn't stop. Had to keep going.

Matthew. She had to find him and couldn't think of anything else.

Her eyes were blurring with exhaustion when she spotted the dark cloud in the sky. She frowned. Rain. Just what she did not need. She hadn't taken anything from Gil but his rifle and horse. If she found Matthew, she'd need the horse, for Gil had driven Matt's horse away. "In case he didn't die," he had told her.

As she crossed the huge expanse of land between the two streams, the dark cloud grew closer. She frowned. The sky on either side was a pale blue with a hint of color from the sun that was just starting to drop behind the horizon.

The horror of that cloud hit her. They were birds. Lots of birds. Big, black birds. Birds of death. A cloud of death hanging over the land.

"No!" She screamed Matthew's name and spurred the horse faster. When she drew near, she saw a horse. A golden-yellow horse standing still and silent, as though guarding something.

Movement on the ground stopped her. The birds were on the ground as well, trying to get close to something beneath the horse's feet.

Lifting the rifle, Brenna pulled the trigger.

Renny knelt in the shelter. Blood was everywhere. She shook her head. "Where is he? Where could he have gone?" They'd searched the outside and found Matt's saddle. There was no horse.

"Please, let him be all right," she prayed. "And Brenna. Let her be safe with him."

Renny held the bloody shawl in her hands.

Tyler came back inside. "Found a trail."

Renny jumped up. "Let's go."

Before they could mount their exhausted horses, the blast of gunfire shattered the quiet.

Renny ran around Tyler. Behind her, Tyler yelled her name. He grabbed her, pulled her to the ground. "You can't go running out there."

"Let me go, Tyler. We have to go see if it's Matt!"

"Renny, look at me." His voice was gentle.

Tears were streaming down her face. "I'm scared, Tyler."

"I know, baby. I know. We'll go see, but let's be a bit more cautious, all right?"

Renny nodded. As they stood, she grabbed his arm. "I love you, Tyler. No matter what we find."

"You're not alone, Renny. Not ever again." Tyler wiped the tears from her face.

Renny nodded. "I believe now," she said.

Tyler got slowly to his feet. "In spirits?"

Renny held on to him for a moment. "I believe in you. In us."

"Thank you, Renny." Tyler took her by the hand.

Drawing a deep breath, Renny started forward. "Let's go."

Matthew drifted in and out of consciousness. The cloud of death was hovering over him. When he opened his eyes, he saw the birds and knew that they were waiting for him to die.

"You're not going to die," a sharp voice said.

Matthew didn't open his eyes. He knew that voice. "Old Man," he murmured.

"You will hang on. She is coming for you." The voice faded into the wind.

"Who?"

There was no answer. "Old Man. Do not leave me!"

He heard the flap of wings but didn't have the strength to even wave his arms. A shadow fell over him and he felt the soft muzzle of his horse on his face.

He thought of his sister. Renny. She'd love that horse. Too bad she'd never see it, for he knew he'd never see her, or the rest of his brothers and sisters, ever again. He figured dying would be hard, but all he had to do was close his eyes and go to that other world. So easy. Yet something was holding him back.

A voice. Distant. Frantic. It called to him, then all he heard was the sound of thunder above his head. The dark cloud whirled, the birds around him flapping.

He tried to move, but fell back; his last thought was of Brenna. His biggest regret was not telling her that he'd loved her since the first day he'd set eyes on her.

"Brenna," he whispered.

Chapter Twenty-two

Renny leaned over Matthew. It had taken some time to get him back to the shelter. Her heart was still racing, her skin clammy. She was shaking as she tended to Matt's side. The ugly gash was red and festered, and required her to open it, clean it and draw the pus out.

But Matthew was alive. They'd found him in time. She glanced up at Brenna, who stood in the doorway. She was white as a ghost, her dark eyes filled with the horrors of her ordeals.

For a long moment the two women stared at one another. One with fear, one with compassion. Renny didn't know everything, just enough of the story had been told to answer the basic questions.

"I'm sorry, Bre," she said. And she was. Gil had been a friend.

Brenna drew in a shaky breath. "I'm so sorry for what he did, Renny. For what we all did." Her gaze went back to Matthew. She pressed her fingers to her mouth.

Renny recognized the anguish and love in her eyes. After packing the wound with the medicines and herbs both Renny and Brenna had with them, she stood and handed Brenna a clean cloth. "Bathe his face and his body. We need to cool his skin."

Brenna clutched the cloth in her fist. "You trust me alone with your brother?"

Renny turned at the entrance to the shelter. "Yes, Brenna. I trust you. You came back. You did the right thing."

"But I left him to die." Brenna's hands shook as she ran the strip of cloth over Matt's face.

"No, you left him to give him life." Brenna had been hysterical when they'd found her crouched protectively over Matt. It had taken Brenna a while to even recognize Renny and Tyler.

Renny left her brother to Brenna's attentions. Outside, Tyler held out his arms. When sobs shook her body, he lifted her and carried her a short distance away.

Under his soothing voice and gentle fingers combing through her hair, Renny cried.

She cried for her parents, she cried for Mattie and Collin. She cried for all the pain Patrick O'Leary had put them through, and for his betrayal.

She cried for Matthew, and even for Brenna, for Renny understood the need to protect her loved ones at all costs, even that of your own soul.

In her head, she thought about all the things she was crying over. She cried even for Tyler, his losses and the pain she'd caused him.

Finally, she'd purged herself of all the guilt. The

pain was less now, and she knew she'd start to heal. It would take a long time. She and Matt both needed to heal: him on the outside, her on the inside. But she had hope now.

Lifting her head, she looked at Tyler. His eyes were clear, and full of love. "Better now?"

Her lips trembled in a smile. "Yeah. Feel like—"

Tyler smiled. "I love you, Renny." He bent his head.

She wrapped her hands around his neck. "Yeah. I love you, too," she said.

They kissed. A slow, gentle kiss that conveyed much more than words ever could. Their kiss linked their hearts and souls.

Tyler lifted his head. "Don't want you to stop," Renny pouted. She loved this man so much.

"Neither do I, but I think we have company." He stood and pulled her to her feet.

Renny glanced around and gave a happy cry when she saw the rest of her family approaching.

She ran to them. In minutes everyone was laughing and talking and asking questions. After the initial excitement died, they sobered and each of them filed into the shelter to see for themselves that Matthew was alive.

They each spoke, and touched him. Though he was unconscious, they wanted him to know he was not alone. They were there with him. No one questioned Brenna's presence or asked what had happened. There was time enough for that later.

One by one they sat, forming a tight circle around Matt.

Renny reached over and grabbed Tyler's hand with her right hand. Her left, she offered to Brenna.

Slowly, Brenna took it. One by one, each person joined hands. Brenna reached down and took one of Matt's hands. Reed guided Matt's other hand into Mattie's.

They were linked. Joined by more than their hands. Tragedy brought them together. Love would keep them together and erase the painful past with a happy tomorrow.

A slow chant fell around them. It seemed to come from the top of the trees. Without questioning, they each joined in until the low chant filled not only the shelter but their hearts.

It died slowly. And they dropped their hands. Mattie went into Reed's arms and he led her out of the shelter. Caitie went with them.

Renny went outside with Tyler. By unspoken agreement they walked along the river. Renny wasn't surprised that in the confusion of everyone arriving, Maze had disappeared.

"I wonder if we'll ever see her again," she said. She'd told Tyler of her dreams and of Silver Star, a spirit by the name of *Mazaska Wicahpi*.

"I have a feeling she's up there now, watching over us." Tyler was eyeing the stars overhead.

Renny smiled. "You've taken all this pretty well."

Tyler sighed. "I'm guessing I'd better get used to this. Yours is not what I'd call a normal family."

Laughing softly, Renny agreed. "We're not. Wait until you meet the rest."

Tyler looked horrified. But he was smiling. "Can't wait," he said.

Renny didn't tell him that it would be soon. She figured they were closer to their Uncle Wolf's home than Pheasant Gully. They would go there and stay until Matthew was well.

She sighed with contentment. "It sounds like everyone has gone to bed."

Tyler tipped her back in his arms. "You tired?"

Renny shook her head. "No, but I'm hungry." She slid one hand over the back of his neck.

Tyler bent down. "Me, too." He kissed her, then stood.

"Tell me what you want."

Renny leaned into her sheriff. "I want you. Now."

Tyler grinned. "Think we'd better take a longer walk."

"Whatever." She nipped his lower lip. "You're mine. All that matters."

Tyler slid his hands down over her curves, gliding over the buttery soft dress. He bunched it in his hands and pulled the garment up until he could slide his palms over warm, bare skin.

"Who do you want, Renny?" He pulled her hard against him, letting her feel his need for her. "Say my name."

Renny lifted herself on tiptoe. She nibbled at his ear. "I want you, Tyler."

Feeling Tyler sigh, she stepped lightly on his

foot. "I also want my mother hen and nanny. I want all of you," she said. Her body yearned to get closer. "Are you done talking yet?"

His soft laugh made her shiver as she stepped onto his other foot so she was standing on him.

Tyler trailed his mouth down the side of her neck. "You got something else in mind?"

"Yeah. I do. Take me away, Trowbrydge Tyler Thompkins Tilly."

Tyler started walking, his hands holding her firmly to him. "Gonna go too far one day, Renny."

She tipped her head back. "Yeah, that's what you keep telling me, Sheriff Troll. Guess when I do, you'll just have to go with me."

"That's a promise, Miss O'Brien. That's a promise."

EPILOGUE

Two months later, Renny woke beside Tyler. In the early morning light, she lay, sleepy and content. Her head, pillowed on Tyler's chest, rose and fell with each deep slow breath.

They'd arrived at her Uncle Wolf's place near the Missouri River. Matthew was healing under Brenna's care, and Brenna had been accepted into the family without question. Later today, both Matthew and Brenna and Tyler and Renny were going to be married by another of her uncles, Striking Thunder, who was chief to their tribe.

She sighed. Life was good, she thought. Two months with her favorite aunt and uncle had done wonders for them all, and today, the rest of the family would arrive. Her fingers trailed absently over Tyler's chest. She loved the warm feel of him. His hand shot up and grabbed hers.

"Keep doing that and we'll be doing something else really quick," he said, his voice gruff with sleep.

Lifting herself onto one elbow, Renny grinned

down at him. Her fingers spread out until her palm ran across his broad, hard chest. "Promise?"

Tyler grabbed her hand. "Minx."

"Troll." Renny flung herself onto him. "*My* troll," she breathed as she kissed him.

Tyler rolled her over. His eyes were wide awake and filled with love. He agreed: "Only yours, sweetheart. Only yours." He leaned down and kissed her gently.

A shout outside made them both turn toward the open window of the barn loft. Renny grimaced. Kealan was up early. She pulled Tyler back to her.

"Ignore him," she ordered.

"Happy to oblige," Tyler murmured in her ear. He kissed her, following the line of her jaw from ear to ear. Renny melted.

"Feels so good," she groaned.

"Yeah, baby, it does. But I don't think we're going to be able to stay up here long enough to finish what you're trying so hard to start."

Renny wrapped her hands around Tyler's neck and held him tightly to her. "They can wait," she said.

Her beloved laughed softly, then groaned when a small pebble came sailing into the room. It was followed by a chorus of voices outside the window, calling her name and Tyler's. He rolled off their bed and began dressing.

"Come on, the gang isn't going to wait much longer."

Renny found her clothing and dressed with a sigh. "No, I guess not," she agreed.

"Hey, don't sound so glum. It's our wedding day!" Tyler took her back in his arms. "Today, you become Mrs. Tyler Tilly."

Renny leaned back, a mischievous grin on her face. "As long as you're the only troll in the family." She snickered and slipped out of his arms and went to the window. The wooden shutters were open as she and Tyler had spent the evening bathed in moonlight, starlight, and the heat of each other's arms. As she bent down to glance out, a small stone cleared the opening and hit her.

"Hey! They really are going too far," she muttered to Tyler. She popped her head out, ready to let her brothers and cousins know that enough was enough. "No throw—"

Her voice died as she stared down. Her younger brothers were there, as were Wolf and Jessie's brood, but there were others. Many, many others.

Her gaze settled on a man with an arm swung back, a small pebble clutched in his fingers. The rock-thrower was none other than her mother's brother, Striking Thunder. "Leksi! Uncle!"

"My niece!" Striking Thunder grinned, dropping his rock. His hands went to his hips. "You've been in bed long enough. We arrived hours ago. Come down or I send the children up to rouse you from your bed."

Renny laughed, her eyes eagerly searching the crowded yard below. She spotted a woman with hair a shade darker than her own.

"Emma!" Renny turned. "Tyler, Emma's here!" Her voice rose with excitement.

Tyler joined her at the window. His gaze went wide with shock. "Who are all those people? I thought we were waiting for two aunts and two uncles?"

Renny sighed with contentment. "And my cousins. And I guess the rest of the tribe decided to come as well." She eyed the cone-shaped tipis going up wherever there was space.

"There is my uncle. He's a chief, and he's going to marry us." They would also be married when they got back to Pheasant Gully, so there was no doubt in anyone's mind that they were well and truly man and wife.

She added, "My sister is the one with red hair."

"Would never have guessed," Tyler said dryly.

Renny swatted him playfully. "Down over there is my Uncle Jeremy and his wife, Dove." She sighed with contentment as she eyed a large group of children standing directly below. Her own brothers and sisters stood among them, their red heads standing out like copper pennies.

"And those are all my cousins," she said. The children ranged in age from ten down to newborn, and she had no idea who belonged to whom at this point. Shades of hair ranged from reddish brown to the blackest black, showing the mixed heritage of the family.

Renny turned and headed for the ladder.

"Who are all the rest?" Tyler asked as he followed.

Renny glanced up at him. "Family," was her reply. Her extended family and friends.

"Hurry up," she called as she jumped the rest of the way down. Without waiting for him, she ran out, right into her sister's outstretched arms.

The two women laughed and hugged. It had been years since Renny had seen Emma and the rest of her Sioux family.

"Renny. It's so good to see you!"

Renny didn't want to let go, she'd missed her sister so much, but she finally stepped back—and found Tyler there, her rock, her anchor, her love.

"I have someone I'd like you to meet," Emma said. She turned to her husband and accepted a tiny bundle from him. "This is our newest daughter." She placed the sleeping newborn in Renny's arms.

"Oh, Emma!" Renny said softly as she stared down at her newest niece. "She's beautiful." The infant's hair was thick and soft. It was a reddish blond, and Renny fingered a blond curl. "It's almost like our grandmother's."

Emma leaned against her husband. "That's why we're calling her White Star. After Striking Thunder's mother, and your mother."

Renny's eyes filled with tears as she stared down at the infant. Never in the presence of The People would White Wind or Star Dreamer's name be said aloud.

As Renny held the tiny, helpless infant, she asked herself if life got better than this. Watching the baby's eyes blink sleepily, and the small, round, rosebud mouth make sucking movements, she didn't think so.

Warm hands closed over her shoulders. She looked at Tyler, saw his misty-eyed look. There was also an intense look of yearning. She turned and placed the infant into his large hands.

Suddenly, seeing his big, strong hands cradling the baby so gently made Renny cry. He glanced down at her. In his eyes, she saw his heart's desire, and she knew he was thinking of Gracie, and remembering the love he'd given to his baby sister and how cruel Fate had been in taking her from him.

"I want to give you a daughter," Renny whispered.

"We have time," Tyler replied. "I don't want to rush you. I can wait."

Renny grinned and took the baby back, needing to hold the tiny infant. "What if I cannot?"

Uncaring of their audience, Tyler pulled her close and kissed the top of her head. "Then we will have a child right away."

Renny handed White Star back to Emma. She grinned and wrapped Tyler's arms around herself, bringing his palm down over her abdomen. Then she admitted, "Yes, we will have a child. And sooner than either of us planned."

Cheers went up all around them. Tyler's shocked cry of pleasure was drowned out. Striking Thunder ushered his children and his many nephews and nieces away. "Let's get this wedding started," he cried.

Hours later, in the low afternoon sunlight, Renny and Tyler stood facing each other as Chief Striking Thunder wound ribbons over their hands, binding them forever to one another. As the couple turned to face their family and friends as man and wife, Renny's earlier question returned.

Did it get better than this?

The answer was no. There were no guarantees in life. There would always be death and sickness and other tragedies, but there would always be love too. Those who loved her, and those she loved. As long as she had love, she had all she needed.

Her hand crept down to where new life grew. Was it a son or a daughter? She smiled. It didn't matter to her. The child was a gift. It was a sign that life went on, that light followed darkness around the wheel of life.

Tyler leaned down. "I love you, Renny."

She leaned into him. "I love you, Tyler. Forever."

"Promise?" His breath was warm on her cheek.

"Promise." She enjoyed a quick kiss before her family gave a round of cheers and descended upon them.

LETTER TO THE READER

Dear Readers,

After a lot of thought, I am ending the White series with *White Vengeance*. Perhaps in the future we will go back and revisit the friends we have made. I've enjoyed my time spent with them and will miss them.

I've included two lists below. One is the title of each book and the order it came out; the other is my recommended reading order, which many of you have requested.

Thank you so much for your support over the years.

—Susan Edwards

Titles by published date:
White Wind
White Wolf
White Flame
White Nights
White Dreams
White Dove
White Dawn
White Dusk
White Shadows
White Deception
White Vengeance

Susan's recommended reading order:
White Dawn
White Dusk
White Shadows
White Wind
White Wolf
White Nights
White Flame
White Dreams
White Dove
White Deception
White Vengeance